SPELLBOUND WITH SLY

SHELLEY MUNRO

MUNRO PRESS

Spellbound With Sly

Print ISBN: 978-1-99-106386-1
E-book ISBN: 978-0-9951026-3-7

Editor: Kelli Collins
Cover: Kim Killion, The Killion Group, Inc.

Munro Press, New Zealand.

First Munro Press electronic publication October 2017
First Munro Press print publication May 2025

DEDICATION

For Paul, my husband, partner in crime, and fellow adventurer. Every day is a good day.

INTRODUCTION

A princess with a nefarious plan abducts him from his home...

Feline shapeshifter Sly Mitchell is an unwilling participant in his family's fantasy capture business. His preference—to work the land as he did on Earth, but familial loyalty runs strong. An unusual meeting with a beautiful mystery woman makes his attitude more accepting. Captivating and alluring, the woman makes Sly break every one of his rules to steal a kiss. Finally, a woman he'd love to capture and keep.

Victim of a curse, Cinnabar is fated to spend most of her life as an owl. A spy and reluctant accomplice for Princess Iseabal of the Seelie folk, Cinnabar's mission is to watch the man the princess intends to steal as her husband. But Sly doesn't deserve his fate. His kiss steals Cinnabar's heart, yet she's stuck in the middle of an impossible situation.

A handy spell sucks Sly into court life at Seelie. Drugged and unable to remember his family, he's suspicious and wary, yet the beautiful woman in the white, wine-stained gown lessens his unease. The attraction between them sizzles with dangerous erotic tension. Tantalizing kisses turn into more, but they have no future, not with the selfish princess holding the reins. The princess has her goals, and nothing less than a power grab will do. Woe betide anyone who stands in her way.

Contains an intelligent farmer with callused hands, a shy lady-in-waiting who wears feathers with aplomb, friendship and steamy love, and an evil witch of a princess who wants everything her way. She's not above stacking the odds in her favor, so let's see how these cursed lovers jolt a kingdom in their quest for happy-ever-after.

CHAPTER ONE

S ly Mitchell reached the brow of the rolling hill half a step ahead of his brother Joe and halted, scarcely out of breath. Instead of green trees and the sunbaked paddocks of Middlemarch on Earth, the tropical pink and green foliage of Ione Island on the planet of Tiraq spread out before them.

Their reality—a new Middlemarch far from Earth.

From their viewpoint, a ribbon of water glinted as it wound between the mass of trees and exited to widen into a swimming hole.

Closer, their grapevines, brought from Earth, stood in soldier-straight lines. Healthy green leaves showed they thrived. He and Joe had nursed them from cuttings, and pride filled him at the accomplishment, considering grapes shouldn't flourish in this tropical climate.

"Feel like a swim?" As Sly glanced to his right, he grinned

at the satisfaction radiating from his brother, an echo of his own pride, and not surprising, given they were identical twins. They'd worked hard to establish these and other crops and nurture the cuttings brought from Earth. Now, it was time to purchase animals. Unfortunately, Saber—their oldest brother and leader of their people—had informed them they lacked funds for livestock. Every penny needed to go to their capture resort. *That* was their priority.

"Last one in is a rotten egg." Joe took off with a celebratory whoop, sprinting down the hill at breakneck speed.

Sly hurtled after his twin, running flat out, his delight resounding and scaring a flock of colorful crimson-and-green birds from their perch in a copse of trees with black trunks and hot-pink foliage.

They hit the grassy bank of the swimming hole, each flinging off footwear and clothes. He and Joe splashed into the cool water together, too close to call the winner.

Sly dived beneath the surface and came up grinning, his hair plastered to his skull. He floated on the surface, relishing the freshness of the water after the sweaty toiling on their budding farm. The grassy bank reminded him of his and Joe's bedroom during their teenage years, with the explosion of colorful clothes and footwear.

Joe popped his head up from the water beside Sly, his green eyes and knitted brow communicating his frustration. "What are we going to do?"

Sly didn't dissemble, knowing his brother's mind. "Saber won't change his position. He needs to keep upgrading the resort. I get that, but it won't make our farming operation more viable."

"I asked him again," Joe said. "After you stomped off."

Sly groaned. "You didn't. Did he shout?"

"He went iceman. You know how his voice goes quiet and low and his eyes narrow. When he'd finished telling me about resort repairs, new capture attractions, and the money for building houses in the village because our people deserve a few luxuries after uprooting their families to come here, I felt like a worm. Lower than low."

"But we're growing food and contributing to the kitchen." Sly stood on the gravel bottom and grimaced. He hadn't wanted to leave Earth. Joe hadn't either, but they'd departed with their family and friends because of the feline virus that had decimated the shapeshifter population in New Zealand.

"Not enough. Saber said if we discovered another way to earn money, he might reconsider."

"Huh!" Sly snorted. "It's not as if we have time when we have to romance the guests."

"At least Saber isn't forcing us to take part in the captures now." Joe pulled a face. "That's something."

"Yeah. The dancing is bad enough." An identical expression to Joe's dug into Sly's features and tightened his facial muscles. "I've got a big bruise on my arse where that group of green women kept pinching me. I forget where they come from, but damn, they're intense. Did you see their teeth? Only a madman would put his dick near them."

"You should've shifted and shown them *your* teeth," Joe said.

"I considered it, then thought about Saber's reaction. And Ma's reaction. That knocked sense into me. I removed the hands and asked someone else to dance."

Joe laughed, an abrupt bark of irony. "Have you seen anyone interesting in the latest arrivals at the resort?"

"Nope. Can't remember the last time I had excellent sex," Sly said.

"I can. On Earth with Melissa."

Crap. "Hell, Joe. I know you liked her. Bloody virus screwed up everything."

Joe squared his shoulders, lifting his chin as he unburdened himself. "I was certain Melissa was my mate."

Distract. "Jodie Campbell wants you."

"She has kids." Joe held up his hand before Sly responded. "Hell, that's not a bad thing. I don't mean it that way. It's just...I want what Saber, Felix, and Leo have. They've found strong mates who help them, challenge them, stand at their sides. I refuse to settle for second best with Jodie."

"I get it. I—" Sly broke off, the hair at the back of his neck prickling. "Someone or something is watching us."

Joe continued to splash lazily, but he'd come to attention. "Yeah. I sense it too. Is it one of those big-arse birds?"

Sly scanned the sky and the fluffy pale pink clouds. Clear of giant raptors. "Nah, the smaller birds and animals would've warned us. Besides, we haven't had a sighting for a while."

"Better not be Jodie and her friends trying to ogle my naked arse." Joe scowled as he studied their surroundings. "If I catch them, I'll spank backsides. And it won't be pleasurable for them. Still can't see anything. You?"

Unease rippled through Sly. "You still sense it, though?"

"Yeah, something's out there. I hope it's not a new neighbor, or worse, a predator. Saber reckoned there wasn't anything else dangerous out here on the island. Casey agreed."

Casey was Felix's mate, and she'd traveled for her military job before settling down with their brother. During her service, she'd amassed info on alien races and their habits.

"We should get back to the resort, anyway," Sly said. "There's a new batch of women arriving."

"Don't remind me." Joe perused the trees and vineyards one final time before wading from the pool.

Sly followed and dressed rapidly, despite the water on his skin. He'd dry. As they strode up the hill toward the resort, the sense of someone spying persisted, and he made a mental note to report it to Felix and Saber.

Princess Iseabal MacAsgain of Seelie watched the men frolic in the water, intrigued by two things. One, they were twins. Identical twins, which made them like her and her twin sister, Katrina. And two, they made her breath catch in a way no other man of her acquaintance had since Trevelyan. Their striking physiques and playful manner grabbed attention. At this moment—hers.

She cocked her head and owned the smile pushing for display. Her lips curved until her cheeks ached, ambition sparking to fiery life.

This—one of these twins—presented the solution to her problem.

A man.

A husband.

She'd make her ailing father happy and secure her position at court. The first steps to full power.

She studied the men. Black-haired and sound of limb. Too far away to view clearly, yet their laughter deepened her exceptional mood.

"*Ooh, Cinnabar,*" she gushed to the russet-colored owl perched on a nearby rock. "One of them will make a fine husband. The one on the left, I think. The other seems quieter. Unhappy." She nodded decisively. "I will take the one on the left. A husband will strengthen my position. Go closer and listen to them." She wiggled in a gleeful, happy dance. *Power and the crown.*

Before Cinnabar took to the air, the two men waded from the pool.

"Huh!" Iseabal muttered, disappointment a sharp stab in her chest. "I wish I was closer. Follow them, Cinnabar. I want a report. Who are they? Their names. Is there a woman in my way? Any information to help make a marriage happen."

The owl observed her with big blue eyes. They always appeared faintly accusing, but Iseabal sniffed and shrugged off the smidge of remorse that zapped her like a magical spell.

"Don't return until you have the knowledge I seek," Iseabal ordered as the owl rose into the air and sped after the delightful twins.

She scrutinized the two men until they'd disappeared, with Cinnabar following on the wing.

"Mystery man, you will be mine," Iseabal whispered as she retraced her steps to the secret entrance to Seelie. Trevelyan could stick his proposals and kisses. "You will be my husband and my path to power."

CHAPTER TWO

C innabar Taithligh hesitated, eyeing Princess Iseabal in the hope she might change her mind. How was she meant to acquire answers while stuck in this feathered form?

Finally, wary of the princess's changing expression, her thinning lips, and narrowed eyes, Cinnabar flapped her russet-colored wings and lifted into the air.

On the plus side, this was freedom of a sort. She'd enjoy her time away from the princess and her uncertain temper while she spied on the two men who'd caught Princess Iseabal's interest.

The twins hurtled up the hill, and Cinnabar hustled to catch them, flapping her wings harder and faster to arrow through the sky. Normally, Princess Iseabal ordered Cinnabar to stay near. Even when the curse relaxed at midnight and she reverted to her true form, her options for exercise were limited. She was paying for the lack of fitness now, her heart drumming against her feathered breast.

The pair laughed as they walked, their jocularity relaxing Cinnabar and making her wish for the power of speech. Owl screeches were restricting. They slowed at the top of the hill as if reluctant to reach their destination. This gave her a chance to scrutinize them more closely. Both tall with black hair, they possessed muscular bodies and held themselves in the same manner. Twins. Of course, the pair *would* intrigue the princess. She'd think their discovery was kismet, something meant to be.

Once Cinnabar passed the brow of the hill, she saw they were headed for the old resort. The place had changed since she and the princess had first left Seelie long ago to explore. The buildings were no longer unkempt and unloved. Someone had repainted the bungalows in white with red trim, replaced the roofs with new thatch, and tamed the tangle of colorful plants and vines.

Now, a selection of variegated leafy bushes lined the paths, their vivid blue and white flowers perfuming the air like exotic market spices. Tall trees with bright coral-colored trunks and green-and-coral foliage cast shade over the gravel walkways. A group of women lounged around a pool, fruity drinks at hand. Appetizing meat snacks had Cinnabar's stomach rumbling. A shiny new fence encircled the entire resort.

Inside the resort enclosure, the two men parted. Cinnabar followed the one the princess had picked, something about his confident stride differentiating him. He stopped to speak with a dark-haired man and a petite woman. A brother? Her quarry hugged the woman, laughing when the other man grumbled in protest.

Cinnabar landed in a tree above their heads, and the threesome glanced up. Surprise froze her in place. No one noticed her unless she perched beside the princess in the castle grounds.

"An owl," the woman said. "I've never seen one here before."

The two men regarded Cinnabar with interest. Yes, brothers.

They had short black hair, similar features, and the same green eyes. Handsome men, while in contrast, the woman appeared plain. Interesting.

A small boy ran down the path, and the woman's face bloomed with the joy Cinnabar used to see on her parents' faces when they were still alive. One of the men patted the boy on the head, his love as visible as the woman's. Their obvious regard lightened Cinnabar's heart, and she wished for a visit with these people, under more normal circumstances.

She listened to their chatter and discerned nothing of interest. Cinnabar flitted to another tree nearer the pool to eavesdrop. The women hailed from different planets, as evidenced by the variations in hair, body, and skin tone. Some of the races were familiar from knowledge she'd acquired from visitors to Seelie, while others—especially the ones with green skin and pointy teeth—were new to her.

"Has anyone been captured yet?" a Tigrus woman asked, her gold and tan skin stripes on display, since she wore nothing except a brief loincloth.

A green woman spoke. All babble to Cinnabar. The other women understood, though, and laughed. Confused by the foreign language, Cinnabar flew to another tree and snooped on a separate set of women and the unhappy twin.

"Over here, waiter." A tall, thin woman with waving tendrils instead of hair signaled the employee. "When will the captures take place?" the thin woman demanded, snapping her fingertips imperiously.

Cinnabar clacked her beak. A bird form of *tsk-tsking*. Rude woman. She wouldn't last long around the princess.

The unhappy twin turned back to the guest. "The captures take place at any time, miss. Our capture committee likes to have a surprise element to make our guests' experiences more real."

"Any time?"

"Yes," the twin said with a brisk nod. "Do you have further questions?" He waited a beat before hurrying to the next group of women to take drink orders.

Captures? The women came to the resort for this purpose? Intrigued, Cinnabar moved on to spy on other employees and guests.

"I'd love to get captured and spirited away for some hot s-sex," a buxom lavender-colored woman shouted. She hiccupped her last word, obviously tipsy from downing too many colorful drinks.

A second shapely lavender woman sipped her purple beverage, listening and nodding to her friend. Their physical appearance reminded Cinnabar of their neighbors from Unseelie, although those from Unseelie were cobalt rather than lavender. Generations ago, they were outcasts from Seelie—enemies—their skins turned blue to differentiate them from the golden-skinned Seelie residents. These days, they lived in peace and aided each other in the season changes.

Cinnabar concentrated on the women's conversation.

"My friend was captured during her resort visit. She said the sex was magnificent, and she had trouble walking when she left. Best experience ever, she told me. She encouraged me to take my break here. There are so many attractive, fuckable men around this place." The lavender lady leaned closer to her tipsy friend and jerked her head in a direction to Cinnabar's right. "Him, for instance."

Cinnabar shot to attention. *It was him.* The confident twin. Robust with muscles sculpted from physical labor, he made her breath catch. Self-assured, with a swagger that drew every female eye in the vicinity, the man possessed enough attitude to attract Princess Iseabal. Charm and kindness, too, Cinnabar noted with disappointment.

The man was too *decent* for the princess.

Princess Iseabal didn't deserve a man like this, yet she'd have him, whether the man agreed or not.

Her eyes widened as a large black leopard trotted up to the confident twin. The twin straightened and followed the big cat away from the pool area. Curiosity prompted Cinnabar to flit after them.

The pair took a path, through an internal gate, past signs indicating the area was private, and entered a large bungalow. Several other bungalows clustered around the large one, and as Cinnabar watched, a number of dark-haired men and black cats arrived. Some of the men strolled up the path with women. The clear intimacy between the pairs indicated couples.

Brothers. They had to be, given their resemblance. Ah, a family. At least two of the women bore a resemblance to the men.

Cinnabar needed to listen to their conversation but entering the building... Dangerous. She settled for a window ledge and cocked her head, fascinated by the strangers. Perhaps it was the change in her monotonous routine, or maybe just determination to complete her assignment that grabbed her. After all, she had a slim chance Princess Iseabal might reverse the spell confining her to owl form if she completed her task.

More than anything, she wished for a return to her normal life. She'd never complain about lady-in-waiting duties again. *Never*. Not if she had two hands to work with and a voice with which to express herself.

A group of six men arrived, plus three more black leopards. They knocked and were invited into the building. The big cats...were they pets? Strange how they listened intently to the conversation.

Cinnabar's curiosity grew. She must get closer. She needed to listen closely to answer Princess Iseabal's questions.

One of the dark-haired brothers stepped forward and spoke. Unfortunately, despite her excellent hearing skills, Cinnabar was perched too far away.

Those who she'd decided weren't family spoke one at a time,

before everyone discussed the points raised—or at least that was what Cinnabar assumed. She had to get closer. She glanced at the door. Still open.

Before the next thought formed, she was inside the building.

"Where did that owl come from?" an older woman asked, breaking into the conversation.

Silence fell, and Cinnabar quivered, her heart speeding. Had she placed herself in danger?

"I saw it earlier in one of the trees near the swimming pool," Confident Twin said.

"Are owls bad luck if they fly inside?" a tall woman asked.

"Only if they poop," the older woman said dryly.

"Should we try to herd it outside, Ma?" another tall man with green eyes asked.

"No, leave it until we're finished. Maybe it will fly outside by itself," Ma said. "What do we think about the latest guest arrivals? Is there anyone worthy of a true capture?"

"There is a big lass who interests me," a bulky man with blond hair said. "She is kind and has a sense of humor. My feline likes her. I do too. Her name is Rachel." When no one else spoke, he continued. "I would like to keep her. Has anyone else noticed her? She has blue skin and pretty blue eyes."

"He's gone," someone from the back teased.

"I trust my feline." Creases of humor formed at the edges of the blond man's eyes. "She's beautiful."

"Anyone else?" A stern man, also with black hair and green eyes, scanned everyone.

Fascinated, Cinnabar listened as they planned to kidnap—capture—the woman named Rachel. It sounded as if they intended to keep her here, rather than let her leave once her holiday ended.

The stern man nodded. "All right, Greg. This is what we'll do. Scarlett can dig deeper into Rachel's background while you spend more time with her. You need to be sure, because once we take the next step, there is no going back. Are you all right with that?"

The blond man nodded decisively. "That sounds fair, Saber. I might ask Rachel to go on a picnic with me on the private beach."

"Entice her to go skinny dipping," one of the other men who Cinnabar thought was a brother suggested.

"That is a clever idea," Saber said. "What do you think, Ma?"

"Romance her. Learn more about her yourself. Her job. Her life. Where she comes from. Talk to her and listen. Make her feel important and half your job is done. You're a good man, Greg. Rachel will be lucky to have you as a mate."

"All right," Saber said. "Are there any other problems?"

"Yes," another brother said. "Those green women and their pointy teeth. Can we assign them to the holo rooms, for a capture that way? Let them have their way with the sex-bots, because no breathing man *or* his cock is safe near those teeth."

There was a moment of silence.

Ma broke it with a saucy chuckle. "Felix!" She chortled, humor lines fanning from her eyes. "Joe. Sly. You should see your faces."

"Ma," the unhappy twin—Joe—said, "Sly and I danced with them last night. Our backsides are bruised. We had to be nimble to keep ahead of them and their quick fingers."

Confident Twin—Sly—rubbed his backside, which set off more jocularity.

Cinnabar remained perched on top of the curtain rail and listened to their teasing. At least she was learning their names. The twin she was interested in—*no*, the one Princess Iseabal intended to steal, was Sly. A strange name.

Confident she'd learned enough to appease the princess, Cinnabar exited the room and flew toward the private portal to Seelie. Her Seelie being sensed the opening and, once closer, a faint blue shimmer outlined the arched entrance. Cinnabar flew at the doorway.

Smack!

Stunned by the collision, Cinnabar dropped and hit the ground with a croak. A wheezy screech emerged from her beak. It took long seconds to right her aching body and gingerly stretch her wings. Nothing broken. Ruffled feathers poked out at odd angles though. Her head rang. *Ding. Ding. Ding.*

She limped closer to the portal and pressed one clawed foot against it. The solid surface refused to give. Desperate, she attempted to mind-speak despite her success rate being nil.

Her mind remained silent.

Cinnabar screeched, stamping her right talon as she reached a horrid conclusion. She was stuck here until Princess Iseabal decided to open the door to Seelie for her.

Evening came, and Sly wandered the resort, as did the rest of his brothers and staff, on the lookout for women on their own. As time passed, the clock ticking on toward midnight, he danced with several of the loners, using charm and gentle flirtation to make them glow with happiness. Saber grimaced at him from the dance floor, his partner one of the green women. Her pastel-green hair bore forest-green highlights, and her right hand slid down his brother's back.

When Sly winked, he received the big-brother frown, the one that said he needed to shake a leg and ask one of the green group to dance. With a quick mental prayer, Sly picked the nearest green lady. This one wore her hair piled on top of her head, her beam displaying pointy teeth as he firmly placed her hand on his shoulder.

Obviously, Joe and Felix had received the same silent order, along with several of their staff, because the dance floor became crowded with green ladies in slinky dresses.

A pair of fingers slid down Sly's shirt-clad back and smoothed over his arse. His partner pinched his butt and he jumped.

"Stop doing that," he snapped.

"But it would be rude not to express my thanks," his partner said, the green of her compound eyes brightening with an inner light.

Sly froze. "That's your way of saying thank you?"

"Yes. It is also a sign of friendship."

Her teeth flashed, pointy and white. Sly barely suppressed a shudder when his thoughts veered to sex. *So not gonna happen.* Why the hell hadn't Scarlett discovered this pinching custom during her research?

"Why do you pinch so hard?" he asked.

"Yes. Yes. The male of our species has armor to protect him from our teeth. We have to pinch hard to get through his hide."

From the corner of his eye, he glimpsed his sister. Her hands covered her lower face, and she stood with difficulty, leaning weakly against the wall, her shoulders shaking.

Suddenly, everything was clear. She *had* known of this custom, but decided not to tell her brothers or the rest of the staff.

He'd let Saber deal with their sister.

"None of us has armor, and your pinches cause us pain. If you wish to express your thanks during your stay here, can I suggest you pat my shoulder, like so?" He demonstrated with a quick rub of her shoulder. "Or smile and dip your head? This way." He showed her what he meant by performing the action. "And say thank you."

The green lady caressed his shoulder, smiled, and dipped her head. "Thank you."

"That's perfect," Sly said, while attempting to hide his cringe at those white teeth. "Would you mind passing that on to your friends, please? If they do this, they're more likely to receive requests to dance and make friends with the men here at the resort."

"Yes. Yes," the woman said and went through the sequence again. "Thank you."

The music ended, and Sly escorted his partner back to her seat and the rest of her chattering green friends.

"Wait," his partner said. "Yes. Yes. Let me demonstrate the correct method. Yes?"

Sly nodded as the woman spoke to her friends.

"Yes. Yes," she said, turning to him. "This is the correct manner." She performed the actions and offered her thanks. "Yes. Yes. Wait. They will want to practice."

Great. He intended to take his break after this. A walk on the beach, where hopefully he wouldn't meet any lecherous women intent on groping his arse.

Aware of his brothers' gawks, he stood stoic while the entire group of females practiced saying thank you.

Half an hour later, he scanned the room for Saber and found him with Eva, his mate, discussing supper, which was eaten at midnight when everyone needed a break from dancing. He checked and realized it was almost time now.

"What was that about?" Saber asked.

"My dance partner pinched me, and I asked her why they did that. Evidently, it's a sign of politeness and civility on their planet. I showed her a better way of expressing gratitude. Scarlett knew all about it but didn't tell us. I saw her creep into the room and laugh so hard, she was having trouble standing."

Saber's brows drew together. "I'll deal with Scarlett."

"Good, because my butt is bruised," Sly said.

"Mine too," Saber said gruffly.

"Poor baby," Eva cooed, her eyes full of laughter. "I'll give you a massage later and kiss it better."

An arrow of envy struck Sly even as he backed up, his hands clapped over his ears. "Please, spare me. I don't want images of a naked Saber popping into my head."

"You'd better not," Saber growled, but his eyes gleamed as he wrapped his arm around Eva. "Take a break, Sly. You deserve it. Masterly job."

The praise brought warmth to his heart, but he merely nodded.

"Collect a plate of food from the kitchen before you go," Eva said.

"Thanks." Sly lifted an arm in farewell. The scent of chocolate and cinnamon wafted to him as he neared the kitchen, plus hints of spicy tomato and cheese, or the Tiraq equivalent. His belly rumbled in anticipation.

Sly halted on the threshold and searched for his mother. Not there.

"Hey," one of the workers said, his brows rising then drawing closer in a frown. His jet-black hair flopped forward, and he flicked it away to reveal light purple eyes, narrowed in irritation. "You can't be here. 'Tis busy."

"Eva told me to collect food to take with me."

The kitchen hand's expression cleared to a grin. One of his front teeth was missing, creating a gap-toothed smile. "Miss Eva said?"

"Yes."

"Okie-dokie. If Miss Eva said, it be all right. Stay there. I be right back."

Sly obediently remained inside the kitchen door and out of the way. Someone had a crush on his sister-in-law. Saber had said she'd hired more staff from Dalcon, since none of their people wanted to work in the kitchen. They preferred the other jobs on offer around the resort.

"Here you be," the kitchen hand said, producing a basket. "Manfred told me to pack a drink for you too. Who you be?"

"I'm Sly Mitchell." Hard not to be charmed by this kid. "Eva is mated to my older brother."

"Ah, Mr. Saber. I knows him. He be leader."

"Yes, he is," Sly confirmed. "What is your name?"

"Taiaha," the kid said. "Miss Eva give job, room to live." He rubbed his flat stomach. "Food and currency. Like it here."

"I'm glad," Sly replied.

Eva had grown up in a poor part of town on Dalcon, and she'd found a way to help other youngsters who labored under the same disadvantages. His sister-in-law had a big heart. "Catch you next time, Taiaha." With a wave, Sly hustled to the beach while he wondered what Joe was up to right now. He considered searching for him, so they could play hooky together. In the end, he turned away from the center of the resort, unwilling to lose this slice of freedom.

The gravel path crunched under his boots, and insects hummed, the sole sounds until he heard a masculine murmur and a giggle. He stepped off the path and into the shadows to avoid the approaching couple. An amorous pair.

A feline snarl—sharp and full of warning—gave him a clue as to the identity. It was Greg and his blue lady. Rob...no, Rachel. Sly waited until they'd passed before stepping back onto the path.

The gentle swish of waves lengthened his steps, and soon he stepped onto the sand, now dark but bearing a faint pinkish tinge during daylight. In fact, many things—plant and mineral—on this planet were pink. Something to do with the soil. The seawater, though, was a stunning jade green.

Sly scanned the beach, and the faint tension in his shoulders released. Not a single enamored couple. *Perfect.*

He set the basket down to check his bounty. A blanket filled the top and he pulled it out, spreading it across the sand with a flick of his wrist. Starved, he opened a tin and pounced on the savories, consuming one then another. They went down with a quick swallow of crisp pastry and chunky meat in a rich gravy.

From where he sat, faint and romantic music drifted from the function room. Colored lights added ambience, and the floral scent from the gardens seemed stronger at this time of the evening. He didn't know the identity of the blue and white flowers, but their fragrance reminded him of cookie spices.

A woman wandered along the path, the whiteness of her dress snaring his attention. Her face and hair hid in the shadows. She was behaving like a new arrival, her focus flitting from the sea to the gardens to the sand. As she drew closer, he heard her humming to the lilting music that drifted on the air. She started dancing, twirling closer and holding out her arms as if she had a partner.

The moon peeked from behind the cloud cover, allowing him a better glimpse. Red hair, long enough to reach the middle of her back. Her white dress bore a large red stain on the front, but the mishap, presumably from a spilled drink, didn't seem to bother her.

Coming to a decision, Sly stood. "Would you like this dance?"

She jumped, her hand pressing to her breast, her steps faltering.

Blue eyes. She had blue eyes that reminded him of the owl he'd seen earlier, and her hair—it was the shade Ma described as strawberry blonde. He called it red. His first glimpse of her aroused his curiosity.

"Please, dance with me." Sly held out his hand.

Her blue eyes widened to match her mouth, and a chuckle tickled his tongue. Instinct told him to hold back the burst of humor. He'd hate to scare her, and he'd learned a thing or two from watching his brothers' interactions with *their* mates...

Holy crap. He shot a glance at the woman, his feline stirring in interest, in *more* inquisitiveness, in dazed wonder.

His hand remained stretched between them, and a howl of victory pressed against his chest as she extended her fingers. *Don't scare her.* He tamped down his relief, noting her shy glances. He wrapped her hand in a gentle grasp and drew her closer. The scent of fresh flowers drifted to him. Not the same as the ones in the resort gardens, but something more delicate. More like the wild flowers of Earth.

"Ready?" His voice emerged gruff because the muscles of his chest had tightened. He—his feline—suddenly wanted to pounce.

"Yes," she whispered, her smile timid.

He sensed she'd flee if he made the wrong move. Best behavior. He could do that. Sly listened to the music and waltzed, guiding his mystery woman around their sand dance floor.

"What is your name? My name is Sly. Sly Mitchell."

"Cinnabar Taithligh."

"I haven't seen you around the resort. What happened to your dress?"

She glanced at the splotch of wine-red on her left breast and the skirt of her white gown. "An accident," she said, her voice strangely hollow and despondent. "It was an accident."

"We can find my mother. She might be able to get out the stain for you."

"Thank you, but it's all right. I think my dress is past hope. I wanted to enjoy my time here. The peace and the beauty."

The music ended, and another song commenced. Sly kept dancing, his interest aroused by this lovely waif. Some women who stayed at the resort were wealthy and brought servants with them. Was Cinnabar a servant? A Cinderella who wasn't allowed to attend the ball? Full of questions, he drew her closer and enjoyed holding her, enjoyed her floral scent, enjoyed spending his free time with this mystery woman.

This time, when the music ended, he drew back but retained his grip on her hand. "I came here to spend time alone and eat a picnic dinner."

"Oh. I'm sorry. I've interrupted your peace."

"No, come and eat with me. Join me."

When she hesitated, he tugged her hand.

"Thank you."

Sly led her to the blanket he'd spread on the sand. He poured her a drink in his sole beaker and handed her two savories. Her stomach gurgled, and he laughed. "You're hungry too. Eat. The kitchen staff packed plenty of food. I'll never eat it all." A lie. He could demolish this and more, but he'd grab food later. Right now, he wanted to spend his time with Cinnabar.

"Do you have family here? I've noticed men who resemble you."

Sly took a savory and reclined, his elbow propping him up. "I have four brothers and several cousins with the same coloring as me. One of my brothers is also my identical twin. Do you have family?"

"No. Not any longer. Are your brothers older or younger than you?"

Sly shrugged inwardly. She didn't seem to want to talk about herself. He'd listened to his sister and his brothers' mates prattle. He knew how to chitchat if necessary. "I have three older brothers. My twin and I are next in line, then we have a sister. She's the youngest."

"Are you the oldest twin?"

"I am," he said in surprise. "I'm four minutes older."

She nodded. "I don't think you've been on Tiraq for long."

"No." Sly studied the springy red curls framing her face, the anxious press of her pink lips as she worried about his reply. Why did he get the sense she was pumping him for information? He hesitated, then decided none of the answers were confidential. Anyone at the resort would have ready answers. "We come from a planet called Earth, and no, we haven't been here long."

"I visited the resort before when the owners had left it to grow wild," she admitted. "I live on the Tiraq mainland. You've done wonders with the place."

"We've worked hard to make it a success," Sly said. "We've talked a lot about me. Where exactly on Tiraq do you live?" He sat up and handed her a piece of nectar fruit, watching her white teeth bite into the golden flesh. The juice ran down her chin. "Wait."

She froze like a fuzzy zylon, alert to danger as he leaned closer.

He'd intended to use his fingers to wipe away the juice, but her enticing scent and her sharp intake of breath dragged his thoughts off Good Intention Road. Instead, he turned onto Temptation Alley...and used his lips in a gentle kiss.

This close, he heard her rapid breathing, felt the pounding of her pulse, but she didn't shy away from his touch. This was fast, maybe too fast, but unable to resist, he removed the remaining nectar fruit from her trembling fingers and tossed it aside. He eased her onto her back then trapped her with his chest and arms, telling himself she'd come to their resort for romance and the hope of a capture.

Her blue eyes rounded again, and she quivered, but she never offered a protest as he lowered his head and made clear his intentions.

Then he was kissing her again, tasting her gently, savoring her curves pressing against his chest—and then everything in his world went topsy-turvy.

CHAPTER THREE

H e was kissing her.

If the princess learned of this, her fury would rattle the kingdom of Seelie.

Sly Mitchell was kissing *her,* and Cinnabar never wanted him to stop. His firm lips were softer than she'd imagined. Gentle and cajoling, enticing her to participate in the intimate caress. The instant she responded, he increased the pressure, and the kiss transformed from incredibly sweet to more demanding.

Despite the possible repercussions, she wrapped her arms around his neck and threw herself into the moment. For so long, the princess's spell had bound her to the form of an owl. No one had touched her or held her or offered comfort.

Oh, the princess kept her safe and fed her micelets because it amused her to witness Cinnabar's disgust of the wriggling gray creatures. A form of silent gloating, because she'd cast a spell on

Cinnabar and not one of the residents of the royal court had guessed Cinnabar's fate. Everyone believed she'd left Seelie to run off with a group of visiting players from Unseelie, who had entertained the court.

Wandering thoughts. No. *No.* Concentrate on the man kissing her. Sly Mitchell. The lazy stroke of his tongue. His talented make-her-forget-everything lips. Savor the remaining time before the curse dragged her back to owl form. She ran her fingers through his black hair. Silky and fragrant. She approved of cleanliness in a man. Yes, she must treasure this moment snatched from her boring routine and try not to feel too guilty about lying to him.

His touch gentled while his hand glided over her shoulders and upper arms. He lifted his head, his dancing green eyes glowing in an unworldly way. His breath caressed her cheek as she stared, mesmerized by his face and the sensual emotion etched into his features. An unusual rhythmic vibration accompanied their muted breaths.

"You're beautiful," he whispered.

"Me?" She gaped at him while ripples of shock battered her mind. He meant it. Certainty filled his voice, and that stole her breath, stalled her protest. He truly considered her beautiful. Princess Iseabal taunted her, told her she was lucky to be an owl since she'd never attract a man. *You suit feathers.*

Frying fungus! She refused to let Princess Iseabal spoil this moment for her.

"I'm not beautiful," she whispered. "But thank you. I shall treasure the compliment."

He stroked her cheek, his lopsided grin pushing her pulse to speedy. "Maybe not in the traditional sense. But your smile is bewitching. I love your red hair, your bouncy curls. Your sensual lips that entice me to touch and stroke. And you have pretty eyes. They're kind and radiate honesty."

Guilt kicked her in the rear end. There was nothing honest

about her visit to Middlemarch Resort. She came to reconnoiter, to spy for the princess, to betray this man.

"When did you arrive?" He brushed a lock of springy hair from her eye.

"Today." In this, at least, she could offer honesty.

"I didn't see you with the new arrivals."

"Some of them were very eager," Cinnabar said carefully. "I skirted the trampling hordes." This was also true. She'd witnessed the new arrivals and their shocking behavior. The pushing and shoving. The sly pinches and displays of selfishness amongst the women, as if they thought they might miss out on something important. It was behavior she saw every day at court amongst the bored courtiers. Power and prestige didn't go hand in hand with decency and common sense. This she knew, to her cost.

Oops, and there she went again. Spoiling this special treat by letting reality intrude.

"The women are...pushy," Sly said in understatement.

"I think you're diplomatic."

He grinned, his joy wide and bright and reaching his green eyes to make them glow. Before she knew it, she was returning his smile and laughing, suddenly much lighter of mind.

He lowered his head and kissed her again. The contact started slow, somehow more intimate, as he pressed her into the blanket with the weight of his muscular chest. It was sweet. It was tender. It was exquisite. He explored the recesses of her mouth with his tongue, and her stomach went into a wild swirl. Need crashed down on her, pulsing through her body and prickling her breasts.

Gentle kisses.

Deep, drugging kisses.

Urgency.

Emotions gathered and eddied through her mind. Pleasure. Oh, yes, there was much pleasure in this encounter. But also helplessness at her situation. The knowledge that in a brief time, the spell would work its wickedness, and once again she'd become an owl with no future, a puppet to do as the princess willed.

A tear welled and trickled down her cheek. Another followed, and another in quick succession.

Sly reached for her hand and gently squeezed her fingers. "What is it? What's wrong?"

Cinnabar shook her head. Even if she told Sly the truth, he couldn't change her life. And despite her guilt, she knew when the princess chased a goal, she never surrendered until she won her desired prize. Soon she'd seize Sly, turning his life into a nightmare. It was what Princess Iseabal did. No one ever checked her when they feared the possible consequences, her magic too strong for minor nobles or servants to counteract.

Other residents had disappeared from the princess's entourage. Rumors flew as fast as dragons winging across the skies of Narenda.

"Cinnabar? Please let me help you."

She stared up at Sly, his earnest expression. This man would help if she asked. This man, who was essentially a stranger, offered his aid when not one of her people would lift a finger. But the particulars of Princess Iseabal's spell prevented Cinnabar from blabbing about her misfortune. She'd warned Cinnabar that telling others would have dire consequences, although she hadn't explained further. Cinnabar shivered. The warning was enough.

No, only the princess had the power to break the curse.

"I'm sorry." Cinnabar swallowed the obstruction in her throat and attempted to circumnavigate further questions. "I've had a difficult day. It's nothing I can talk about," she added. "I'm sorry. I didn't mean to spoil your evening."

"You haven't." Sly used his thumb to brush a tear from her cheek. "My day hasn't exactly been stellar." He sat up and rifled through his basket of food. "Ah. The kitchen staff packed fruit tarts for me. Would you like one? They're my favorites."

"No, I won't take one. They're meant for you."

"They'll taste even better if I know you're sharing them. Honestly, Cinnabar. Meeting you has made my day so much better. Here, wipe your eyes and share my fruit tarts."

He handed her a tissue, and she blotted the moisture from her eyes.

"Thank you. Can you tell me about your day?"

He studied her for a moment, his green gaze dissecting her, his intelligence obvious in that one glance. Too much man for the princess. Honesty and integrity. Then, there was that kindness. It wasn't a characteristic common amongst Princess Iseabal's friends.

"You truly want to know? Most women who visit Middlemarch Resort are only interested in sex. We could get to the fun, sexy stuff instead of eating and talking."

Cinnabar gawked at his bluntness. "You want to... With *me*?" She was used to men ignoring her because she blended with the background, or at least she had until she'd spilled a drink on the princess and ended up cursed.

A shudder tore through Cinnabar as she recalled the princess's order to aid her in changing. Once they'd reached privacy, the princess had suffered a meltdown at the stain on her new gown. She'd thrown her own goblet at Cinnabar before chanting her spell; the reason the dress Cinnabar wore bore a red stain during her fleeting return to human form.

Sly barked out a laugh and took her hand. "Contrary to what the women here might think, I do not go around kissing the guests unless I want to. I refuse their sexual offers because none of them attract me. You're different. I wanted you from the moment I saw you dancing in the moonlight."

"Oh." No. No, no, *no*.

She'd never be able to hide the truth from Princess Iseabal. She jerked her hand from his touch, away from temptation. This man enticed her to act against common sense. Another of Princess

Iseabal's spells aimed her way might kill her. "I thought you were going to share your fruit tarts with me." A definite improvement on squeaky micelets. Cinnabar's stomach churned, nauseated by the way her owl form devoured micelets without a blink.

She swallowed rapidly. Once. Twice. Forced her thoughts from owl food.

"Here you go." Sly held a tart to her lips.

Almost too pretty to eat. The red fruit lay in slices over the surface of the tart. A shiny substance kept the fruit in place and made it glisten.

Cinnabar took a bite and moaned.

Sly chuckled and urged her to take another bite. "I knew you'd fall under the tart spell. Eva is the best cook, and she trains her helpers well."

Cinnabar savored the burst of sweet and bitter and swallowed. "It's delicious. Can you tell me about your day? What went so wrong?" It was better than answering his questions, such as where she came from. She accepted the last bite with a moan of appreciation.

He studied her while he ate a tart in two bites. "Joe, my twin, and I want to run a farm rather than work in the resort. I'm tired of getting groped and propositioned and objectified by the female guests who come to the resort. I know Saber—he's my oldest brother, and the one everyone turns to for leadership—is doing the best he can with our resources, but Joe and I want different things. Our crop of grapes is doing well, and I think we'll have a bumper crop to make wine for the resort, but we want to expand to animals. We want cattle, but Saber says the profits must go into the resort and advertising, provide houses for our people. I understand that. I do. I sound ungrateful, but I want to follow my interests. Joe thinks the same way."

Ah, the grapes must be the crop that grew over the land of Seelie. That would contribute to the health of the plants, not that she'd admit that. Most Seelie people kept to themselves unless the outside world intruded or necessity made it so. Apart from Prince Liam, of course. He made his own rules.

"Saber says we can buy stock if we make the money ourselves. But even if we could, Joe and I haven't heard of any cattle for sale."

"Describe cattle for me," Cinnabar said. "Maybe I can help." Seelie residents might be isolated by choice, but they weren't uninformed. Thanks to the prince, they traded with outsiders, and external gossip flowed in to the kingdom. Listening to Sly's ambitions, his passion for doing something he loved, pushed aside her self-pity. "Yes, tell me of these beasts."

"They have four legs and... Wait. Why don't I show you pictures? Would you walk with me to my room? Joe and I have pictures of our prize-winning cattle from Earth. We had to sell them before we left, and it was one of the hardest things I've ever had to do."

Aware of the passing time, the curse ticking like a fast-running clock, she nodded.

Sly stood and held out a hand to aid her to her feet. Such a gentleman. Gallant and strong. Her mind jumped ahead, thinking of a future with a man like Sly. With a regretful huff of breath, she watched Sly tidy the contents of the basket. He folded the blanket and tucked it under his arm, seized the basket, and offered her his free hand.

The physical contact had her breath catching, her pulse bounding ahead like an eager pet-pup.

"It's not far," Sly said. "We'll take the private paths, so we don't meet anyone."

"Okay." In Seelie, wandering with a single man was dangerous, especially for a woman of little consequence. Anything might happen—attacks or worse—and rumors would fly.

Sly gifted her with confidence, a sense of safety. She instinctively trusted him, since he didn't scrutinize her in the same way she peered at her micelet dinners. That probably made her a fool, but the truth was, nothing much could happen in the brief time before she morphed back to owl.

They strolled through beautiful gardens and under towering trees. Giggling carried from behind a hedge, and Sly paused, his big body freezing. She stilled, fascinated by the change in him. The stunning man at her side vibrated with menace. This new facet of him didn't scare her, but instead, intrigue bloomed.

A black cat prowled from the shadows. One she'd seen earlier. The creature stopped in the middle of the path and sat, its attention wholly on her. Cinnabar edged closer to Sly, and he slipped his arm around her waist. The big cat cocked its head then leaned closer to sniff Cinnabar's fingers. A rough tongue swiped across the back of her hand.

"That's enough," Sly said and pushed the cat away.

The cat rubbed his head against Sly's hip and let out a big purr before stepping clear of him.

"Go away. No, don't you dare." Sly wagged his finger, but the cat sidled closer to her.

The giggles they'd heard earlier grew louder. The cat growled and slinked off, melting into the darkness.

Sly tugged her in the opposite direction. "We don't need to meet anyone else."

"Who does the cat belong to?"

"No one."

"Oh?" She stumbled because she was staring in the direction of the giggles, and he caught her weight before she fell to her knees.

"Careful. Not much farther to go. This is a shortcut so we don't run into any half-naked giggly guests."

Cinnabar grinned. "Does that happen a lot?"

"You have no idea," he said with feeling. "If we were the ones without clothes, that I could deal with, but after considering sweet-talking you out of that pretty dress, I've decided to go slow.

We have time to learn about each other first. I want to savor you like an exciting Christmas present."

"Oh." Cinnabar's cheeks heated. She didn't understand half of what he'd said, but his meaning was clear. He wanted her. *Her*. She embraced the wonder of it for an instant before folding it away and stuffing the astonishment and awe to the back of her mind.

Sly would never belong to her.

She'd never own the right to observe him unclothed.

"This is the bungalow I share with Joe. I have an old tablet that runs on solar power."

Cinnabar nodded, aware of the passing minutes.

He opened the door. "Lights on," he ordered.

She followed Sly into the dwelling and peered around with interest. The room was tidy, with a long, comfortable seat, much like the one she'd noticed in the big meeting room. Pictures of various people covered the walls. A cooking area took up the far corner. The doorway to another room stood open, and she caught sight of a bed.

Sly strode over to a wooden table and scooped up a black square. He hit a button on the side, and the square lit to reveal a picture. Sly tapped several buttons and swiped his finger across the surface. "Ah, here it is. I knew I had photos on my tablet."

Cinnabar peered at the picture. "Coos," she said. "There are none on Ione Island, but on the lands to the west, they grow beasts like that there. You need to visit the Scothage people who live in the Highlands. Two, maybe three cycles' journey from here."

Sly's face lit with excitement, his green eyes mesmerizing her with their open joy. "Two or three days? That's nothing. We don't have suitable transport to get them here, but knowing where to purchase them is a start. I've asked in the market on Dalcon, but no one understood. Eva said she'd heard people speak of cattle, but she didn't know where to find them."

"If my memory is right, and it *is* only two or three cycles away, you should be able to drive them here. When the tide is at a low point, there is a causeway on the far side of Ione. Although you would need to drive them through the savages' territory."

"The savages?"

"Their king wears a bone through his nose. They cook everything they find in a big pot on a fire, or so the rumors go."

Sly laughed. "I believe Saber and Eva have met them."

"No, it might be better to take the long route. The Frogish clan is friendlier."

"Logistics," Sly said. "We can work that out later. Knowing where to find the cattle—coos—is a start. Thank you." He tugged her closer and settled his lips on hers. The kiss was too brief, but still enjoyable.

A bell-like noise drew them fully apart.

Sly cursed under his breath. "Reality intrudes," he said. "I'd better get back to work before Saber comes gunning for me. Can we meet once my shift is over in the morning and get to know each other better? I'd love to know about your home on Tiraq. I'm so glad you live nearby."

"Yes. N-not far from here." Oh! Frying fungus. Thank the goddess he hadn't asked for too many details earlier. Sly had driven every scrap of common sense from her mind, but now that they no longer touched, Cinnabar became aware of the prickles of magic forging through her veins. She had to leave before the spell dragged her back to owl. She didn't want him to learn of her curse for fear of Princess Iseabal's reprisal. The woman had no conscience. No soft side. No mercy when someone crossed her.

"I-I'll wait outside for you." She slipped outside before he replied, and none too soon. She cleared the door and turned right before the magic claimed her, and she transformed to owl.

34

The next day, staff dining room, Middlemarch Resort

"Did you find her?" Joe asked.

"No." Sly barked out the answer and it rang with temper and frustration. No, he hadn't found Cinnabar. If Joe hadn't seen her too, when he met them in cat form the previous night, he might have suspected he'd hallucinated and imagined the entire encounter.

"Have you asked Scarlett? Checked the bookings?"

"Yes." Sly bit back his anger. It wasn't Joe's fault Cinnabar had vanished. Perhaps he hadn't dazzled her as much as she'd amazed him.

Cut off at the knees, more like. He'd never experienced such a visceral response to a woman. Not even on Earth.

"Well, what did Scarlett say?" Joe prompted.

"I don't know Cinnabar's family name, but Scarlett checked our bookings. Not one of our guests has the name Cinnabar. I described her, since Scarlett worked on reception during the latest guest arrivals. She didn't recall her."

"What about her scent track? Did you check that out?"

"I did that straightaway, but it was the weirdest thing. Her scent stopped right outside our bungalow. It was as if she'd vanished."

"Teleportation?"

Sly shrugged, tamping down the anguish threatening to bury him. "I haven't heard of any locals using that method of transportation."

Joe frowned. "What about the Ghost race?"

"I thought of them, but from what Saber, Felix, and Leo have told us, they don't leave their area unless the population grows too high. Even then, they never travel alone."

"Yeah, that's what I thought. Besides, she didn't give off the ethereal vibe."

Sly recalled her firm curves beneath his questing fingers. No, nothing ghostly about Cinnabar.

Scarlett, the youngest Mitchell and their only sister, sashayed into the dining room and made a beeline toward them. She yanked out a chair and plonked onto it. "Did you find Cinderella?"

"Cinnabar," Sly snapped.

Scarlett flapped her hand, unconcerned by his burst of temper. "She disappeared, didn't she? Wait. Did she leave a slipper?"

Sly didn't try to contain his feline snarl.

"Are you sure Cinderella isn't a figment of your imagination?" Scarlett spoke over his growls.

"Enough teasing," Joe said. "Cinnabar was here last night. I saw her with Sly."

"Where did you meet her?" Scarlett asked.

"Saber gave me time off, so I grabbed food from the kitchen and walked to the beach. That's where I met Cinnabar."

"By herself?" Scarlett frowned.

"Yes. Someone had spilled a drink on her dress. I invited her to join me, and we ate supper together. We were talking about cattle, and I offered to show her a picture."

Scarlett groaned. "You bored her to death."

"I did not," Sly said, stung by the accusation. "She was interested. Joe, she told me about a place on the mainland to the west. The Scothage people. They have something called coos, which resemble our Earth cattle."

Scarlett rolled her eyes. "Yep, you scared her away with your cattle fixation."

"Who scared away whom?" Ma's gentle voice stopped Sly from snapping at Scarlett. One word from their mother generally stopped family squabbles dead. Saber was with her.

"Sly met a woman last night, but she's disappeared," Scarlett said.

Ma and Saber skewered him with their interest.

He didn't want to discuss Cinnabar. Time for a strategic retreat.

"Joe, we'd better get going if we want to get our farm chores done before we're scheduled to start at the resort."

Joe pushed his plate of half-eaten food away and rose, solidarity between twins. "Let's go."

Grateful for the rescue, Sly turned to Saber. "We'll be back in time for our shift."

"Running away," Scarlett taunted.

Sly and Joe ignored their sister and strode away together. The last thing they heard as they left the dining room was their mother chastising Scarlett for her cheeky attitude. That made Sly brighten—until he recalled Cinnabar had vanished.

Someone must know her. He'd keep asking until he found answers, or his name wasn't Sly Mitchell.

CHAPTER FOUR

ROYAL COURT, SEELIE

"Where the devil is Cinnabar?" Princess Iseabal stomped from her tower chamber, down the winding stone stairs, along the long passage, past the chambers of the ladies-in-waiting, to the last one—Cinnabar's. She flung open the wooden door without knocking and wrinkled her nose as she scanned the narrow bed, the clothes hooks on the wall bearing two shabby brown gowns. A sneeze erupted, and she stepped back. Gah! Nothing but dust in this cupboard.

No one had bothered to clean or gather Cinnabar's possessions after she'd supposedly run off with the group of players. How had Cinnabar withstood the lack of space? No matter. She had plenty now. *Too much freedom, since she is missing.*

Iseabal stamped her right foot and stormed toward the Great Hall. Cinnabar should've returned from her assignment by now.

She'd attempted mind-speak, but it never worked with Cinnabar. As soon as she broke her fast, she'd go in search of the traitorous woman, and if she didn't have a satisfactory excuse, she'd strip her of her feathers. See how she enjoyed nakedness.

Chatter, both male and female, spilled from the Great Hall, along with the scents of grilled slices of meat and fried lark's egg. Her stomach rumbled as she dodged a wriggling pet-pup begging for a scratch behind the ears. She ignored the gray canine and his wagging tail, checked the tables on the dais, and hurried to take possession of an empty chair with her ladies-in-waiting. Katrina, her sister, sat beside their brother Liam. She had no idea where Calum, Katrina's husband, was, but he never left her sister alone for long.

"Good morn," the ladies-in-waiting chorused, chairs scraping over the wooden floor of the dais as they rose to curtsy.

A servant girl, carrying a tray of dirty platters, tripped over Lord Sutharlainn's outstretched leg. Platters flew in all directions. One smashed on the flagstone floor below the dais. Another thumped Lord Sutharlainn's chest, splattering runny egg yolk over his maroon jacket.

"Stupid girl." Lord Sutharlainn flicked his wrist, and Iseabal felt the tug on the ley power as the plates flew back to the tray.

"Thank you, sir." The girl scuttled away with her tray, but not before Iseabal noticed the worms wriggling over the plates. The maid hadn't noticed them yet.

A shriek and a crash came from the passage outside.

Ah, she did now.

Lord Sutharlainn performed more magic to right his appearance, tugging from the ley lines running beneath the kingdom to power his chant. Iseabal sniffed, but hid her contempt. *Fool*. When one used their magic, they depleted their magical strength, and only time righted the problem. She saved her magical talents for the right occasion.

She also practiced each day in the privacy of her tower. Not so, most Seelie residents. They grew complacent. She wrinkled her nose.

Their loss. Her gain.

The delicious honey-nectar fruit and lark's egg pie sweetened her mood. Replete, she pushed away from the table and stood. Plates clattered and cutlery clunked as her ladies-in-waiting scrambled to stand as a show of respect. Iseabal wanted to laugh at the skinny Mirabel, who'd dropped her knife on her gown. The chubby Andry had spilled her fruit, and a bright green-and-yellow stain smeared the full skirts of her robe. They were a gormless lot, with their disheveled dress and careless manners. At least Cinnabar obeyed her orders, even while dressed in feathers.

Most orders, since she was currently missing.

Iseabal tittered. She couldn't wait to feed Cinnabar her next meal. She'd acquired two mouselets. Cinnabar had to eat to survive, but her wide-eyed blinking whenever she was presented with her squirming dinner never failed to boost Iseabal's mood. Such fun. Such entertainment.

Now, where the devil was the owl?

When her ladies-in-waiting would've followed, she waved them away, preferring to search for Cinnabar alone. No one needed to know her pet owl was, in fact, her former junior lady-in-waiting. That was her amusing secret, which she intended to keep for as long as Cinnabar entertained her.

Iseabal wandered to her usual haunts before the truth struck. She clapped her hand across her mouth to contain her chortle, not wishing to attract the attention of the maid cleaning in the family solar. Once the maid had bustled away, duster and polishing cloth in hand, Iseabal dropped her hand to her side. "Oops." She'd forgotten about the portal, which would be locked to Cinnabar.

Now certain of Cinnabar's location, she headed for the secret portal, which allowed an exit from Seelie. She placed her hand on the shimmering surface, and a door opened.

Ah! There she was perched in a tree.

Iseabal stepped forth, enthusiastic, before another obstacle occurred to her.

Cinnabar had no communication skills in this form. The spell was designed that way, so no one else discovered Iseabal's secret. Cinnabar couldn't tell anyone the truth during her time in normal form, either. A backlash spell. It should work well enough, if necessary, although Iseabal hadn't tested it. There was no need when Cinnabar was terrified of what might happen next. Yes, an amusing twist to protect Iseabal's secret, since she knew Liam would never approve.

But for once, the lack of a voice presented a problem.

What to do?

"Cinnabar, to me," Iseabal ordered.

Cinnabar blinked her rounded blue eyes once and soared from the shelter of the tree to a rock to Iseabal's right. Impatience pummeled Iseabal, and she fisted her hands until a solution presented itself. Questions. She'd ask Cinnabar questions with yes or no answers.

"Did you find the man? The twin. Flap your wings if you did."

Cinnabar hesitated.

"I don't have all cycle," Iseabal snapped. "Flap your wings for yes. Blink twice for no."

Slowly, as if she had an inexhaustible amount of time at her fingertips, Cinnabar ruffled her feathers and spread her wings in a flap.

"You did! You found him. I knew you wouldn't fail me. Do you know where to find him again?"

Cinnabar flapped her wings.

"Will it be easy to get him to come here?"

Cinnabar blinked.

"Hmm." Iseabal tapped her chin with her forefinger. "I'll need to go to him to persuade him."

Cinnabar flapped her wings.

"Is he handsome up close? Is he worthy of me?"

Cinnabar didn't react straightaway this time, and Iseabal frowned.

"Cinnabar. Is he worthy?"

Cinnabar flapped her wings.

"Handsome?"

Another flap.

Iseabal clapped her hands together. "Perfect." She needed a plan and the answers to more questions. "Cinnabar, return through the portal to Seelie, and when you revert to your true form this eve, I want you to write me a note. Tell me everything you know and suggest the best way to approach this man."

Once the owl followed her orders, Iseabal skipped back to the entrance to Seelie. Perfect. She'd gain a handsome husband and become more important than her sister again. More important than her father and brother, if things went to plan. Iseabal hummed happily, now that her scheme was coming together.

Of course, she couldn't marry without her father's permission, but she'd take this man to Seelie. Her father would soon understand the benefits of the marriage, while she'd have no problem controlling the man.

Confidence had her nodding and warbling a few notes of her favorite song.

Best plan ever.

Middlemarch Resort, Ione Island, a few cycles later

Princess Iseabal trailed the shirtless man—an employee—down a narrow path that wound between gardens full of blue-and-white flowers and trees with pink-and-black trunks and equally bright fern-like leaves. Her gaze lingered on the man's back muscles, glistening from the heat, and the fascinating pattern in black, which seemed etched into his skin. It also crawled up his right arm. A disease of some type? Nothing about the man suggested an ailing specimen.

Armed with the information from Cinnabar, Iseabal had told her father she intended to spend a few days with Lady Jessika, her friend who lived near the main entrance to Seelie. He'd accepted her words without suspicion, and Iseabal practically vibrated with excitement.

She couldn't wait to meet Sly Mitchell. *Sly Mitchell*. His name tingled her vocal cords as she whispered it aloud.

The man walking in front of her halted and turned to face her. "Did you say something? Did you have a question for me?"

Iseabal—plain Iseabal this trip—smiled even as she appreciated the perfection of the man's bulging muscles. A depiction of a snarling black cat decorated his left pectoral muscle.

"I'm sorry," she said. "I was talking to myself. There is so much to occupy my time at the resort."

The man took her words at face value, returning her benevolent humor and nodding. Several other men wandered past, some with women and others in groups. So many striking men, all way more attractive than those in her circle. Cinnabar had assured her Sly Mitchell was a worthy specimen. Iseabal agreed, since she'd already observed his musculature, albeit from afar.

When the path widened, Iseabal eschewed protocol and hastened her steps so she walked alongside the man. "What would you suggest I do first?"

"Go to either the swimming pool or the resort beach. Order a drink from one of the waiters. Soak up rays from the sun and relax. Get into the holiday mood. Tonight, make sure you attend the welcome mixer. Dance and enjoy yourself. Meet others. Then, on the next day...ah, cycle, have a relaxing massage, spend time in one of the holo rooms with the sex-bots. Have fun." He flashed an impish and knowing grin, closing one thickly lashed green eye in an exaggerated blink.

Iseabal's pulse did a *cha-cha-cha,* and she resisted fanning the heat from her face. "Anything else?"

"Whatever you do, don't miss the ball. Wear your sexiest outfit and arrive prepared for excitement and entertainment. Anything is possible after the ball."

"Anything?"

"Yes, anything. This is your room. You've packed lightly," he added. "You did bring a special dress to wear to the ball?"

"I did." Her magic would aid her in that regard. Success in the first part of her plan was worth a slight power depletion.

The man showed her through her bungalow and left her alone. Iseabal decided to wait for Cinnabar before she left her room to explore. Meantime, she'd adjust her apparel to match with that of the others. With little more than a thought, her flowing gown dissolved, and she wore the clothes that Cinnabar had described to her in one of her many notes.

The owl made an excellent spy, noting intricate details that wouldn't have occurred to Iseabal. She frowned at the scraps of cloth covering her breasts and reached down to tug on the matching cloth that covered her buttocks. She'd gone with bright red, since it contrasted with her long black hair and golden skin. She tugged on the stuff again, but the second she released the fabric it returned to a place slightly higher on her buttocks. Oh well. She intended to sit and observe and try one of the special drinks the man had described.

A shrill cry indicated Cinnabar's arrival. Iseabal hurried to let her into her bungalow. She shut the door after Cinnabar flew inside. Once the owl was perched on a chairback, Iseabal considered the information she required. How should she frame her questions to gain the necessary knowledge?

"Is Sly Mitchell present?"

Cinnabar flapped her wings.

"Will I find him at the pool?"

Cinnabar blinked twice.

"That's annoying. How will I find him?"

Cinnabar didn't move a feather.

"Can you take me to him?"

Cinnabar blinked.

"Why not?" Iseabal demanded. "Wait." She held up a hand to enforce her order. "Will I see him tonight?"

Cinnabar flapped her wings.

Ah. Perhaps he was outside the resort area, as he'd been when she'd first spotted him. It didn't matter if Cinnabar said he'd be present this eve. She'd make her move, then implement her plan into action. No, she'd told her father she would stay with her friend for two cycles. She'd learn more about the resort and enjoy herself meanwhile.

"Go and watch him," Iseabal ordered. "Stay near him and only return to me if something changes."

"Can you sense someone watching us?" Sly asked Joe.

They were preparing the ground for another crop, on a slice of land to the left of their vines. Already, they'd germinated some of their precious seed supply, and the plants were thriving in their private hothouse. Now it was time to transfer them outdoors.

With uneasiness simmering through his belly, Sly scanned their surroundings. "That owl is here again."

"Where?" Joe asked.

Sly pointed out the russet-colored bird. The owl stood upright, talons gripping the branch of a tree, peering at them intently. Big blue eyes dominated its large, broad head. They were the same shade of blue as Cinnabar's eyes.

His Cinderella.

Despite his searches and inquiries, she'd vanished without a trace, without a hint of a shoe to help him discover her whereabouts. His feline gave a breathy sigh of regret, one that Sly echoed.

"You're thinking about Cinderella again," Joe accused.

Sly shrugged, unwilling to admit—even to his twin—how much he missed Cinnabar and craved her presence. "Anyone catch your attention from the latest arrivals?"

"No," Joe said. "I never thought I'd say this, but even the easy sex gets old after a while. I want a woman with intelligent conversation, one I can be grumpy with if something is wrong, and she'll forgive me because she likes *me* rather than my body."

"I know what you mean. They tend to take one glance and get a greedy expression in their eyes. It makes me want to run. You spent time with a woman last month."

"I liked her," Joe said. "The sex was okay, but I didn't like her enough to offer more."

Sly noted the sun and its position in the sky. "We'd better hustle. Saber will be pissed if we arrive late to the welcome mixer."

An hour later, he and Joe approached the noisy function room. Background music played while topless male waiters dispersed fruity cocktails.

"Just great," Joe muttered. "A bunch of boozers. We'll be black and blue tomorrow. Luckily, we heal fast."

While Sly shared Joe's opinion, he didn't comment. No point, since nothing he did would change their reality, not until either he or Joe thought of another way to raise funds to finance their farming operation. He snorted. Things hadn't changed much from life on Earth in that respect.

Joe clasped his shoulder, giving it a quick squeeze of encouragement. "Catch you on the other side. Want to go for a night run afterward? A zylon hunt? Saber mentioned a hunt since the population is rising again."

The fluffy creatures appeared cute and cuddly until they bit—something in their saliva reacting badly with those in humanoid form. For some reason, a zylon bite didn't kill felines, and they presented a sociable sport and an excellent way to wind down after an evening playing affable host with the resort guests.

"Count me in," Sly said. "Leo and Betrys might like to join us. Ma will keep an eye on the kid." Ma loved babysitting Ricci and was always side-eying her three oldest sons, willing them to add to her current count of one grandchild.

"I'll check with Scarlett, too, if I can find her. She's making herself scarce these days. She refused to tell me what she was doing when I discovered her on the other side of our vineyard."

Sly pulled a face. "She was collecting rocks to make jewelry. She called them precious stones, but they resemble common rocks."

Later, as he entered the function room, he noticed the owl again. It huddled on the windowsill, feathers ruffled, and it blinked twice, appearing sad and dejected.

Inside, Sly collected a glass of water from the bar. The main function room was a glorified hall, in truth, but Ma and her helpers transformed it for each event until the space resembled a magical cavern full of flowers and colored lights. After a deep, fortifying breath, he started circulating. Although he disliked making nice with the grabby women, at least their currency had improved the lives of his family, their friends, and relations.

"Hello," a black-haired woman said. She'd turn heads with her golden skin and slim figure, yet Sly felt nothing. She took his hand and laced their fingers together and smiled. "I saw you from across the room and had to say hello. I'm Iseabal. I'm so pleased to meet you."

"Iseabal." Sly inclined his head and fought the urge to rip his hand from her touch. "How are you enjoying your holiday at Middlemarch Resort?"

"It's wonderful." She beamed at him. "I've never visited a place like this before. So many interesting people and new ways."

"I'm glad you're enjoying your visit," Sly said, maintaining a polite manner that would make his mother and oldest brother proud. Gently, he regained ownership of his hand. "Let me introduce you to a few of our other employees." He led her over to a group of his cousins, hoping one of them would take her off his hands. Something about this woman clanged his warning signals, yet he didn't know why. "This is Iseabal," he said. "My cousins Saul, Lucas, Duncan, and Ross."

As Sly had hoped, his cousins found the woman enticing and drew her into conversation. Her sweet laughter followed him as he left the group and searched for someone less pushy. He scanned the clusters of women, hunting for red hair. Cinnabar. The mysterious woman had captured him mind and spirit. He...he yearned for her. Not that he'd mention this to any of his brothers. They'd laugh.

His gaze fell on a group of blue-skinned women, then he intercepted Saber's glower and got the message. Get busy with the social thing.

The joyfulness of the guests eluded him, but he forced a polite smile. "Hello."

"Good eve," a petite blue-skinned woman said in a surprisingly deep voice. She had short blue horns protruding from her temples. "This is a beautiful resort."

Sly eyed the woman warily, gradually relaxing when he realized she didn't intend to attack his person. It was early in the evening though. "Where are you from?"

Saber and Ma had drilled them in polite conversation, and now the words flowed without a second thought.

"I live on the Tiraq mainland," she said.

"Are you here alone?"

"No, my friends are here with me. Five of us. We wanted to visit the resort before Mica mates with a chief from our neighboring planet, Dalcon."

Sly's ears pricked. Not about the upcoming nuptials, but the fact she lived on Tiraq's main land mass. "My brother and I enjoy working the land. We wish to purchase coos. Someone told me the Scothage people breed coos."

"Barbarians," the woman spat.

"Oh?"

"They live in the Highlands in drafty castles and the clans are always feuding. One steals coos from his neighbor, and the neighbor's neighbor steals them and so on, until the coos are back where they started."

Sly grinned at her obvious distaste. "I'm Sly Mitchell."

"Juanite Farstenan," she replied.

"What else can you tell me about the Scothage race? Do they sell their coos to outsiders?" The horns were kinda cute. He hadn't seen a guest with horns before.

"It's possible. One of my friends may know more than me." She craned her neck and let out a huff of impatience. "I hate having no height. Can you see my entourage?"

Sly scanned the function room and spotted Joe. "Juanite, come and meet my brother. We can search for your friends at the same time." He offered his arm as Ma and Saber had instructed. "On Earth, this is a polite gesture," he explained. "It means I wish to escort you safely across the room to discover your friends."

"I can protect myself." But she placed her hand on his arm, and he maneuvered through the crowded room to where Joe stood with a Tigrus woman. His brother was edging away, a smile frozen on his desperate face.

"Juanite, this is Joe," Sly said when he reached his twin.

Both Juanite and the Tigrus woman scrutinized one twin and then the other.

"We're twins," Sly said, stating the obvious.

"Pretty," the Tigrus woman purred. "I want both."

"No," Sly said.

"No," Joe echoed.

"I will persuade you." The Tigrus woman cocked her head, her purr rumbling in her well-endowed chest.

"Friends only," Sly said before the Tigrus woman could pounce. He noticed Joe had edged away, leaving him closest and in pouncing range.

"Stand down," Juanite ordered.

The Tigrus woman bristled, her striped hair lifting and puffing out and upward in agitation. Her feline eyes narrowed to slits, and Sly was certain her tail was twitching from side to side.

"How about a drink on the house?" Joe said hurriedly.

"What would you like?" Sly asked.

Neither of the women paid them the slightest bit of attention, their gazes locked and loaded with challenge.

Without warning, Juanite opened her maw. Her tongue shot out and slapped the Tigrus woman on the face. The force of the blow sent the Tigrus woman flying.

Sly hurried to help her up. Holy hell. That had been...unexpected. Horns and a weird tongue.

Saber arrived, shot him and Joe a stern glance as if they were at fault, and escorted the weeping Tigrus woman away for a consolation drink.

Five petite blue women, all with horns, appeared and fanned out behind Juanite in a silent show of solidarity.

"Problem?" one barked.

Juanite waved a hand in dismissal. "No. No. Taken care of."

"You should have called, Princess," one of the blue ladies chided.

"I am capable of handling an unruly Tigrus," Juanite said with disdain.

"Princess?" Sly asked. "Most of our royal guests have their security teams with them."

Juanite sniffed. "Where is the fun in that? We were searching for you," she told her group.

The five blue women gaped, navy-blue brows arching in unison. Sly worried about tongue action and took a half step back.

"Why didn't you mind-call?" one asked finally.

"I enjoy the slow way of searching." She tucked her arm in Sly's. "I like Sly's company. He hasn't tried to spank me or to strong-arm me to mate with him."

"I-I..." Sly paused and tried again. "I don't wish to mate with a woman. All I require is friendship." *Apart from his mystery woman.*

The five blue women gaped again, giving Sly another glimpse of their bluish tongues. They appeared innocent enough, despite the whopping Juanite had meted out to the Tigrus woman.

Juanite beamed. "I told you this was the perfect place for us to visit. We get a rest from pushy suitors and a chance to rejuvenate and enjoy spirited conversations. Sly and I were discussing coos."

"Coos?" one asked.

A second blue lady wrinkled her nose. "Nasty creatures. Big horns. Shaggy coats. They do taste exceptional though."

"Do you know where we can buy coos?" Joe asked.

"Yes," Sly said. "We understand we'd have to negotiate with one of the Scothage clans."

"Dangerous people."

"Barbarians."

"But do you think they will sell us coos?" Sly asked. "Even a few would be a start."

"We could make inquiries for you when we reach our home," Juanite offered. "You're welcome to visit and stay at our chateau while you transact your business."

"Thank you," Joe said.

Sly nodded. "Yes, thank you. We need to save our currency first. But if we learned more, the cost and how many the Scothage would sell us to start that would be a help."

"We can do that for you. Give us your com direction and we will secure the information you need. Now, what would you suggest we do tomorrow? We are not interested in captures. We can do that at home," Juanite said.

"The beach is lovely. Ask the kitchen to organize a picnic for you and spend time at the beach. Visit the shops. All the ladies seem to enjoy the clothes and shoes on sale," Sly suggested.

"Shoes?" Juanite asked. "I adore shoes. Do they have ones to make me taller?"

"My brother's mate designs clothes, and her aunt makes shoes. If you have something special in mind, speak to Casey. My sister raves about her clothes," Sly replied.

"Any other suggestions?" one of the blue ladies asked.

"Don't miss the food at the ball. You'll get to try delicious Earth dishes. Or go for a tour of the village and grounds. I do those," Joe said.

Juanite clapped her hands together. "I sensed this was a delightful place to visit."

Sly exchanged an amused glance with his twin. He was learning. Introduce the topic of clothes, shoes or food, and most of the guests grew excited and happy. Joe shared a grin of satisfaction with him. They had a solid lead for their cattle. Progress at last.

In his peripheral vision, he caught a blur. Wary of over-exuberant women, he half-turned.

A cloud of golden dust engulfed him in a swirling wave and a blinding flash of yellow light.

Sly gasped, the shimmering particles filling his nostrils, his throat. He sneezed, peered around blearily, yet he saw nothing except eddies of gold and yellow. Every muscle in his body tensed.

Something walloped him in the chest.

The force of the blow shoved him backward. He tried to countermove and regain his balance. His limbs refused to obey.

A wrenching pain jerked his torso. His skin prickled. He wheezed, struggling to inhale. Not enough air. *Not enough air.*

Breathe. Breathe. Breathe, dammit.

His mind grew fuzzy. He glimpsed faces for a brief second. Joe's. Juanite's.

Couldn't speak. Couldn't breathe. Couldn't move.

He was frozen.

Sly's knees crumpled.

He felt himself falling, falling, falling.

His surroundings faded, growing darker, until they reached a suffocating, endless black.

He struck the ground. Groaned, unsure which way was up or down.

Everything was black and full of nothingness.

Empty.

Was this death?

His throat tight, chest constricted, he finally, finally dragged in a breath. It made a sucking sound. He turned, did two slow blinks.

Why hadn't anyone told him death had blue eyes?

CHAPTER FIVE

S aber kept an eye on Sly, Joe, and the group of blue ladies after he'd escorted the weeping Tigrus woman to his mother. His gut bucked and tightened and jiggled, yet he noted nothing amiss. Not a single threat. Sly and Joe were entertaining the group from the Tiraq mainland. His younger brothers spoke with enthusiasm, waving their hands in illustration.

The blue ladies appeared equally happy, listening intently and offering their contributions to the spirited discussion.

Still, Saber's warning antenna buzzed and buzzed. Like a bee in a tizzy, a premonition circled his mind. He scanned the function room. Not one threat visible.

Strife happened. Not unusual in this mix of races. If he didn't stomp them dead, minor misunderstandings quickly switched to large ones. An example—the situation between the blue lady and the Tigrus woman. He'd learned to spot the signs before small situations turned into outright war.

But no. It was happy-happy, joy-joy. Everyone beamed, even the Tigrus woman, who was now chatting with his cousin Sam Mitchell.

Saber scrutinized the room again. Cheerful guests. Sly and Joe and their blue entourage.

Then a burst of golden light erupted, so bright his eyes shut in self-defense. He blinked to refocus.

Crap! He was darting, running, pushing past stunned bystanders even before his vision cleared to twenty-twenty. He skidded to a stop beside Joe as Sly crumpled.

"What the hell happened?" Saber pushed aside a blue lady and crouched next to Joe.

"I don't know! There was a bright light. By the time my sight cleared, Sly was down. He has a pulse. God, Saber. Tell me I'm not imagining his heartbeat." Stark fear shone from Joe, and the same terror beat and slapped at Saber.

"No, you're right. He's still alive."

Leo and Felix arrived.

Felix inhaled sharply. "Is he—?"

"He's still breathing. Joe, help me get him out of here. Felix. Leo. Offer everyone a drink. Tell Ma to organize a party game."

Sly was a dead weight. His skin radiated a clammy chill that reminded Saber of Earth during a cold July winter in New Zealand. His skin appeared bloodless and pale, his chest lifting grudgingly in tiny increments. He didn't show a sign of regaining consciousness.

And still unease buzzed through Saber, the bee still present, still agitated.

He and Joe hoisted Sly to his feet and pretended to walk him from the function room. In reality, they dragged him, using brute force to get him outside.

"Where do we take him?" Joe asked.

"The infirmary," Saber said. "I'll contact Casey once we get there. Hopefully, she'll know what's wrong with him. Did any of those blue women touch him with their tongues?"

"No. We were talking. None of them wants mates. It was a friendly chat."

"Okay." Saber tamped down his worry. The bright light hadn't dropped anyone else. Just Sly. Had he been unlucky, or was it something else?

They huffed and puffed and manhandled Sly along a short path to a squat stone building. Currently empty. Actually, it was usually vacant.

"Hold Sly's weight while I get the door," Joe said. "I didn't realize he was so heavy."

"We'll tell him he needs a diet once he regains consciousness," Saber joked.

They half-lifted, half-dragged Sly to a narrow bed, both grunting as they dropped him in place.

Saber pulled out his com and messaged Casey. She must've been nearby, because he soon heard the *clomp-clomp* of her boots, signaling her arrival.

"What's wrong with Sly?" she asked, her dark hair ruffled from her race to the infirmary.

"We don't know," Saber said. "He's breathing, but he hasn't regained consciousness. There was a bright light, so bright it hurt my eyes. By the time I focused again, Sly was on the floor."

"That's all I saw, too," Joe said. "He dropped without warning. I didn't have a chance to catch him. Have you seen anything like this before?"

Casey ran her hands over Sly's body, then stalked to a drawer. She pulled out a medi-comp and ran it over him. When it beeped, she frowned at the results. "No known cause. According to the medi-comp, he should be walking around."

A former marine, Casey had vast medical knowledge collected in the field during encounters with other races.

Concern gripped Saber. Sly's skin felt cool when his feline genes usually generated warmth. "What do you think?"

Casey worked her bottom lip between her teeth as she repeated her sweep with the medi-comp. "No one else was hurt?"

"No," Joe said. "I'm fine. So are the women we were speaking to at the time."

"I'm sorry, Saber. I've no idea what's wrong with him. I've never come across anything similar. All we can do is watch him, keep him warm. I'll try my contacts for information."

"I have to return to the mixer and do my welcoming speech," Saber said. "Joe, can you come back with me and speak with the blue ladies? Maybe they saw something that one of us missed."

Joe nodded. "I'll do that."

"I'll stay with Sly," Casey promised, and gave Joe a swift hug.

"Thanks." With a last glance at his brother, Saber guided Joe from the infirmary. Worry bounced inside him like a fidgety child. Joe and Sly were close. He'd need to watch Joe, keep him busy while they worked out what ailed Sly.

CHAPTER SIX

S ly bolted upright, his gaze snapping around the room. Bed. A bedroom. Gray-and-maroon cloth shaded the windows. Pictures... No, tapestries covered stone walls, the silk threads gleaming and giving him an impression of an old-fashioned room in a historic house. And the bed. A four-poster complete with gray-and-maroon curtains, carved posts, and—he blinked—nymphs. Naked nymphs doing naughty things.

He glanced down and lifted the sheet covering his lap.

Naked.

He sniffed and smelled nothing more than a floral note. Probably the vase of deep red flowers by the window. Not roses but something similar.

He searched his memory.

Nope.

This wasn't home.

No woman or indication of a hook-up. No lingering scent of sex. No impression on the pillow beside his.

Yet something was off.

A buzz, a scratching of fingers, directed his attention to the wooden door with metal decoration in the far wall.

"Sir?"

"E—" Sly cleared his throat. "Enter." Despite swallowing, his voice emerged with a croak.

A tall, upright man, dressed in gray trousers and a matching short jacket with maroon trim, opened the door and glided inside, a tray in hand. *Weird clothes.* Formal and prissy.

The scent of food distracted him, and Sly's belly rumbled on cue. Chocolate, if he wasn't mistaken. He sniffed again, catching a waft of the aroma from a silver pot. Yes, chocolate. And the food scents...

The dome over the plate prevented visual clues. He couldn't identify the delicious smell or pull the information from his sluggish brain.

"Breakfast, my lord."

The man's bony fingers pushed a button on the silver tray, and it rose, hovering for an instant before gliding toward Sly.

Sly sucked in an astonished breath when the tray halted in front of him and continued to hover.

"Ah, thank you. Ah..."

"Alfric, my lord." His thick black brows pinched together briefly as he removed the dome cover to reveal eggs, some type of meat, a red substance...vegetable? And a crunchy bread roll.

"Thank you, Alfric, but I'm not a lord. Call me Sly."

"Oh, no," the man said, aghast. "That wouldn't be showing my respect. Will that be all, my lord?"

"Thank you," Sly said, his thoughts racing and not finding answers.

The man dipped his narrow head in acknowledgment, giving

Sly a glimpse of shiny skull before he straightened. "I will return with your clothes. It is an exciting day. A betrothal. Your arrival is a surprise, but we are pleased that Princess Iseabal has found love."

Sly frowned. In the end, he remained silent because nothing resonated with him.

"The princess said she intended to show you the castle this morn. It won't do to keep her waiting. Eat. Eat, my lord."

My lord? That still didn't seem familiar. "Thank you," Sly said again, for lack of something better to say. *Princess. Betrothal. Castle.* He picked up a fork and concentrated on the easy stuff. "This is tasty."

Alfric beamed and bobbed a quick bow before leaving the room. The instant the door closed, Sly dropped his fork, shunted the tray aside, and jumped from the bed. The tray continued to hover in readiness. A handy gadget. He sidestepped it and strode to the window.

Nothing seemed familiar.

How did he get here?

He knew his name—Sly Mitchell.

But that was all...

He scanned the green square below, the graceful wings of stone to his right and left, ending in round towers, which told him the castle...castle? He continued his scrutiny. The castle flowed around a grass square with another courtyard farther away. There was an archway below, and several people rode through on strange, shaggy creatures. Other men and women followed on foot.

Beyond the castle walls, trees in different shades of green covered the steep hillsides. The sun glinted off a body of water. Sly pushed open the window. Fresh air tickled his face. Voices drifted to him. A bird with big, round, blue eyes regarded him from a stone perch. Its upright body and large head reminded him of a statue. Until it blinked.

A sense of familiarity claimed him. He'd seen this bird before, yet everything else seemed foreign.

The door opened behind him.

"My lord." Alfric stood in the doorway, his butler-straight posture spoiled by his gaping jaw. Four men carried a large trunk, and a gaggle of women followed, tittering loudly upon noticing his nudity. "Leave the trunk there," he ordered. "Cease your prattling, women. Place the garment bags on the bed and leave. And if you know what is best for you, you won't gossip about seeing Lord Sly." He strode to a wall, waved his hand, and pulled a robe out of a wardrobe that appeared as if by magic.

Meanwhile, Sly stood frozen until the women's comments registered. His hands darted down to cover his groin.

"You do not wish to anger Princess Iseabal," Alfric snapped, and the discussion abruptly halted. The servants hustled to carry out his bidding and then left. "Your robe, my lord. Were you not hungry?"

"No, I—" The rumbling of his belly belied his response.

"Come, my lord. Sit and break your fast."

Sly followed Alfric's urging and applied himself to eating. The eggs and meat tasted delicious, as if he hadn't eaten for a lengthy period. He sipped his chocolate drink but that tasted bitter, so he set it aside.

"I knew you must be hungry, my lord," Alfric said with approval.

Sly caught a faint hoot before Alfric closed the window.

"Step into the en suite and refresh yourself. Your clothes for today are here." Alfric indicated a maroon suit made of velvet and a frilly cream shirt. I will unpack your trunk while you bathe. "It won't take long." He snapped his fingers and the trunk sprang open. Then Alfric waggled a forefinger at the trunk and the clothes within sprang upright and floated toward the wardrobe. They hovered while Alfric opened it then they sailed inside, settling on hangers and in cubbyholes.

Sly shook away his astonishment and focused on the suit of clothes Alfric had set out for him. He winced. Unsure of his reaction, he rifled through his memories. A blank. His mind felt like the green square—surrounded by walls. He pushed, shoved, and bullied those barriers in his mind, but they remained solid and impenetrable.

Weird. Plain weird.

Everything in him screamed with wrongness, yet he couldn't decide what bothered him.

Wait. Observe. Gather facts.

An unknown voice spoke the words in his mind, a voice of authority and reason. It made sense. Even though it was a stranger speaking, he followed the suggestion.

Once Alfric bustled from the room, he removed the robe and wandered into the en suite. Glossy ruby-red tiles covered the walls, and a white bathtub sat against the far wall. A pale green tube filled a corner, and Sly thought the nozzles in the wall to his right looked like a showering system.

He strolled over to the bath. After trial and error, he learned the water ran on voice control. Finally, he climbed into the fragrant bath water. The heat relaxed tight, sore muscles, and he leaned back in enjoyment. After lingering for a time, he decided to get dressed before Alfric returned.

He dried off in the green tube thingy, its purpose discovered by accident when he was searching for towels. Clothes next. He donned a thin pair of black underwear, then thrust his legs into velvet-like maroon trousers. *Whoa!* While loose when he pulled them on, the fabric quickly tightened against his limbs.

Cursing, he grabbed the waistband, but the trousers continued shrinking until they clung to his hips and legs. Then they stopped. Warily, he removed his hands from his stomach. The waistband drew in until it fit snugly against his belly.

Sly waited, relaxed a fraction. The shrinking process had ceased.

He eyed the cream shirt with trepidation. The garment appeared large. Okay. No shirt scared him. He slipped his arms into the cream sleeves and fastened the wooden buttons down the front. Instantly, the shirt contracted in the same manner as the trousers. Sly jumped, startled by the weird sensation. *Groped by a shirt*. Every muscle in his body constricted. Long moments later, he pushed out a shaky chortle.

Surely he should remember this, yet dressing seemed a new experience.

Did they do things differently at his home? Alfric had indicated he'd just arrived. Maybe that accounted for the weird vibes. But his home—shouldn't he remember?

The bell on his door tinkled. "Sly? Are you awake?"

The door burst open, and a woman with straight black hair and golden skin stood in the entrance. She beamed at him, her blue eyes sparkling with happiness, and practically flew the distance separating them. Sly flung out his arms to catch her, and before he knew it, they were in a lip-lock.

Male. Beautiful woman.

Sly did the natural thing and settled in to enjoy the exchange. Her shapely curves melded against his chest. Her exotic floral fragrance surrounded him. With her long ebony hair, the blue-blue-blue of her eyes, balanced features, and golden skin, she was a looker, a woman who drew a man's attention, yet Sly felt...

He felt nothing.

He drew back, forcing a diplomatic smile while his mind jumped hurdles. How had he arrived here? Shouldn't he remember? The reasons? The journey? Hell, where had he come from?

For a fleeting second, another face—big blue eyes and red hair—flitted through his mind, but the recollection faded into mist when he attempted to grasp the memory.

Another layer to add to the confusing puzzle.

"Sly, I've missed you so much. I'm so glad you're finally here. I can't wait to introduce you to my father. He will love you. I know he will. And I'm sure he will give us approval to wed."

Married? This must be the princess Alfric had mentioned. "Iseabal?"

"Princess Iseabal," she chided. "You must observe the formalities."

"Princess Iseabal," he repeated.

Surely, if they were to marry, he'd call her Iseabal? Everything he learned added more doubt to his mind. While the princess seemed familiar, he didn't recall their first meeting or agreeing to visit the castle. Which was where? Where the hell was he?

He clasped his hands behind his back and pinched the tender skin of one wrist. The nip of pain convinced him. This wasn't a dream. More a nightmare with the questions jamming his thoughts and clogging his brain.

Sly opened his mouth to ask a question—which one, he wasn't certain—then he thought better of revealing his bewilderment. His teeth clacked together.

"Are you almost ready? Don your boots and we'll go to meet Father. If we hurry, we can have breakfast with him."

Not a suggestion. An order.

Sly turned away to pick up the knee-high black boots. They didn't seem like his style. Shrugging aside the strangeness of the boots, he sat on the edge of the bed and thrust his right foot into one of the boots. Like the clothes, it shrank to fit. With his boots in place, he grabbed his maroon jacket. This shrinking business disconcerted him, which told him his home didn't enjoy the same technology.

When he stood, the princess hovered by the open door, practically vibrating with impatience.

"I'm sorry to keep you waiting." Sly offered his arm. He'd gather knowledge, fill in the gaps.

She placed her fingers on his sleeve, and her exotic floral fragrance filled his next breath. *Wrong.* Yet he couldn't explain why that raised his hackles.

"Which way?" he asked.

Princess Iseabal tugged on his arm. "We're going to my father's private salon in the west tower."

"Tell me about your father." Sly's fingers itched to tug at his jacket and high-necked shirt. "Will he approve of me? Wouldn't he want you to wed someone of his choosing?" He surreptitiously yanked his waistband with his free hand. The fabric gave at his touch, yet discomfort pervaded, hence the urge to tug, to jerk, to find something less...colorful to wear.

Sly caught a flash of his reflection in a shiny metal urn and groaned inwardly. He looked like an uptight...popinjay—whatever they were. His mind twisted and prodded at the foreign word. Another mystery to add to the pile.

"No. Well, yes." A bell-like laugh tinkled from the princess.

The tuneful glee relaxed something inside him. Sly's shoulder muscles slackened, every instinct telling him to hoist the charm flag. "Which is it? Yes or no?"

"If Father wished me to meet a man, I would. No question, but he values my opinion. I've told him you're strong and loyal. Handsome too. He wishes to judge for himself, although I don't have any concerns. You'll charm him as easily as you did me when we met at my friend's house."

Sly still didn't recall their first meeting but inclined his head and continued strolling at her side while taking stock of his surroundings.

Luxury. Everywhere, the impression of wealth.

It whispered from the elegant marble columns. The paintings. Tapestries. Statuary in alcoves. Fresh flowers in painted vases.

And servants. They passed several maids, who ducked their heads and dipped polite curtsies. As they neared a large and tall wooden door, two security guards straightened, their eyes stern and watchful, impassive expressions on their golden faces. Both wore swords rather than guns. Strange, but then his entire day resembled a jigsaw with ill-fitting pieces.

"The king is expecting us." Princess Iseabal practically skipped toward them, barely pausing in her determined journey.

"Aye, Princess Iseabal," the larger of the two men said. He jerked a thumb at his partner, and they pushed open the door and stood aside for their entrance.

A thin and drawn gray-haired man sat at a table over the far side of the room. It was another of those floating tables. A ray of sun poured through a window, highlighting the pallor of his golden skin, yet his delight shone sweetly when he spotted his daughter.

"Iseabal, it is lovely to see you this morn. And you've brought a guest."

"Father, this is Sly. Remember, I told you about meeting him. I'm so glad he was able to visit. I so wanted him to meet you."

"Sir." Sly inclined his head in greeting. "Ah, how should I address you?"

"I am king of Seelie. You may call me King Fionnghall."

"Sly, I'm sorry. I should've explained things better. Father, it is my fault. I'm just so pleased Sly is here and forgot my manners." She squeezed against Sly's side, an impish grin on her face.

"Father, have you seen—"

The new arrival—a woman—came to such an abrupt halt, the man following in her wake bumped into her and shoved her two steps farther into the room.

Sly's eyes widened. He glanced from the new arrival to Iseabal and back again. Twins. Both had black hair and glowing golden skin. Both possessed blue eyes. But the newly arrived sister wore her gray gown buttoned to the top, her black locks severely restrained, her expression neutral. A drab imitation of the Princess Iseabal, who sizzled with vitality.

"Here you are," the newly arrived twin said. "I've been searching for you. I wanted to discuss Father's medicine with you. The pills and potions the doctor prescribed aren't helping. Calum thinks we should call a specialist."

"Don't fuss, child," the king said. "I'm fine."

But his hand quivered, and his sallow skin and bony appearance spoke to the contrary. It didn't take a medical person to discern an ailing king. Sly waited and watched, still trying to make sense of his position. A guest at a fancy castle. Friend to a princess. Her hand curled around his fingers. *Close friend.*

"Now that you're here," Iseabal said. "This is Princess Katrina, my sister, and her husband, Lord Calum. This is Sly Mitchell. I met him last time I visited Lady Jessika. We got on so well, I persuaded him to visit." She pressed herself against him again and sent him an intimate smile, one that spoke of more than friendship. No, this smile said lovers and a serious stay-at-your-side future.

The temperature in the room grew chilly. Sly kept his polite expression fixed and watched the various players, unsure if he was imagining undercurrents.

"I'm pleased to meet you." Sly stretched out his hand in greeting. Not exactly the truth, but he wanted to create a satisfactory impression, or at least appear normal. Telling everyone that this was the weirdest fuckin' trip he'd ever had and his memory had taken a turn down AWOL Avenue might raise *beware* flags.

At least this Calum dude wore a similar suit. His matched his wife's attire—stark black and white to her dove gray, and he wore his curly blond hair pulled back in a ponytail. Lord Calum stared down his narrow nose, distaste *drip-drip-dripping* off him.

Sly accepted the hint and dropped his hand. His presence was not welcome.

"Come. Sit. Join me while I break my fast," King Fionnghall suggested. "As long as you don't speak of doctors or medicine, we'll have a fine visit."

"Where is Liam?" Katrina asked, ignoring her father. "He should be here for this discussion."

"Only family should be present," Calum stated coldly.

Ooh, a matched couple. Sly had an urge to shiver theatrically, but again—shoddy manners. Castles had dungeons, didn't they?

"Fine," the king said. "We will summon Liam and have a discussion." He reached for a golden bell sitting on the table to his right and picked it up. It rang weakly, hampered by his lack of strength.

Calum stalked over to the table and seized the bell. He rang it vigorously, and the large wooden door at the entrance to the room sprang open.

"You rang, Majesty?" one of the security men asked.

"Summon Liam," the king ordered.

"This is a family gathering. Why don't I go for a walk and explore the castle grounds? Would that be acceptable?" Sly asked.

Katrina sent him an approving glance.

"Thank you," the king said. "That is very understanding of you."

"Let me guide you in the right direction while we're waiting for my brother," Iseabal said, pouting. "I wanted to show you around the castle."

"You can do that once you're finished with your meeting," Sly said. "I'll wander the grounds."

Iseabal beamed again, her favorable mood restored. She slipped her arm in his and led him from the salon. "This might take a while," she added. "It's just like Katrina and Calum to pull this rubbish and spoil your first day here."

"I don't mind." Sly groped for understanding, for answers. If this was his first day in Seelie, where had he resided before?

Iseabal led him along a wide passage, which opened out to a landing. "Go down these stairs and outside. Turn right and you will come to the gardens. Beyond the gardens is the lake, although

I doubt our talk will take that long. I will send a servant to let you know when we are done."

"That's fine." Sly turned, eager to begin his explorations and to answer some of his questions.

"Aren't you forgetting something?"

Sly turned back to the princess.

"You didn't kiss me goodbye. As soon as I speak to my father, our betrothal will become official."

Sly hesitated, feeling critical stares drilling into his back. Eyes. Watching them. Watching *him*. Judging.

"Sly." Abrupt impatience simmered in that one word.

Sly closed the distance between them, wrapped his arms around Iseabal, and kissed her. He kept the kiss gentle, with his tongue barricaded behind his teeth. Nothing suggestive or sexual, but the exchange appeased Iseabal.

She gave him a quick hug before skipping back to join her family.

The sense of being watched again pushed Sly to motion. He needed to leave the castle to find a quiet place to think.

Outside, workers clipped hedges and deadheaded red flowers, making the gardens a busy place. Too full of people.

"Good morning," Sly said. "Can you point me in the direction of the lake?"

One of the gardeners ceased the *clack, clack, clack* of his clippers and straightened. "Follow this path until you come to a red gate. Go through the gate and follow the yellow path. It will take you through the forest and to the lake."

"Thank you," Sly said.

After five minutes of walking past white-and-red flowers and formal hedges in straight lines, he came to the red gate. It was set in the middle of yet another freshly trimmed hedge. The entire garden screamed formal and fussy. *Not him.*

He opened the gate, the contrast between the gardens and the wilderness bringing a low whistle of astonishment.

An owl flew overhead and landed in a nearby tree. The russet-colored bird regarded him with soulful blue eyes and hooted a mournful cry. A memory stirred, and then dissipated the instant he tugged it.

"Fuck," he muttered. And he repeated the pithy word, because it was familiar and fit the situation. "Fuck."

Wait. How did he know the curse? Yet another mystery.

Sly kicked a stone and ambled along the path. The owl followed with a quiet whoosh of its wings. Leaves rustled as the owl settled on a branch. A stalker bird might freak some people, but Sly didn't think it meant him ill. Heck, it might be something as simple as him stirring bugs as he walked, which the owl hoped to catch.

Sly glanced over his shoulder, and when he saw nothing but trees and the owl, he let his breath ease out. Something about this place, the castle, raised the hair at the back of his neck.

The trees thinned and the path opened to showcase the lake. Soaring mountains thrust upward into puffy white clouds. A stream spilled over a cliff face, creating a waterfall at the far end of the lake.

Sly wandered across the stony lakeshore and took a seat on one of the large rocks edging the water. A rush of air and flutter of wings had him turning his head. The owl.

"You're following me," Sly said.

The russet owl settled on a rock beside him and cocked its large head as if it was listening.

"I don't remember how I came to be here." Sly settled more comfortably and picked up a pebble. He tossed it into the lake. "Iseabal...Princess Iseabal said I arrived yesterday. I don't understand. Did I drive? Did I walk? I should know, right?"

The owl offered a quiet hoot that Sly found comforting.

"The princess seems to think we're close. We kissed, and it was like kissing my sister. I get the feeling the princess thinks we'll marry. This isn't my home. These clothes, the castle... They're not familiar. And you know the weirdest thing?"

The owl screeched and took flight, disappearing into the trees.

"The weirdest thing is that whenever I think too hard and almost remember something relevant, the memory dissolves. Yeah. Something is off, but I don't know what it is."

The crunch of footsteps and loud, wheezing breaths had Sly climbing to his feet.

"The princess is finished and requests your presence," the liveried servant gasped out between pants. His face was almost the color of his scarlet livery.

"All right," Sly said, brushing the dust off his backside. "I'll be along in a few minutes."

"She be waiting now," the young man said with a trace of anxiousness. "She don't like to be kept waiting."

"I'm coming," Sly said, holding back his snap with difficulty. He got that Iseabal was a princess, but he was no lackey to order around.

Tamping down his displeasure, Sly followed the servant back to the castle. The young man hustled, yet his breathing came in exhausted gasps.

"Slow down," Sly said finally. "If you don't slow your pace, you'll collapse."

"You don't understand. The princess hates to be kept waiting, and the last thing anyone wants to do is stir her anger. A fierce thing, it be. Scarier than a thunder of dragons flying overhead. People tremble when she loses her temper. Her magic is strong. Rumors say even stronger than the king's. I have none. No means of defense. Please, we must hurry. I-I need this job."

"All right," Sly said. "You go slower and catch your breath. I'll make sure Princess Iseabal knows I was by the lake, and it took you a while to find me."

"Thank you, Lord Sly. You are kind."

Why did everyone keep addressing him as lord? "Sly," he said firmly. "Call me Sly."

"Oh, no, my lord. I can't do that. You are the princess's betrothed. No, I must show you respect or the princess will chastise me."

Sly frowned. The servant's tone made him suspect the chastisement would run closer to punishment rather than a verbal set-down. "Thank you for explaining. I'm new here and catching up with the rules."

"Yes," the servant said, fervent with his reply. "It's best to learn the rules to stay safe."

Sly lifted a hand in farewell and strode ahead, soon reaching the red gate. He stalked through the gate and through the formal gardens.

He heard the shrieking before he reached the steps leading to the massive carved entranceway to the castle. He hastened his pace and burst past the two burly soldiers on guard duty. They seemed relieved, although they remained silent. It was more the loosening of their tight expressions.

Sly spied Princess Iseabal mid-shriek.

"Where is he? I asked a servant to locate him ten minutes ago. Ten minutes! Where is he?"

"Princess Iseabal." Sly bowed, although the action took him by surprise. He didn't think he'd ever bowed to anyone. No...

Damn, the notion disappeared before he figured out his regular behavior.

"What took you so long?" Her words held sharp edges, but she reduced her volume. Her face—all fiery, red-tinged angles and flashing red eyes—had him approaching with caution. Red eyes?

"I'd walked as far as the lake." Sly blinked. Ah. Imagination. Her eyes were blue now. "I headed straight back once the servant found me. Is your father all right? Did your meeting go well?"

Princess Iseabal's face smoothed out, and her golden beauty shone again. "Yes, he seemed better and ate a meal with us. Are you ready for your tour around the castle?"

"Of course. I'm looking forward to it." Sly took her arm, and she dimpled up at him.

"Father liked you," she said with satisfaction. "He approved of your manner and agrees you'd make me a fine husband. He's issued an order. The banns will be called on the next holy day. Soon, we can set a date for our wedding."

CHAPTER SEVEN

C innabar wept inside, at a loss as to how to prevent this injustice. Dejected, she flew through the evening sky and finally returned to the castle, choosing to perch on a ledge near Sly's chamber. Princess Iseabal would never release Sly. No one would dare gainsay her because of her position, even if anyone guessed the truth.

Too quick to anger. Too unpredictable. Too powerful.

The princess had decided she wanted Sly, and no one else would do. Now, Sly would forget his loved ones, his previous life, and become a broken man. Like...like the Creeper zombie race on the nearby planet of Oucie, referred to most by the colloquial name of Ooze, since the residents tended to seep and trickle into the ground to flee visitors. Cinnabar shuddered, and her feathers rustled.

If she met Sly during her hours in her natural form... But no. She'd never gain access to the royal wing. The security men would stop her. And if the princess spotted her inside the castle in owl form when she'd expressly bid her to remain outside... No, that wouldn't work either.

If only she was brave enough to dispute the banns.

An objection to the marriage would stop the princess, yet no one—least of all Cinnabar—dared refute Princess Iseabal.

As she dithered about her dilemma, the right and wrong, and whether she was willing to forfeit her life to correct this debacle, Sly stirred in his chamber. She cocked her head, a thrill of excitement buzzing to life. If he left the castle during the night...

She shifted her weight and stomped her talon against the stone ledge, her eyes closing as resentment pulsed in her feathered breast. This wasn't fair. None of it was fair.

Although the princess took great care with her private punishments, Cinnabar couldn't be the only unfortunate one—cursed or killed because of a mistake or a slight to the princess.

Mayhap it was time to take a risk. At present, she lived a half-life. One of servitude and fear. If she helped one person—Sly—and made others aware of the princess's behavior and abuse of power, her sacrifice might stop the immoral acts. Death would free her, and it might save Sly.

Cinnabar opened her eyes and straightened from her puffball slouch. Her heart beat strong and sure as her muscles tensed. She could do this. Plan. Set her goals. And *wham bam*! Blow the selfish give-me, *give-me* princess from her protective bubble. Show her family, her people, exactly how she abused her powers—both magical and hierarchical. How she'd trained and practiced each morning until spells and chants came to her with ease, how she'd mastered pulling energy from the ley lines with precision.

Observe. Plan. Act.

Pleased with her decision, Cinnabar listened to Sly pace the confines of his chamber. *Thump. Thump.* Curse. Finally, she heard him huff and leave.

Interesting. Where did he intend to go?

Five long minutes later, he exited the castle and entered the gardens. The two security guards on the door inspected him.

"He's a strange one," McRobber, the junior guard, commented.

"I checked with the princess. She said he had freedom to wander within the kingdom, but he couldn't leave Seelie without her," McGuiness, the senior guard, replied.

McRobber knit his brow and tugged on his right ear. "What if he intends to leave?"

"Och, don't fash." McGuiness watched Sly until he disappeared. "The guards on the main gates will hold him, should he decide to flee."

McRobber tugged his ear again to the point of redness. "Why would he *want* to leave? I understand the first of the banns will be called on the next holy day. The princess is pretty and holds a position of power."

"Shush, lad, 'tis not for us to ponder. All we do is follow the princess's orders." McGuiness stepped back into the warmth of the castle. "I think it is time for a warming drink."

With the guards' retreat, Cinnabar winged after Sly. On the plus side, at least the princess hadn't insisted on sharing Sly's bed. She wasn't brave enough to upset her father when patience achieved the same result.

Sly strode through the formal gardens yet didn't stop. He opened the red gate and continued his determined journey through the darkness. His night vision seemed extraordinary, since he never hesitated or stumbled on rocks or tree roots on the path.

Cinnabar followed him to the lake and settled on a large rock to watch. Strong. Handsome. Not a pushover. But something bothered the man. He mumbled as he paced, periodically stopping to pick up pebbles and toss them into the dark waters of the lake.

After a long time, he ceased stalking up and down the lakeshore and plonked his muscled backside on a rock not far from where Cinnabar perched.

To her surprise, he turned to her and snapped, "Why are you following me?"

She blinked. He'd noticed her presence when everyone else ignored or forgot her after a quick glimpse. She issued a low hoot and eyed him warily, prepared to take off if he lashed out or attacked.

"This place is weird," he said. "I feel as if I don't belong here, but I have no idea of my life before today. I feel as if I came from a cabbage patch and a stork delivered me here."

Cabbage patch? Stork? Gibberish words to Cinnabar, but his mental turmoil emerged clearly. The princess had ripped him from everything he knew, stealing his memories, his family, his world. She stared into his mesmerizing green eyes and wished she possessed the ability to speak. That power might be denied her, but she would find a way to help. Even if it was little more than creating a disturbance at the last reading of the banns. Objecting with every screech she could summon before Princess Iseabal killed her for disobedience.

The time passed, and even Sly's mumbles ceased. Cinnabar wondered if he was asleep, but she heard his sudden intake of breath when a white stag emerged from the trees and walked to the water to drink.

"Beautiful," Sly whispered.

Cinnabar's insides fluttered with the same breathless awe. She'd not seen or heard of a recent white stag sighting. Normally, it was an omen of death. A shiver rippled through her body, setting her feathers on edge. Her belly tingled, and the vibration spread as she watched the stag lift its regal head to observe them. Long seconds passed before the stag trotted away into the trees.

The tickle continued to plague her, and a distressed hoot escaped as the truth swept over her in a magical rush. She'd lost track of time with all that had happened and everything on her mind. An instant later, she toppled from her stony perch onto her well-padded arse. Her white skirts flipped up, covering her face but revealing her lower limbs.

She froze, terror flooding her mind.

The princess had promised—threatened—that if she ever told anyone of the spell, she'd die, and she'd suffer a far worse fate if she informed Sly of the truth.

"Cinnabar?" Sly jerked his head back, his body going rigid.

A thrill rushed through her as she righted her skirts and attempted to stand. He was beside her in seconds, aiding her to rise. He remembered her name. How was this possible?

"Cinnabar. It *is* you!" His warm arms slipped around her waist, and he gave her a quick hug before pushing her back to search her face. "Why didn't you shift before and speak to me?"

Cinnabar blinked, her mouth opening, closing, opening. "I transform at midnight for three hours. The rest of the time, I'm an owl."

He frowned. "You're not a shifter?"

"No."

"Then why do you have two forms?"

Cinnabar hesitated before lifting her chin in decision. She'd leak a few things without confessing the entire truth. "It's a spell."

"Why?"

"A punishment."

His hands tightened on her waist. "Who did this to you?"

"I can't tell you."

"For fear of reprisal?"

Her shoulders hunched, and she hugged herself. Close enough. The truth—Princess Iseabal had included the condition as part of the spell. She couldn't tell anyone *exactly* what had occurred, but it seemed she'd skirted the truth well enough.

"So we have three hours? Do you know how I got here?"

"Yes." She cleared her throat, desperate to survive, to savor this time with Sly. What to do? "I can tell you some things, but not everything."

"You're telling me I need to phrase my questions carefully?"

"Yes."

"Will I stay here forever?"

"Once the banns are read, and you are married." Regret knifed straight through Cinnabar's heart. Her fingers crept to her lips. He'd kissed her when they first met, the memory of it bringing heat to her cheeks. Longing.

"Tell me about Seelie." He brushed a curl from her cheek and smiled down at her, the kindness in his green eyes pushing her pulse to fast and choppy.

"Seelie is a kingdom ruled by King Fionnghall MacAsgain. The queen died many years ago, but they had three offspring. Prince Liam, and the twins Princess Iseabal and Princess Katrina. Princess Iseabal is the oldest twin. Princess Katrina is married to Lord Calum O'Gadhra. Prince Liam is next in line to succeed, followed by Princess Iseabal, but only if she marries. Currently, Princess Katrina is next in line to Prince Liam."

"Ah, which is where I come in as Princess Iseabal's betrothed. Everything's becoming clear. But surely the king would arrange his daughter's marriage?"

"That can be done, but the princess can suggest a candidate. That is the Seelie way. No one will object unless you're clearly unsuitable."

"This explains why Lord Calum treats me like a bug beneath his foot. I present yet another person between him and the king, and by extension, to his power." He stepped away from her, but before she had a chance to miss his touch, he reached for her hand and twined their fingers together. "Let's walk. It helps me think. Will anyone else come to the lake at this time of night?"

"I don't believe so. The security men are more interested in staying warm. To continue with Seelie...the king is ruler of the summer court, and as such rules the season."

"Are there kings for the other seasons?"

"There's a winter king. When the two kings meet, the seasons combine to make spring or autumn, depending on the kingdom in which they meet."

Sly's brows drew together. "I haven't met Prince Liam yet. He's been busy with his duties and didn't dine with us. What is he like?"

"Prince Liam is popular with the people. He is slowly changing things. The kingdom is no longer as isolated, thanks to him. He works hard and is often away from Seelie, brokering deals to sell our wool and cloth. I'm sure you will like him."

"Can I leave Seelie?"

"There are two ways out of Seelie. One is for royal personages, and no one else has the power to open the portal. Security staffs the main entrance, and those with passes may enter or exit. The princess has ordered the security force to detain you should you try to leave, with magic if necessary."

Sly rolled his eyes. "Great. Do you possess magic?"

"Basic skills. Most of the servants and lower classes possess low-level magic we're taught by our parents or employers. Nothing close to the powers of the king, his family, and the courtiers. They're schooled from an early age, and have the time and money to keep up their training."

"I have no magic." Sly scowled. "The magic system seems unfair." He halted, stared across the shimmering waters of the lake. "I don't belong in Seelie, yet the instant I attempt to grasp my stray thoughts, they dissolve. It's frustrating."

The idea of not seeing Sly made her chest ache, but she understood his desire to return to his home. "The princess has likely spelled your food or drink to keep you confused. She won't have spelled all the food, since you ate with the royal family this eve."

Sly's eyes narrowed. "Perhaps the hot chocolate I drank this morning. It tasted weird."

"Ah, that might explain why you're aware there's something wrong. Beware of taking food or drink that isn't eaten by others. Drink your hot chocolate only if the princess is watching. As soon as she leaves, dispose of the drink, and your mind will remain clearer."

"Will my memory return? Of my life before I arrived?"

"I'm not sure." Cinnabar frowned. "I believe that is part of the spell. Your memories will remain locked away until you can break free of Seelie or the princess reverses the spell. Which she won't. She's stubborn."

"I haven't seen much magic occurring."

"You haven't been here long."

Sly nodded. "True. So, magic is another strength or ability to you all. It's a common power, and royals have the greatest magic and therefore supremacy over everyone."

"Yes. That is an excellent summary."

"Can you do magic now?"

"No. The curse that transforms me into an owl has blunted my magical ability. I can do nothing to break the spell placed on me."

"That makes us equal," Sly said. "I'm at a disadvantage too. What type of wool do you produce in Seelie?"

"We call the creatures kashmore. They are about this high." She held up her hand at mid-thigh height. "They have horns and grow a fleece that is shorn. The male of the species is smelly and can be mean. It takes a skilled farmer to deal with them."

"Ah, this animal seems familiar to me, although I don't recall their name. I haven't seen any animals. Where are they kept?"

"The queen refused to have them near the castle. Most of the animals are kept, and the weaving is done on the other side of Seelie. Most of the population lives in the village there too."

"I'd like to see these animals. Do I have a family?"

"Yes." Cinnabar froze, eyes wide as she waited for an invisible axe to fall. When nothing happened, she breathed again.

"You're trembling." Sly tugged her closer. He wrapped his arms around her and held her, the silent comfort bringing tears to her eyes.

The last person to hug her had been Sly. Before that...she had to dig deep in her memories. Her mother used to hug her before she died. Her father, a distant cousin to the king, had spoken kindly but never demonstrated his love. He'd died not long after her mother.

"It's all right. Nothing happened." Sly drew back and smoothed his hand over her hair. "Perhaps the princess rules by fear."

"Not just fear. I have witnessed demonstrations of her anger. When my father first brought me to court, she turned a servant into a bug, then crushed her underfoot."

Sly gawped until Cinnabar tapped his chin. His teeth clacked together as he straightened, his expression dumbstruck.

Shock. Cinnabar recognized the emotion well. She'd spent her first year at court with terror holding her in its clawed grip. Yet she'd learned to hide her reactions and consider her words carefully before she spoke. Unfortunately, she hadn't learned to control the clumsiness that came with nerves and that had been her downfall.

"Doesn't anyone check the princess?"

"Her mother used to keep a close eye on her, and her father often lectured her on kindness and respect. Everything changed after the queen died, and now the king rarely appears in public. Princess Iseabal is older now. More careful and controlled."

"She sounds like a keg of dynamite about to blow," Sly said.

"I know not what this dynamite is, but I take your meaning. The princess has little restraint when her temper rises."

Sly wrinkled his nose. "Now that you mention it, I have no idea what dynamite is either." Irritation flared in his eyes, yet he didn't scare her like the princess did with her tantrums.

She pressed against him, offering silent comfort until a groan rumbled through his chest. Surprised, she glanced up—and what she saw had her breath catching. The displeasure had shifted, leaving plain heat.

Instinct had her tongue darting out to moisten her lips, and he groaned again, seconds before he swooped.

His lips captured hers, and Cinnabar's body hummed under the raw male desire she'd unleashed with her innocent attempts to console. She opened to him, and he took instant advantage, sliding his tongue against hers and deepening the contact. The eager pressure of his mouth shoved pleasure through her body. Her heart thundered, and she shuddered, soaking in every bit of the wonderful physical contact. He was touching her willingly, his groan telling her he was enjoying the sensual exchange as much as her.

Her breasts prickled against the plain syncotton chemise beneath her gown. Heat curled to the secret place between her thighs, growing, growing, growing until she whimpered and attempted to push closer to Sly.

The kiss inflamed. It consumed.

Cinnabar had experienced nothing like it before and greedily wanted more. As if she'd stated her desire aloud, Sly moved his hands. One slid down her back to cup her backside while the other slipped between them to cup a breast. The twists of sensation grew sharper, her cries needier, and when his fingers teased her nipple, the ferocious heat became too much to bear.

"Please," she begged, not knowing what she pleaded for, just that Sly must fix this white-hot conflagration burning her body.

"Shush, sweetheart." He lifted his head and scanned their surroundings. Seemingly satisfied with his perusal of the scenery, he drew her into the shadows thrown by a pile of boulders. "Let me make you feel better."

He paused, seeming to want something from her. "Cinnabar?"

"Oh." Permission. He wanted permission. "Yes."

She might not be a stranger to the act of sex, since she'd witnessed the princess take lovers and had acted as watchman—or owl—but she had never understood the attraction or wanted to participate.

Sly leaned against a boulder, drawing them even deeper into the shadows. He pulled her against him, his chest to her back, and nuzzled her neck while one hand dipped beneath the neckline of her white gown. Fingers to flesh.

Everything inside her melted and her pussy bloomed with heat and moisture. Her nostrils flared, every sense working overtime to catalog sensations. He tugged sharply on her nipple and heat flowed like molten honeycomb from her breast to her sex.

"Let me touch you," he whispered against her neck.

"Yes." A million times yes.

With his free hand, he lifted her skirts to bare her to the air.

"No panties," he murmured.

He sounded approving, so she didn't answer.

A moan of satisfaction, of frustration and excitement, echoed on the air, the hoarse sound escaping from her throat.

"No pubic hair either," he said as his fingers smoothed over her mons. "Part your legs for me, sweetheart."

She widened her stance, her heart thumping against her breastbone as she waited.

Without haste, he traced the seam of her folds, his thick finger stirring a deeper pleasure. She trembled in his arms.

"Don't stop," she pleaded. "Please."

"You do please me, Cinnabar. I searched for you."

He was remembering things. She was so pleased for him. While she had no means of escape from her curse, maybe he did. Cinnabar bit her lip, not wanting to interrupt since it seemed when he relaxed, so did the hold on his mind.

His finger curled and pushed into her opening. She gasped

at the new sensation, the sounds, and the smell of him as he drove her body, her senses. She felt the uneven thumping of his heart, the purring sounds of approval coming from him as he stroked her, teased her, drove her higher. He massaged, finding the perfect spot inside and out. His teeth at her neck became sharper, almost painful as they scraped her flesh. All the feelings, all the sensations combined and writhed together, stirring passion and breathlessness. And pleasure. So much pleasure, she ached with it.

He thrust his finger deeper, and her skin heated all over. She trembled deep inside, the pleasure knife-edge sharp. Awe-inspiring.

She wanted to tell him to stop. She wanted to tell him to continue.

A whimper she couldn't contain rang out, her hips gyrating, the walls of her sex pulsating. She moaned, and he slid his sharp teeth over her neck. He nibbled, then slid his tongue over the spot and danced his fingers over her aching flesh. Up, up, up she went, until one more stroke snapped the tension. She exploded, her channel clasping his finger, the enjoyment stretching for long seconds until she hung boneless in his arms, her breathing rapid.

"You are so beautiful," he whispered.

He removed his hand and let her skirts fall back into place. A croak of protest burst free, but before she spoke, he turned her in his arms and kissed her with a desperation that eased her vocal complaints.

When he finally lifted his head, he was breathing hoarsely, and his man part—his shaft—pushed against her hip. She reached for him, knowing enough from watching the princess's encounters about what to do to ease him, but he stopped her.

"No," he said. "This time was for you."

Before she replied, the familiar prickles of the curse had her yanking from his touch and stepping away. "Thank you, Sly. That...you...mean so much to me."

Scarcely had the echo of her words ceased when the curse dug in its claws, transforming her into a bird. She took one final glimpse of Sly and flew away over the forest.

Chapter Eight

The Next Morning

A *ring-a-ling*, followed by a scratch at the door, dragged Sly from a heavy sleep. Groaning, he pushed upright and focused blearily, blinking twice before his vision cleared. "Yes?"

Alfric entered, carrying a tray bearing a white mug and a jug of hot chocolate. His thick black brows resembled a caterpillar as they squeezed together, a stark contrast with his sparse gray hair. "Your morning beverage, my lord."

"Thank you, Alfric." Sly forced his attention from the fluffy brows, yawned, and tensed as Cinnabar's warning stabbed his sluggish thoughts. "Just set it there, and I'll drink it in a moment."

"Should I prepare your garments for today? The princess indicated she would meet you in the royal salon once she completes her magic study."

"Yes, please." Sly figured the man would have a better idea of what he should wear. "Will the rest of the family be present?"

"Yes, my lord." Alfric strutted across the chamber and opened the wardrobe. It was filled with a variety of colorful clothes. Bold reds and greens and yellows and blues. Alfric's fingers ran across the different items of apparel. Finally, he pulled out an emerald-green suit, of a style like the one Sly had worn yesterday.

Sly grimaced. At least he'd blend with the plants in the garden when he went exploring.

"Do you require help dressing?"

"No, thank you. You get on with your chores, Alfric. I am quite capable of dressing myself. When should I arrive in the royal salon?"

"As soon as you are dressed, my lord."

Nodding, Sly climbed from bed and stretched.

Alfric's eyes bulged, his brows arching to give the caterpillar a curl. "My lord! Where is your nightshirt?"

A prude. This servant, or whatever his job description, was a prude. "Sorry," Sly said, and reached for the robe Alfric hurriedly plucked from his wardrobe. He thrust his arms into the sleeves and belted the garment around his waist.

He walked over to the hovering tray and poured steaming hot chocolate into the pristine white mug. When he noticed Alfric watching him, he paused. "Was there something else?"

"Ah, no."

Sly narrowed his eyes even as he fought to keep his expression pleasantly neutral. Again, Cinnabar's words flooded his mind. *Take care with what you eat.*

Sly picked up his mug and lifted it to his mouth, but didn't take a sip.

Was that relief? Yes, Alfric knew something. He might as well have a banner floating above his head. That was the face of a guilty man, which made Sly wonder exactly what other duties the princess ordered Alfric to undertake.

Sly set his mug back down on the tray without taking a sip. "Perhaps I'll shower first."

When Alfric pulled a face in protest, Sly unbelted his robe and let it drop to the floor. He hid a smirk as Alfric took one horrified glance and backed away.

"You are correct," Alfric said. "I have tasks to complete."

Once Alfric left, Sly picked up his mug and took a pretend sip. If the princess had Alfric spying on him, she might have other methods of keeping watch. He wandered into his en suite. Darkness greeted him. He was about to order lights on when inspiration hit. He let rip with a curse. "Fuck! That was my toe." He tipped his mug and let the contents pour onto the floor.

"I do not recognize that command," a feminine voice said.

Sly grinned. "Lights on."

Instantly, illumination showed him the puddle of hot chocolate.

He stepped closer to the red-tiled wall and the part he thought was a shower. "Water on."

Freezing water bombarded his chest. "Crap! Warm water. Warm water!" he ordered. At least the hot chocolate problem was taken care of. He scanned for soap, but saw nothing obvious. "Soap."

The texture of the water pouring over his head and body changed and bubbled as it hit his skin. Wow, if it weren't for the aching gap in his memories, he'd enjoy this experience. As he washed his hair, he pondered the best way to arm himself with information. Not Princess Iseabal. That's for sure. He'd gained the impression of a self-centered woman who used others to get what she wanted, and he didn't think he'd spent much time with her before yesterday.

He thought back to the last thing he remembered. Waking in this room. But prior to that? An ache speared his temples, a jagged pain that told him whatever the princess had done to him came with vicious side effects. She didn't intend him to resume his regular life.

"Rinse," he ordered. "Warm rinse."

Cinnabar flitted into his mind. Cursed to remain an owl. What kind of life was that for such a beautiful and kind woman? He liked her. A lot. A satisfied grin formed as another memory surfaced. Cinnabar in his arms.

He did not want the princess, despite her beauty and prestige.

It was the mussed Cinnabar he craved, with her stained white gown and bare feet.

Aware of time passing, Sly commanded to halt the water and entered the drying tube. He dressed in the hideous green suit, although the looking glass told him it matched his eyes. Scarlett would say they popped.

He stilled. Turned over the name in his mind.

Nope. Nothing. Who the fuck was Scarlett?

Irritation and impatience simmered through Princess Iseabal as she waited for Sly Mitchell to arrive. She shouldn't have rushed her abduction, but those blue ladies had attracted his attention. She'd needed to act immediately. She peered at the doorway. Although tempted to summon Sly with magic or to send a servant, she bided her time and confined herself to crumpling a piece of bread.

"Not hungry, child?" her father asked.

"I ate a roll and fruit earlier in my chamber," she said. "You seem better today, Father."

"My head has ceased aching. Where is that young man of yours?" His haggard expression dug deeper into his lined face as if he suspected a problem.

"I'm sure he'll be here soon." Iseabal strove for calm. It wouldn't do for Calum or Katrina to witness her agitation.

"I'm beginning to think this man of yours is a mirage," Liam said.

She bared her teeth at him and forced herself not to check the entrance to the royal salon again. Sly had better arrive soon, or she'd have words with Alfric. And perhaps a love potion to boost her spell. Something to back up the drug in his morning drink.

Just when her anxiety was about to force her from her seat, Sly appeared with a servant. He said something in a low voice and grinned. Every ounce of tension vibrating inside her dispersed. Ah, his smile. It lit her day, made her think of triumph.

Sly sauntered toward their family group and bowed his head to her father. "Good morning, King Fionnghall." He turned to her. "Princess Iseabal."

"I was about to send out a search party for you."

He rolled his eyes. "I'm still learning my way around the castle. A search party would've proved helpful. Somehow, I ended up in the kitchen, and one of the girls volunteered to show me the way here. I think I've memorized the route and shouldn't suffer further problems."

"Really," Calum muttered in an aside to Katrina. "I don't know where your sister found this bumpkin but she should send him back."

Fury had Iseabal curling her hands into fists, although she ensured they remained hidden beneath the tablecloth. Sly Mitchell would make a perfect husband. He was handsome. He was strong. And most important of all, she controlled him. The last thing she needed was a bossy husband with aspirations to become the next ruler.

"Sly, this is my brother, Prince Liam."

Sly smiled in a pleased-to-meet-you way and held out his right hand.

Oh, no. Iseabal's breath caught in alarm. She should have explained more about the protocol at the castle. No contact unless invited first. Her cheeks heated as she caught bits and pieces of

SHELLEY MUNRO

Calum and Katrina's whispering.

Liam rose from his chair, and panic unfurled in Iseabal. Liam could injure Sly with a blink of his eye, his power on par with her own—if he practiced more.

But her brother shocked her. He grinned and clasped his hand with Sly's.

Iseabal puffed out her relief—and almost laughed aloud at the abrupt break in Calum's jeering whispers.

"I'm pleased to meet you," Sly said. "I understand you've been away from Seelie to trade wool."

"Yes. A necessary chore, but one I enjoy," Liam said. "Come and sit by me."

"I'd love to hear more about your wool. I understand it makes beautiful garments," Sly said.

"Who told you that?" Iseabal demanded.

Silence fell, and she became the center of attention. *Shoodlepoppers.* Too pushy. Too strident. She'd give away her game plan if she wasn't careful, but she must regulate Sly's activities. She must control him at this stage.

"I noticed the servants have beautiful fabric in their garments. When Judith guided me to the salon, she told me about Seelie's main export. She and the other servants are very proud of Seelie's success. Your wool brings in money, which makes everyone's lives better."

She'd overreacted and drawn attention.

Stupid. Stupid. *Stupid.*

If she didn't ease off, her plan *would* fail.

"I'd enjoy learning more of your farming methods," Sly said.

Curiosity glowed in Liam. "Are you interested in farming?"

The instant the question registered, Sly frowned, and Iseabal's stomach churned with foreboding. She'd never had this problem before. Sly was strong, his mind, his will. *A challenge.*

"Yes." Sly blinked rapidly. "I like to learn about different practices."

"You can come with me after we've broken our fast," Liam said, and approval shimmered in his invitation.

Iseabal popped a piece of roll in her mouth and chewed. This might not be a disaster after all. Liam's opinion held sway with the castle residents. If he approved of Sly, then the people would accept her marriage.

Yes, this might aid her plan. Soon she'd marry Sly, and her power base would grow, and in the meantime, she'd do everything within her scope to ensure Sly's history remained deeply hidden.

Soon, his past would begin and end at this castle.

Castle Seelie.

CHAPTER NINE

MIDDLEMARCH RESORT

J oe Mitchell completed his chores before returning to the room he shared with his brother.

Normally, they fought over who took the first shower. Normally, they whined about having to don dressy clothes and attend the resort functions. Normally, they bitched about the lack of funds allocated to their farming enterprise.

This wasn't normal.

Sly lay on his bed, asleep and unmoving. He'd been unconscious for days and seemed paler than he had this morning, but that was the only change.

Joe removed his muddy boots and padded to Sly's bedroom. Low voices told him his mother and at least one of his older brothers were with Sly. Ah, Saber.

"Hi," Joe said. "How is Sly?"

Worry shaded Ma's blue eyes. "No change. He's breathing normally. He isn't losing weight, so Casey doesn't think injecting him with nutrients is necessary. But he's so cold."

"Has Casey discovered anything from her medical friends? Has anyone else gone through the same thing?" Saber asked.

"No," Ma said. "I...we don't know what to do next."

Joe approached the bed to stand by his older brother. Sly appeared asleep, his naked chest rising and falling with each breath. Yet he wasn't rousing from his slumber.

"I got a pin," Joe said. "I jabbed it into his big toe, and he didn't react."

"Joe," his mother snapped in horror.

Saber laughed. "I have to admit. That is something I might have done myself. Good to know. We'd better tell the others in case Felix, Leo, or Scarlett come up with the same idea."

Joe gripped his brother's shoulder and lightly squeezed. His skin was icy, but it warmed at his touch. "Ma, Saber. Touch Sly and tell me what you feel."

Both his brother and mother did as he suggested.

"The instant someone touches him, his skin warms," Saber said.

"Yes." An idea formed in Joe's mind. Audacious. Unusual. But it might be the way forward—for him *and* for Sly.

Of course, Sly would probably kill him once he regained consciousness.

He trailed his fingers over his brother's chilled cheek. The skin grew warmer, and there was a distinct difference in color between one side of his face and the other he'd just touched. "Sly's pale, but when I touch him, healthy color returns to his skin."

Saber cocked his head. "What are you saying?"

"We should run further experiments, but I think physical contact is keeping Sly alive, keeping his blood flowing. If this continues...we could use his situation to make additional currency." Joe bit back a nervous laugh. God, Sly *would* kill him once he'd regained consciousness. "Tout Sly as a Sleeping Beauty and charge the resort guests for the chance to awaken him. Publicize the old fairy tale. Do a special reading or something. Charge them to kiss Sly. It might at least help his blood circulation. It's not as if he'd want his family caressing him all day." He slid his hand down Sly's arm while he waited for Saber's reaction.

"We do always require additional funds," Saber mused.

"No," Joe blurted. "Sly and I need to increase our farming operation. If we decide to do this, *he* should receive the funds."

Saber started to argue, but Ma spoke first. "Saber, that is fair if we decide to go forward with Joe's suggestion."

"Sly won't like the idea," Saber said.

"He'll hate it, but we need to try something. Everything else has failed." Tears glinted in Ma's eyes. "It's a matter of keeping Sly alive while we seek a cure."

"I agree, otherwise I wouldn't have suggested it," Joe said.

"I can't believe I'm considering this wacky idea, but I'll speak to Casey," Saber said. "If she thinks physical contact will help Sly, we'll proceed."

CHAPTER TEN

CASTLE SEELIE

S ly ate sparingly, eating and drinking only the items Prince Liam devoured. He wasn't the man he'd pictured after meeting the rest of Iseabal's family. Oh, his clothes were of superior quality, but his black hair was unkempt and needed a cut. His face was carved along harsh lines, and his golden skin held a bronzer hue, perhaps because he spent time outdoors. This was a man who listened before he acted, a man he'd instinctively offer friendship.

After they finished their meal, Sly turned to the prince before Princess Iseabal made demands on his time. Even though she seemed pleasant at the moment, Cinnabar's warnings rang in his mind.

"Are you busy today?" Sly asked Prince Liam. "I'd enjoy seeing your farming region."

"Oh, but I thought to introduce Sly to my friends," Princess

Iseabal protested.

"I'm only out for the morn," Prince Liam said. "I'd enjoy the company. Issy, don't pout. I'll have Sly back in time for the midday meal. You can spend time with your friends this afternoon."

"Very well." Princess Iseabal smiled, but her chin lifted and her eyes glinted red for an instant.

Sly blinked. No, he'd imagined the red thing. Her eyes were the same cornflower blue. He stiffened. Cornflower. Now that he thought about it, he didn't know what this flower was or the source of the memory.

Princess Iseabal touched his arm. "Something wrong, Sly?"

"Clothes," Sly said, seizing the first excuse that came to mind. He glanced at Prince Liam's austere black. "Iseabal, I require something else to wear."

"Princess Iseabal," she snapped. "Your clothes are fine. All my male friends dress this way. Do you want everyone to poke fun at you?"

"Like they do Prince Liam," Lord Calum said with a trace of smugness.

"No one wishes to dress like Liam," Princess Katrina agreed with a wry shake of her head.

"Peasant," Lord Calum snapped.

Prince Liam's eyes flashed a red warning. "Who are you calling a peasant?"

Yep. That red eye thing wasn't his imagination. Red eyes equaled temper. Something to file away and remember.

"Enough," the king said without warning. He'd remained silent throughout much of the meal, and now he struggled to rise.

Sly shot to his feet. "Let me offer my arm, King Fionnghall." He extended it to aid the king's tottering balance.

"Thank ye, lad," the king said.

The prince and princesses gaped at Sly. Lord Calum's eyes did that freaky red thing.

"I'll come with you," Prince Liam said, standing.

He hurried to his father's other side, and together they directed the king from the salon, letting him walk on his own but offering balance and strength to keep him upright.

"I have clothes you can borrow when you go out with Liam," the king said.

"Thank you, Your Majesty, but perhaps I'll wear the clothes I have on now. I don't wish to upset Princess Iseabal."

"Wise man," the king said, showing unusual spirit. "But I'll give you the clothes anyway. I'll send them to your chamber with my valet."

"Thank you."

"Father, do you wish to return to bed?"

"Bah," the king said.

His tetchiness reminded Sly of his grandmother. Her flashing green eyes and... The thought faded, leaving frustration in his wake. "How about we pull a chair over to the sunny spot by the windows? You can enjoy the garden and watch your subjects from there."

The king's gaunt face filled with eagerness. "Yes. Yes. Do that. I tire of my four walls."

"Which chair is your favorite?" Sly asked.

Mischief chased across the king's face. "The faded blue one behind the screen over there. Its shabbiness offends my valet."

"I'll get it for you." Sly waited while Prince Liam took the king's weight, then hastened to retrieve the chair. With the chair situated to the king's satisfaction and a blanket over his lap, Sly and Liam left the castle via a back entrance.

"I'm still learning my way around," Sly said. "I didn't realize this entrance was here."

"It's coded only for the royal family." Liam pressed his hand to a panel Sly hadn't noticed, and the door slid open to reveal a large courtyard.

A burly man held two shaggy beasts with stocky barrel bodies, both saddled. An unkempt hump, much like a camel's, protruded in front of their decorative leather saddles. Their heads were long and narrow, reminding him of a... His mind went blank when he tried to source the information, but he continued to study the animals with interest. Their long shaggy ears were rounded at the tips, and they possessed stubby tails.

"Do you ride?" Prince Liam asked.

Sly frowned. "I think so."

"We'll soon find out. Take the one on the right. She is younger and hasn't bonded with any rider yet."

The prince took the reins of one of the creatures. The burly groom held the beast and waited for Sly. Now that they were closer, Sly heard the throaty rumbles coming from the prince's mount. This should be interesting. Some animals didn't like him—something about his dual nature...

As usual, the memory disappeared when he attempted to follow it, and frustration slammed into Sly's head with a fiery spear of pain. He winced and focused on the present.

"What do you call these creatures?"

"Cambeests," Prince Liam said. "They are common on the planet Viros. Other planets in that sector, too, although these days we breed our own stock."

Sly sprang onto the saddle and placed his feet in the stirrups. Surprise glinted in the groom's eyes as he looped the reins over the creature's head and handed control to Sly.

Prince Liam pressed his legs around his cambeest, and it danced in place, surprisingly graceful on its three broad toes, before moving forward.

The animal quivered with restless energy beneath Sly. He copied Prince Liam, and his mount shot straight forward, bucking and twisting as it attempted to unseat him. Instinct took over, and Sly gripped with his knees and thighs, letting his body move with the cambeest instead of against.

Prince Liam grinned from his mount. The groom sported a broad smirk, his beefy arms folded across his chest as he watched the show.

He'd been set up. Too busy for anger, Sly spoke quietly to the cambeest and urged it forward. Gradually, the hijinks ceased, and the frenetic pace slowed to a steady trot.

"Decent job, my lord," the groom called.

"A test?" Sly asked drily when he rode abreast with the prince.

"One you passed with flying colors. Brigitte doesn't enjoy leaving the stable this early. Watch her when you dismount. She'll try to nip your arse. Cambeests aren't known for their sweet disposition."

"Thank you for the warning."

The prince grinned, a wide, friendly beam that told Sly he might have made a friend. "Ready to ride?"

"Bring it," Sly said.

"Where are you from? I haven't heard that expression before."

"I come from..." Damn, it had been on the tip of his tongue. "My memory has been faulty recently," Sly said, unable to watch the man's face as he confessed this weakness.

"No mind," Prince Liam said. "You are here now. You showed compassion with my father, and I thank you for that."

"No thanks necessary. He reminds me of my grandmother. Feisty, despite his apparent weakness."

"I thought to give him some entertainment. You were in a spot visible to him."

"I knew there must be a valid reason," Sly said wryly. "I'll be prepared next time."

"You ride like a natural."

An owl flew in front of them and settled in the sturdy lower branches of an emerald-green tree. Prince Liam's cambeest took exception and shied, almost unseating the prince.

"Turnaround is a bitch," Sly said cheerfully once Prince Liam regained control of his mount. He grinned at the owl, which hooted twice in a weird squawk of amusement.

Prince Liam chortled. "You speak weird words. I like them."

They rode to the far south of the island, not far from the departure gate for Seelie, passing the lake, albeit a different part from where he had met Cinnabar. Once they exited the trees, green fields dotted with white animals filled the horizon.

"Our herds," the prince said. "My father owns this land and the animals, but there are a dozen other large landholders to the west and the north who own larger herds."

"And to the east?"

"The mountainous region. It's not suitable for farming. A waste, really, but Father says we must retain the wilderness area to remain in harmony with nature. The families of high standing wish to use magic to change the topography of this land."

"And what do you think?"

"I agree with my father. He allowed development in the southern region, and the land hasn't done as well. The seasons in the south are extreme, despite the combined magic of one of our most powerful families. Calum's family," the prince added.

"It doesn't pay to fool with nature," Sly said. "To me, it makes better sense to work with the natural climate and the land."

"I agree."

"What are we doing today?" Sly asked.

"I need to sort through this season's offspring and decide which ones to keep. My head shepherd can do the work, but I enjoy keeping busy."

"I understand. I dislike sitting around with cups of hot chocolate."

"I wouldn't tell my sister that." Prince Liam chuckled. "Treading dangerous territory. Be wary of my sister's temper. She has a nasty one, and she isn't happy about you coming with me this morn."

"I'm aware, which is why I thought to take her a small gift on my return. I hoped you would help me choose something suitable."

Prince Liam's face held approval. "You are a smart man. We're almost there. What say you to a race?"

"Bring it," Sly said, even as he silently urged his mount to greater speed with a shift of his body weight and a squeeze of his thighs around the shaggy flanks. He shot forward with a loud, "Hey-ho!"

They raced neck and neck, their mounts appearing to enjoy the furious race to their destination.

"This way," Prince Liam shouted and veered to the right.

The small outcropping of buildings and ramshackle yards wasn't what Sly was expecting, but he didn't judge. They slowed as they entered the yards, and several men appeared from a hut. They blinked upon seeing Sly's bright green magnificence.

"You're early, Prince Liam," a tall, slender man dressed in black said.

The prince dismounted, and Sly did likewise. He handed over his reins and noticed the owl had followed. She appeared unhappy today, her feathers ruffled and her small body hunched as she huddled on the gutter of the nearest building.

"What do we do first?" Sly asked.

"Introductions," the prince said. He pointed at each man and told Sly their names and their main duties.

"Pleased to meet you," Sly murmured, aware he stood out like a bright bird amongst a flock of sparrows. Maybe he should've changed before he came, but he'd hesitated to anger Princess Iseabal further. Cinnabar had warned him, and now the prince. He needed to tread warily until his memory returned. More details popped into his thoughts all the time. If that kept occurring, he had hope. Then, he'd know what to do next.

"We capture each kashmore and run the scanner over it to determine its pedigree and health. We also do a manual scan and decide if the animal will join the pedigree herd or if we'll on sell."

Sly nodded.

"One more thing," the prince said.

Prince Liam's wide grin sent warning signals through Sly. He backed up, but the prince was too fast for him. He scooped up a handful of mud from the nearest puddle and flung it at Sly. It splattered onto the middle of his chest.

Sly reacted on instinct. He grabbed his own mud and chucked it at the prince, taking the man by surprise.

The laughter of the men cut off without warning, and each backed away as if expecting danger.

Given their reaction, Sly froze, watchful.

Prince Liam barked out a laugh and threw two missiles of mud in quick succession. One hit Sly, but the other missed and struck a worker.

"This is war," Sly cried, pelting the prince and one of the workers who wore authority like a cloak. "A hit!"

The worker eyed his trousers, already covered with dirt, and the big splatter on his pale gray shirt. His features firmed in decision, and warily, Sly backed up. The man stooped to pick up mud, and Sly stood close enough to witness the evil glint in his eyes.

Soon mud flew in all directions, thumping against his chest. Striking his face. Pummeling his head. Wet and cold, it soaked his emerald-green suit. It dripped over his hair and down his neck.

"What are you doing?" The horrified voice of a new arrival shouted over the yells and laughter. "The prince will arrive soon. What will he think?"

Chuckling as he wiped mud from his face, the prince appeared from behind Sly. "Ah, Flint. You're here. We were wasting time while we awaited your arrival. Are you ready now?"

Sly bit back a belly laugh. "Look at his expression."

"That was fun," Prince Liam said. "But Flint is correct. We must start our task if we intend to finish it before noon."

The men set to work, manhandling each animal for Flint and the prince to scrutinize and scan. Hard and sweaty work, and Sly enjoyed every moment.

Hours later, dirty and fatigued, Prince Liam and Sly rode toward the castle.

"I didn't realize it was so late," Sly said. "I was meant to be back at the castle to spend time with Princess Iseabal."

Prince Liam shrugged. "Issy will get over it."

"Where have you been?" Iseabal screeched. Overreacting. She knew it, but stopping proved difficult. She planted her hands on her hips, thankful her friends had left without meeting Sly. She'd heard their furtive whispers. Their sniggers behind their hands. Her so-called friends had pitied her, thought she was lying about her impending marriage.

"I've been helping Prince Liam," Sly said.

"That was this morn. You said you'd return to meet my friends."

"Ease off, Issy," Prince Liam said. "We truly have been working all day."

"After you had a drink at the pub," she said snidely, her breasts heaving as her temper rose again. He'd left her to make explanations, made her look stupid. She stamped her foot, straining to hold the worse of her ire. "You had time to have drinks."

"You're right," Sly said. "I'm sorry. I hate to renege on my promises, so I'll try to do better next time. Forgive me?" He slid off his mount and handed the reins to a waiting stable boy before whipping a small package from his jacket pocket. "A gift."

"Yes, well," Iseabal said. No one apologized for their behavior at Seelie. They just did what they wanted. "We've been invited to a party tomorrow eve. I'll have the tailor send you a suit."

"Thank you," Sly said. "I'll enjoy meeting your friends."

Lie. She didn't know how she knew but didn't blame him. Her

so-called friends had shown their true colors today. An appalling mistake, and one they'd regret.

Sly and Liam strode toward where she stood on the steps. A noxious smell wafted from them, becoming stronger as they approached.

Iseabal accepted the parcel from Sly and backed away. "What exactly have you been doing?"

"We told you," Liam said. "Checking the kashmore and deciding which to keep for breeding stock."

She pinched her nose between her finger and thumb. "You've been rolling around in the mud."

"Farming is a muddy business," Sly said, winking at Liam.

Iseabal stiffened. They weren't telling the truth again. She'd ask questions, expand her spy network. Ah, even easier, she'd already ordered Cinnabar to keep an eye on Sly and leave a note for her this eve. That would suffice.

"You need to bathe," she snapped, backing away when Liam approached her. "No! Don't touch me." Her temper rose, and with it her magic, always more unstable when her emotions were high. Her hair stirred, and wind whipped up from nowhere.

With a laugh, Liam raised his arms and backed up. "You have no sense of humor, sister. It's just mud."

Iseabal wrinkled her nose. "Smelly mud."

Sly seized her brother's arm and yanked him away. Iseabal braced herself to act in case Liam took exception to the manhandling, her hair lifting with a consolidation of magic. She did not intend to lose Sly at this stage.

"Don't upset Princess Iseabal," Sly ordered. "Come, let's clean up. You said your father will want a report. Can I come with you? Is that okay, Princess Iseabal?"

To Iseabal's relief, Liam didn't seem to mind Sly's behavior. Her hold on the ley lines relaxed.

"Why don't you call her Iseabal?" Liam asked, cocking his head.

His gaze flitted from her to Sly and back with curiosity.

Easy to discern Liam's thoughts whirring. He knew. No, he didn't know. He guessed she'd done something, because he hadn't been here when she'd arrived with Sly. Sly had little in common with other men and women of their age. He was kinder than most, which made him vulnerable. He listened to people—her father, for instance. Liam liked him. That in itself was unusual.

"Respect," Sly said.

Liam nudged Sly with his shoulder. "Are you going to call her that once you're married?"

"No, I'll probably call her baby or snookems," Sly retorted.

Startled silence throbbed between them before Liam threw back his head and roared with laughter.

Sly grinned, the sort of smile that made a woman's pulse beat faster and thoughts of hot sex dance through her head. Bed sport with Sly... Oh, yes. Something to anticipate. A pity she couldn't indulge before they wed, but she wanted nothing to impede this marriage. For once, she'd wait and play by the rules.

"Where will you be?" he asked. "I'll come and find you once I've cleaned up."

Mollified by his reaction, Iseabal graciously dipped her head. "I'll go and spend time with Father. Come and find me in his tower salon when you're done."

"Won't be long," Sly said and walked off with Liam.

Iseabal stared after them, deep in thought. They were friends. Sly had won over her older brother without breaking a sweat. He'd done the same with her father.

This might not be as difficult as she'd believed.

Later that eve, Cinnabar flew to the lake to wait for Sly. The princess expected her to write a note about Sly and what he and Prince Liam had done during their jaunt away from the castle.

She'd scarcely settled on top of a rock when she heard footsteps. Oh no. Prince Liam had come with Sly. Her chest tightened with disappointment, and her eyes ached, but not a tear fell.

Owls didn't cry.

"Can I come with you tomorrow?" Sly asked.

Prince Liam brushed hair from his eyes. "You don't want to spend time with Iseabal?"

"I can still spend time with her," Sly said. "I'm not used to sitting around and drinking cups of hot chocolate."

"So, what do you do instead?"

"I spend time with my brothers. We have a farm..." He drifted off, and Cinnabar's misery lifted. Sly was suffering too, and she couldn't tell anyone.

A coward. If she were a better person, she'd square off with the princess and tell everyone what she'd done—about her years as an owl and how she'd kidnapped Sly. He didn't belong here. He'd suffer and become a puppet. Bah! They were both puppets now.

Prince Liam gestured at the rock where she perched. "Your owl is here again. The creature trails you."

A fleeting smile passed over Sly's face before he turned his attention to Prince Liam. "I have a way with animals. Both Joe and I do."

"Who is Joe?"

"I...I..." Sly stuttered to silence, shook his head, frustration visible to Cinnabar in his tight jaw. His hands opened. Closed. Opened. "I have no idea." His words held a raw edge of confusion.

"I might leave Seelie next week to attend a sale of our wool. Perhaps you'd like to go with me?" Prince Liam asked.

Hope rose in Cinnabar, only to dash against reality. The princess wouldn't let Sly leave Seelie, at least not until she had taken him as husband. Once married, it wouldn't matter because the princess would have Sly trapped, and if she was smart, soon a child would follow. Silken webs. Since neither Prince Liam nor Princess Katrina had offspring, a child would mean greater power for Princess Iseabal.

"Yes, I'd like that," Sly said. "I enjoy learning new things."

"Is Joe your brother?" the prince asked.

"Yes," Sly said without hesitation.

"I look forward to meeting him." The prince stooped to pick up a pebble and tossed it into the water. "Can you skip a stone over the water?"

"Easy," Sly scoffed, and he picked up a handful of the smooth pebbles. He scanned them, discarded several then threw one. It skipped across the lake's surface, striking the water five times before sinking from sight.

The prince chose his stone, flicked his wrist and sent it skipping across the water. "Five times," he said. "Equal. Where do you come from?"

"Earth," Sly said and skipped another stone. This throw didn't go as far.

Clever, clever man. Cinnabar hooted in soft approval then wished she hadn't, because she drew the prince's attention. Interest shone in his bright blue eyes, and it remained when he turned back to Sly.

"I haven't heard of this place Earth. Where is it?" he asked Sly seconds before he fired off another stone.

Sly stilled, his broad chest scarcely moving. "Earth?" His brow wrinkled in confusion. "I don't..." He flung the remaining pebbles in his hand into the lake. Water splashed, then the surface settled. "I have no freakin' idea why I mentioned the place."

"No," the prince said. "Doesn't matter. It's not important. Sly, are you ready to return to the castle?"

"No, Prince Liam. I think I'll stay here for a while. Maybe walk along the shore."

"Call me Liam," the prince said. "I'll meet you in the Great Hall in the morn." He strode away without waiting for Sly's response. "Forgot to tell you," he called over his shoulder. "I reminded Father about the clothes. His valet will deliver several suits of work clothes to your chamber. Iseabal has no taste when it comes to what real men wear."

Cinnabar watched the prince until he vanished.

Sly approached her. "He asked me to call him by his first name. He must like me."

Not surprising. Sly was easy to like.

"I enjoyed today. Riding the cambeests. Our mud fight." His green eyes sparkled as he recounted his day. "Sorting the stock. I made suggestions about improving the yards, and the prince—Liam—seemed interested in my ideas. I'm going out with him tomorrow. The castle...I don't like spending time there. Everyone is watching me."

His concern was understandable. The princess had spies everywhere, within the castle and farther afield. She would do well to remember that.

The shimmers and tickles that preceded her change back to her natural form had her flitting off the rock to stand on the ground at Sly's side. An instant later, her balance wavered, as it always did until she adjusted to a different center of gravity.

"Cinnabar." Sly swept her into his arms and kissed her, taking control of her mouth, her body, her soul. He tangled his hand in her hair and deepened the caress. His tongue rasped over hers, and when she responded in like, a rough growl vibrated in his chest.

When they finally parted, Cinnabar gasped for breath. "This is dangerous. What if the prince returns?"

"I can't not kiss you. I know it's risky, but something inside me seems to take control."

"I don't want to control anyone," Cinnabar cried.

"Shush." Sly cradled her head, his action tender. "It's not like that. I look at you and can't think of anything else except touching and stroking. I want to see you naked. And the idea of kissing your breasts, your sex, and sliding my body against yours... I crave that as desperately as I want food when I'm hungry. When I'm with you, I'm whole and centered." He pressed his forehead against hers and closed his eyes.

Cinnabar swallowed, her throat thick with emotion. "No one has ever said anything like that to me before."

He straightened, his green eyes narrowing a fraction, his chin lifting. "You think I'm not sincere?"

"I never said that."

"You thought about it. Not that I blame you. You've had a challenging time. You were right about the princess drugging me." A sliver of sharp pain stalled his breath, and he gave his temple a cautious rub, his mind in turmoil. No way would he accept this without a fight. "I think it's the hot chocolate my valet brings in the morning."

And he was answering some of Prince Liam's questions. If he didn't struggle with his thoughts, some of his memories slipped through the fog like stealthy hunters after prey.

"I still can't recall my days before I arrived at the castle."

Cinnabar studied her fingers, frowned and nibbled on a ragged fingernail. "You mustn't let Princess Iseabal know you're remembering your past. She is determined to do things her way and hates losing."

Obvious concern rubbed away any hint of her delightful cheer. Sly missed her gentle smile, her shy manner as she observed him with those serious blue eyes. He stared back at her boldly, his mind taking a different route. When she noticed, she blushed, the tide of heat showing against her golden skin. Sly reached for her hands, the physical contact jolting him. Happiness? He wasn't sure. But whatever the emotion, urgency screamed through him—a sense of a ticking clock.

"Forget about the princess. We have three hours. I want to make love to you, Cinnabar. Please let me love you. We should enjoy ourselves while we can." *Before it's too late.*

Cinnabar's shoulders fell forward in a despondent slump. Her gorgeous eyes filled with tears and alarm had him tugging her closer. Something inside him—a certainty, a sense of rightness—drove him to claim her, to stamp her with his ownership.

He snorted. And wasn't that like the caveman Scarlett had called him? Delight weighed on the scales with alarm. His memory had more holes than his Ma's old tea strainer, but he refrained from chasing the fleeting memories. That was the road to frustration.

Sly shook himself and concentrated on Cinnabar. "I'm sorry. I shouldn't have asked. Taking this step will place us both in danger."

"No." She released his hands and placed her warm palm on his cheek. "It's not that. I've been cursed to live in feathers for so long. No one acknowledges me. I have no physical contact. Touching you, knowing you want to touch me in return... It's everything, Sly. Yes, it's hazardous, but I want this so much. If you're willing to step into danger, I intend to stand at your side."

"We're moving fast. If I'm going too fast or pushing you, tell me."

She swallowed, and one of those slumbering tears leaked free. "We don't have the luxury of time. The first of the banns will be read this coming holy day."

"You need to tell me more about this banns crap. The concept isn't familiar."

"Of course." Cinnabar swiped her cheek. "The banns are read three times on successive holy days."

She had a smattering of freckles on the tip of her nose and a few on her cheeks. Cute. He drew her closer and pressed a quick kiss to the tip of her nose. "Later," he murmured. "Tell me later."

He pulled back and drew off his jacket—this one blue and about four shades darker than Cinnabar's eyes.

"I wish we had the entire night," Cinnabar whispered. "I must leave soon to complete a task for the princess."

"It won't always be this way," Sly promised. "I won't let it." Big words. His gut cramped at the thought of a marriage with the princess. A forced marriage. At least he'd made a friend in Liam, although he couldn't trust him. Not when he was Princess Iseabal's brother.

Sly spread his jacket on the ground and turned to Cinnabar. "We can do a quickie. It will still be outstanding."

"I haven't done this before."

Sly cocked his head. "Maybe we shouldn't—"

"Hush. Sly, I trust you. Our acquaintance might be short, but you have demonstrated more kindness than I've ever known."

Stung by her words, he said, "I don't need sex in payment."

"No, silly. This is for me. This is pure selfishness."

Sly studied her for an instant longer, then swung her into his arms. He placed her on his jacket, took a second to loosen his trousers, and joined her. Her arms came around him instantly, her lips met his, and he was gone, sinking into passion and desire.

Need.

Something worthwhile to combat his sense of helplessness, the growing fear that his life was running out of control.

He slipped his fingers beneath the neckline of her gown, savoring the warmth of her skin, loving her gentle floral scent. The friction from her shapely contours drove back his anxiety and filled him with peace. Desire stirred, his blood flowing south to stiffen his cock. He ended their kiss and nuzzled the graceful curve of her neck, his mouth lingering at the hollow of her throat.

"Sly," she whispered, the tension in her limbs communicating the need for haste.

His hand settled over one breast, and he toyed with her nipple while he dipped his head and kissed the valley between. He pinched her nipple and captured her groan with his caress.

"I love your lips. I can't get enough of your taste."

Cinnabar flicked her tongue against his in pure provocation, and his joy and happiness rang out. Sly repositioned his body and lifted her skirts. She parted her legs for him, and his heart thundered at her easy acceptance.

He moved farther down into the V of her thighs and lifted her to his mouth. Her flavor exploded on his taste buds as he tongued her slit and settled in to tease her nub. She quivered and cried out as her clit spasmed beneath his touch.

Sly continued until the vibrations tailed off, then he rose up her body and jerked his trousers down enough to free his dick.

"Are you okay, sweetheart?"

"Yes," Cinnabar whispered.

"I'll try to go slow, but this first time will hurt."

"I don't care. At least I'll feel alive. I want this. You."

Sly nodded, thankful for her confidence. Pacing himself, forcing himself to go slower, he kissed her again, wanting her soft and wet and needy for him. He caressed her clit again, pleased when she arched into his touch, silently demanding more.

"I want to fuck you so much," he whispered.

"Do it," she urged. "I want you to."

"But what if—"

She slapped a hand over his mouth. "I don't care if this is all I have. All *we* have. This time with you is the best thing that has ever happened to me. I want it all." And she kissed him, smothering his response.

They kissed for a long time, until raw need had him trembling like a green boy, and his balls drew so tight they became painful.

He fit his cock to her entrance and hesitated.

Her nails dug into his biceps, and he drew back.

"No," she pleaded. "Don't stop. Please."

He studied her face, her already familiar features for an instant, then forged deeper into her seductive heat. She gasped, froze, and clung as he pushed past her resistance until he plunged balls deep. He stopped moving, just embraced the heat, the clasp of her hands clutching him tight.

"Is that all?" she asked.

Sly laughed, kissed her, and thrust. She rocked against him, and a rough growl vibrated in his chest. Hot pleasure bubbled in his balls, the violent enjoyment stealing his breath. He came as he feasted on her mouth. Yeah, she stole his breath, his heart, his life.

Suddenly, Saber's words made sense. He'd know when he found the right one.

Never were truer words spoken, but who the hell was this Saber bloke?

CHAPTER ELEVEN

MIDDLEMARCH RESORT

Joe walked into the room they'd set up for Sly, past dozens of plants in black pots. Their red-and-white flowers perfumed the old storage shed with cinnamon and ginger. He and Saber had painted the walls a deep, rich red, and once the paint dried, they'd hauled in a bed—about the size of a large single, and not too big that the guests got the idea of climbing in with Sly. Casey contributed by sewing ruby-red curtains for the windows, and Felix had designed a frame to turn the bed into one fit for a fairy tale. Pure white sheets and a white duvet added the finishing touch.

Everything was in readiness for Sly.

He and Saber had developed a special package, which cost the ladies extra. In the end, they'd decided to embrace the obvious and name the new attraction *Sleeping Beauty*.

Joe snorted, his lips twitching. Sly would loathe this if he was conscious. But still, surely he would understand. Joe hated seeing his brother this way, so pale and still. He scanned the room in a final check. Hopefully, this wacky plan helped Sly regain consciousness.

Half an hour later, the room smelled like a floral bouquet while Sly lay on the bed, dressed only in boxer briefs, although the visiting ladies wouldn't realize that, since they'd covered his lower body with the white linens. A large basket sat next to the bed, full to the brim with flowers.

He ran his fingers down his twin's bare arm, a new habit he'd developed because, without Sly around, he felt as if he were missing a limb.

Almost ready to open for business.

He checked on Sly a final time and did a double take. "What the frak?"

Joe blinked and scanned Sly's face. His brother wasn't awake. He touched his arm again. Still cool to the touch, although he warmed when Joe's fingers lingered.

"Saber!" With a scowl at Sly, he strode to the door. "Saber."

His older brother came running at his call. "What is it? Has he woken?"

"No," Joe said—and pointed at Sly's groin.

Saber's eyes widened, and they shared a glance before turning back to gape at Sly's ginormous boner.

"What are we going to do? We can't let the ladies in here with him in this condition," Joe said.

"You didn't notice this when you entered the room?"

"No," Joe snapped. "It's kind of obvious. I would've noticed. It just happened."

"Maybe we should get Casey to—"

"No way, Saber. That's all kind of wrong. First, Felix won't be happy if he learns you asked his mate to examine Sly's dick. You'd hate Eva checking out another man's junk."

A menacing growl broke free from Saber.

"Exactly," Joe continued. "And Sly wouldn't be thrilled exposing his dick to his brother's mate, either. Go and tell the women there will be a ten-minute delay."

Saber grimaced at the tented covers. "What happens if ten minutes isn't long enough?"

"Then we'll have to check with Casey, I guess." Joe cupped his twin's shoulder, anxiety filling him at the coolness of Sly's skin. "Sly needs physical contact. He seems colder than yesterday."

Saber placed his palm on Sly's chest and frowned. "You're right. Okay, ten minutes. The line isn't long, anyway. It will take time for the word to filter through. There are so many other activities on offer."

Saber strode to the door and exited. Seconds later, he shot back inside. "Joe, we might have a problem."

"What?"

"The line is already longer than when I came in here."

"How much longer?" Joe peeked out the door, his eyes widening upon seeing the excited women. The blue ladies who didn't want mates stood in the front.

"We're eagerly anticipating this," one of the blue ladies called.

"I hope Felix and Leo made sure these women watched the movie about the correct way to kiss," Joe said with a frown.

Saber laughed. "Scarlett came up with the idea of making them kiss a balloon once they watch the movie. Anyone who pops the balloon with their tongue or teeth has to watch the movie again and go to the back of the line."

Joe gnawed his bottom lip, indecisive. Was this right? Sly was his best friend. He was closer to his twin than anyone else, and guilt roared through him. Was he doing this for himself or his brother? He straightened his shoulders. No, it was for both of them. He and Sly would have their cattle.

His gaze darted back to Sly's groin. "Saber, I think we're good now. Give me five minutes, then send in the first three women."

Saber stepped outside and closed the door. Joe took a deep breath and gripped Sly's forearm, willing his body heat into his brother.

Sly's chest barely moved. He was ashen now, and Joe's throat thickened every time he glimpsed his twin. He'd been unconscious for almost three days, and Joe missed talking with him, having a joke, and griping about Saber and his lack of foresight regarding the farm.

"You ready?" Saber asked.

Things were back to normal with Sly's dick, so he nodded. "Yep, send in the first three women.

"First lady," Joe said briskly. "Kiss him gently, like you kissed the balloon. If you wake him, you win a private date with Sly."

"I can do it," the blue lady said with confidence. She bent her head and pressed her lips to Sly's.

Joe watched carefully, but she played by the rules. She stood back, and Sly remained still. "Come stand by me," Joe said, placing her hand on Sly's arm. Might as well fill Sly with extra heat.

The second lady kissed him. Nothing.

The third. *Nothing.*

Joe sent the ladies out after plucking flowers from the basket and tucking one each behind their ears. A consolation prize. Saber sent in the next three ladies, and they repeated the process for an entire hour.

Not a single kiss woke Sly, but at least he was warmer now.

CHAPTER TWELVE

THE CASTLE, SEELIE, A WEEK LATER

S ly dressed in a flash suit—the silver and ruby-red garment given to him by Alfric, as per Princess Iseabal's instructions. He stared at his reflection and snorted. He looked like a friggin' girl with all the lace and frills.

"Here is your hat, my lord," Alfric said.

"Do I have to wear that?" Sly turned the silver three-pointed hat in his hands. It sported a perky red feather. "Ah, what is it?"

"A tricorne, my lord. It is part of the traditional dress worn during a banns reading."

He pushed out a sigh, fought back the dozens of smart-arse comments tickling his tongue, and plopped the tricorne on his head. Transformation complete.

"You're running late, my lord," Alfric intoned.

"I'm going now." Sly strode from his room and headed toward

the Great Hall. Evidently, the chapel was in a room off the hall. His footsteps slowed despite his tardiness. He should recall offering marriage to Princess Iseabal. A life event like that *should* stick with a man.

Once he reached the Great Hall, a steady stream of people pointed him in the right direction. The chapel. Princess Iseabal waited by the entrance, a dark glower on her golden face. Wisely, Sly blurted an apology before she started to speak. "Sorry I'm late."

"This is the first reading of the banns," Princess Iseabal whispered in a fierce undertone. She wore a red gown with silver trim, which made them a matching pair. "You are making me look stupid. The priest is ready."

He was having trouble breathing. Sly surreptitiously tugged at his collar as he offered the princess his arm. He guided her into the chapel.

"We sit at the front," the princess said.

Sly ignored the flurry of whispers and guided the princess to an empty pew at the front. Lord Calum, Princess Katrina, and Prince Liam were already seated. Sly settled Iseabal and slid onto the pew beside her.

A woman wearing a red robe, her hair covered by a hood, glided to the front of the chapel. She raised her hands in prayer and began a melodic chant. The rest of the congregation joined in. Sly kept his gaze down and remained silent. He expected the woman would stop after a while, but the chanting continued. He didn't comprehend a word. Peculiar, since he understood everyone as a rule. The incantation went on and on and on. Sly yawned, then grunted at the elbow in his ribs from Princess Iseabal.

Sly swallowed a disgruntled retort. He didn't want to be here and didn't understand how he'd found himself betrothed.

The vocalizing ended on an exuberant hum. Finally.

Sly straightened as silence fell.

"Now, for my final duty for today. It is with honor that I publish the banns of marriage between Princess Iseabal MacAsgain and Lord Sly Mitchell. This is the first time of asking. If you know any reason in law why they may not marry each other, you are to declare it. We pray for Princess Iseabal and Lord Sly as they prepare for their wedding."

No one uttered a word.

Sly swallowed, everything in him protesting. *An objection. Do it.* But his protest remained unspoken.

"Thank you," the priest said. "I will see you next holy day."

Princess Iseabal turned to him with a beatific smile, her golden beauty dazzling in that moment. Her face glittered with happiness, with triumph, while Sly struggled with the how and the why. He forced a smile, tried to project pleasure and excitement, but a heavy weight crushed the unwilling emotions flat.

This betrothal business trapped him, beat him down, snapped around him like a steel trap, and he felt as if he should try to gnaw his way free, but he had no idea of where to start.

The next day

Another interminable event with Princess Iseabal and her friends. This afternoon it was a tea party out in the gardens and singing. Sly scowled at the woman currently trilling vocals. The sort of singing that built raging headaches. Liam had left Seelie to attend a sale. Sly had wanted to go, but Princess Iseabal had created a fuss. Such a fuss, he'd agreed to stay and attend her stupid party. Huh. *Screaming tantrum, more like.* That boded well for future harmony.

The diva came to the end of her song, holding the last shriek for an excruciatingly long time. She bowed, and Sly applauded, glad, *so glad*, she'd finished.

No one else clapped.

Heads turned. Several of the ladies, young and interchangeable in his mind, giggled behind their hands.

"Barbarian," Lord Calum said, and flicked his wrist in Sly's direction.

Energy tugged and pulled, lifting the hair at the back of his neck. Big, fluffy gloves puffed onto Sly's hands, muting his appreciation. The titters grew louder. Sly snorted and slipped off the lilac gloves. He stuffed them under his chair.

"I beg your pardon," he said. "I assumed everyone would show appreciation of the singer." He rose, conscious of the sniggering expressions of Iseabal's friends. *Excuse me. Princess Iseabal's friends.*

"Where are you going?" Princess Iseabal demanded.

"I require fresh air," Sly said, backing up.

"But we're outside."

Yeah. *Fresh air.* "I will return soon."

Another step backward sent him into a collision. He froze as drinks and tiny cakes flew in all directions and dropped to the ground. *Ping. Ping. Ping. Crash.*

A feminine grunt sounded behind him.

Sly whirled to view the carnage. The maidservant sat on the ground. Her tray—upside down—glittered from the garden. The rainbow-colored cakes had splattered gowns and velvet suits, pristine tablecloths. Silver goblets had disgorged their contents, mainly on Lord Calum.

"You imbecile!" Lord Calum sprang to his feet, fury contorting his golden face.

"It was an accident—" Sly said, breaking off when he realized the direction of the lord's fury. It wasn't at him.

Lord Calum's hand flashed, and black spots broke out on the servant's face. "Clean up this mess. By hand," he spat. "No magic."

He tugged his wet jacket away from his torso. "My clothes are ruined."

Someone behind Sly snickered, and Lord Calum's face turned puce. The servant swallowed, panic stripping the color from her features, the black spots standing out in stark relief.

Sly offered her a hand to help her up, but before she rose, Lord Calum kicked her in the ribs. The girl—and she was a young girl—cried out in pain.

Some of Princess Iseabal's friends laughed.

Lord Calum kicked her again.

"Enough!" Sly roared and shoved the man away. "It was an accident. My fault. Not hers."

"You touched me!" Lord Calum gritted out.

"Duh," Sly muttered.

Lord Calum's blue eyes narrowed, then flashed red. His nostrils flared, and he lifted his hand, muttering a few words Sly didn't catch.

Pop. Pop. Pop.

Sly's cheeks stung. His chin. His jaw. He touched a sore spot. It felt shiny and raised.

Ah, spots. How old were these people? Ten? He ignored the laughs and chortles from the bystanders and helped the maid to stand. "Are you all right?"

She winced but nodded quickly.

"I'm sorry I caused you trouble. Let me help you."

"I-I can do it, Lord Sly."

Sly ignored her and bent to gather the tray from the garden. He placed it on the ground and scooped up empty goblets and cakes. Pink cakes. Red cakes. Purple cakes. Ugh. Who the heck ate purple cakes?

"Stop," Lord Calum ordered. "She dropped them. She can clear the mess."

"Sly, let the maid do it." Princess Iseabal clicked her fingers.

"More singing."

The chatter rose in volume, whispers behind hands. Sly ignored the gossip to continue plucking cakes off the ground. He dumped a handful on the tray. A pained cry had him straightening.

"Stop that, you bully." He shoved Lord Calum away again, removing Lord Calum's foot from the maid's hand. The moron had stood on it on purpose, and now the girl cradled her hand against her stomach.

"Don't interfere," Lord Calum snapped. "It's my right to discipline the servants." He zapped the maid with another burst of magic, and she grew a set of cat's whiskers.

Sly gaped at the girl. Tears poured down her face as she awkwardly collected the last of the goblets. Princess Iseabal and her friends had lost interest and were chattering and making rude comments about the new singer. He spied another cake and had to consciously relax his hand to pick it up.

"Let her do it," Lord Calum snarled.

Sly stood to his full height and turned slowly to face Lord Calum. "Cretin, you're abusing your power. It's not right."

Lord Calum twitched his fingers, muttered something, and suddenly Sly had his own set of cat's whiskers.

Anger exploded in Sly, a fury so great, it cried for release.

Sly led with his fist and struck the lord's nose dead center. His second quick punch made a satisfying crunch, and blood splattered both him and the bully lord.

Lord Calum hit the ground and curled up with a pitiful whimper.

The caterwauling from the singer ceased. Silence fell, and everyone stared at Sly with varying expressions of pity and glee.

Disgust curdled his stomach. He had to get out of there. Sly commandeered the tray from the maidservant. "I'll carry this for you."

"Sly, where are you going?" the princess asked in a frosty tone.

"Away from here!" Sly snapped.

"He hit me," Lord Calum whined.

Sly rolled his eyes and walked off, herding the maidservant away from the selfish and entitled lords and ladies of the court.

Without warning, a flock of scarlet birds dive-bombed them.

"Bloody prats," Sly muttered and urged the maidservant to hustle. With his free arm, he protected his face and head as best he could. Cupcakes dropped to the ground, and the birds scooped them up like treasures. He flung a handful away and most of the birds left to feast, but one or two determined attackers pecked his hands and chin before retreating.

Sly strode into the steamy kitchen. "Where do you want these?"

"Lord Sly." The head cook was a tall, hefty man with a paunch that declared his love of food. "What happened?"

"It was an accident," Sly said. "I was clumsy and backed into your maid. She dropped her tray. Lord Calum took exception and blamed her. Well, you can see what he did. The idiot kicked her and set birds on us."

"Let me magic away your spots and whiskers," the head cook said. "Maud, get some cloths to cleanse their wounds."

"Thanks," Sly said. "The help is welcome, but leave my spots. Fix your maid's face and check her injuries. Let her work in the kitchen for the rest of the day to stay out of Lord Calum's way."

The head cook nodded. "Thank you for helping her."

"You shouldn't—" Sly broke off as his legs moved without orders from his brain. "What the fuck?"

"A spell." The head cook scowled. "Don't fight or you'll cause yourself pain."

Grimly, Sly let his legs direct him back to the party, to the empty seat beside Princess Iseabal.

If she thought to rule him with magic, she should think again. He was his own man and would behave as he thought fit.

Fuming, Sly ignored Iseabal, ignored the singer, ignored the smart-arse comments sent in his direction. He sat in his chair, not reacting until the weight of a stare prodded him. Slowly, he turned to meet Lord Calum's red gaze.

If looks could kill...

Later that eve, Sly studied his reflection while dressing for dinner. Black spots and a set of white whiskers. Huh. He'd set a new fashion trend. Alfric had set out a red suit for him to wear to the evening meal in the Great Hall. *Red.* He was not a red kinda guy.

Sly stalked over to the wall and waved his hand to open the wardrobe. Some sort of sensor thingy. He froze. What the hell?

Red.

Every single item of apparel.

"Well, I might wear a red suit to dinner."

He dressed in the suit Alfric had left for him and strolled from his room. Late. Too bad. Rather than spend time with the princess and her self-centered friends, he'd prefer to skip dinner, walk in the gardens, and hang out by the lake with Cinnabar. He dawdled along passages, startling a laugh from two female servants he met.

"Lord Sly." A buxom maid with golden hair to match her skin blinked at him. "You have whiskers."

Sly fingered his cat whiskers. Strange, but they didn't seem as weird as they should. "I didn't have time to shave," he said.

"We heard of your troubles. Thank you for standing up for Leeza," the other maid, a chubby brunette, whispered. "Would you like us to magic them away?"

"You can do that?"

"Those of us with magic can undo basic spells. It doesn't deplete much power."

"I think I will leave them." Let Iseabal and her friends snigger.

He loathed the way they treated the servants. Someone needed to take a stand on their behalf. "They're dashing with my red suit."

The chubby maid tittered. "No one will miss you."

Sly bent in a bow. "Have a good evening."

A few minutes later, he walked past two security guards and into the crowded Great Hall. Silence fell as he strode toward Liam and the only empty seat. Heat sizzled through him without warning, and a glance showed his red suit had acquired a series of back spots to match his face.

Liam grinned as Sly took a seat beside him at the high table. "Who have you angered? I'll magic them away for you."

"No, I wish to make a point," Sly said, and nodded at the young lady on his other side before turning his attention back to Liam. "Lord Calum was picking on a servant this afternoon. She tripped and spilled a tray of drinks on him because I accidentally collided with her. I'm tired of the people around the 'court'." He paused to do air quotes. "And the way they bully and treat the servants. It's not right."

Liam straightened, lost the grin. He waved his hand, and a transparent bubble covered him and Sly, cutting off the chatter from the rest of the Great Hall. "What happened?"

"He gave the servant spots and ordered her to clean up the mess by hand instead of using magic. He took exception to me helping her, and we both ended up with spots on our faces. I hit him. Popped him in the nose. For that, a flock of birds dive-bombed me. The cook and several servants have offered to fix me, but I declined. Explain this magic system to me. I don't get it."

"Ah, do you mind if I change the color of your suit? It's hurting my eyes."

Sly snorted. "Every piece of clothing in my wardrobe is this color."

"You've made yourself an enemy. Lord Calum holds a grudge."

Sly shrugged. "If he's picking on me, the servants might get a break."

"Is it really that unpleasant?" Liam scowled. "I hadn't realized. I should have, since with Father ill, I am in charge." He flicked his hand, and Sly experienced a faint vibration as his clothing turned from red to black. "Most residents can perform basic magic, and those from wealthy families tend to study the subject from an early age, which gives them a greater ability. Our magic is performed by tapping into the energy—the ley lines—beneath Seelie."

"Can't the servants retaliate or work together to stop the bullying?"

"No. They can undo trivial things—the spots on your face, your whiskers. They can use magic to shift heavy loads, to clean. Simple one-action chores. A complex spell, such as decorating an entire chamber or making a meal of many ingredients, requires greater skill. Anytime one uses magic, it depletes our power. It's the way we use the ley lines, and only time replenishes our magical ability. That's why you'll see more pranks than serious stuff."

Sly thought of Cinnabar. "What about a curse? Or causing a death?"

"My father or I possess ample power. Maybe my sisters. Some of the high lords."

"What about undoing a complex spell? Can you do that?"

"That is where things get tricky. Each spell is individual to the person doing the casting. Undoing another's magical spell is difficult. Mostly impossible. And a complex spell can leave the spell caster vulnerable. Once again, that will vary and depend on the spell caster's skill level."

"Boredom is a terrible thing," Sly commented.

Liam's eyes narrowed. He resembled Princess Iseabal in that instant, and every muscle in Sly tensed for flight. "Are you telling me I need to mend my house?"

"I'm telling you vulnerable people are getting hurt and ridiculed because others are selfish and entitled. Not naming names. Just letting you know. Many of your servants spend their working hours terrified of making a mistake."

Liam lost his royal hauteur. "Thank you for telling me. I must think about this."

"Speak with your royal guards. They do their best to help, but interference dumps them in the firing line."

Liam nodded, offered a wry grin. He murmured a few soft words, and the transparent bubble vanished. The noise level rose to the normal Great Hall din.

"What were you discussing?" Princess Iseabal demanded.

"Farming matters," Liam said. "I wished for privacy."

"I saved you a seat," Princess Iseabal said.

Not true. The only empty seat at the high table had been next to Liam.

Princess Iseabal clicked her fingers at him. "Come. Your place is at my side." She stalked back to the other end of the high table.

"She treats me like a pet," Sly muttered. And even more telling, she hadn't made one comment about his appearance. The spots. The whiskers. The clothes that had turned red again. Frustrated with his position, Sly stood and ambled over to the empty seat beside the princess.

He was no man's dog. Princess's dog. Whatever.

He was his own person, his own boss, and somehow, he'd teach the princess this truth.

The days passed and fell into routine. The banns were read a second time, and it felt like a trap was closing over his head. He spent his mornings with the family, breaking his fast, part of the day with Liam, and the rest with Princess Iseabal and her friends. The latter the most challenging part of his day. His late evenings he spent with Cinnabar, talking and making love.

Someone scratched at his door an instant before it opened, and Alfric shambled inside, following a floating tray bearing his hot chocolate.

Sly yanked back the covers and slid out of bed, naked as usual. Grinning, he sauntered over to the tray and poured half a cup of hot chocolate while Alfric averted his eyes. Sly's preference for sleeping naked bothered his elderly valet.

Sly pretended to take a sip. "Ahhh," he said. "The first sip always tastes perfect. I'll take the rest of my cup in the bathing room."

Alfric gave a nod, yet stared at his feet. "Shall I choose a suit for you?"

"I'm going out riding with Liam. We're checking the kashmore at the west farm."

Alfric *tut-tutted*. "Very well, my lord. I'll place an appropriate suit out for you."

"If you wouldn't mind, pick one for me to wear upon my return, too, Alfric. Not red, if possible."

"Of course, my lord. Will there be anything else?"

"No, I'll dress myself. You go ahead with your duties." One of which, according to Cinnabar, was to report to Princess Iseabal.

"Thank you, my lord."

Sly took a moment to top up his cup before wandering into the bathing room. He set the cup on the counter and turned on the water. He'd dispose of the contents as soon as Alfric left.

About half an hour later, Sly strode toward the royal salon.

"Good morning," he said to a maid dusting the china and sculptures in the alcoves along the passage.

She jerked up her head, stared at him, then offered a shy smile. "Good morn, my lord."

He continued to the salon, whistling a tune. He had no idea what it was or where it came from, but the melody cheered him.

"Hello," he said to the two security men on the door.

"Good morn, my lord," the senior one said.

"Have the family arrived?"

"Just Prince Liam," he replied.

"Thanks," Sly said and continued with his whistling. "Hey, Liam. How's it hangin'?"

Liam blinked double time, the back of his throat visible, so big was his goggle.

"You're inviting bugs to explore the interior of your mouth," Sly said, smirking.

Liam offered a nonplussed grin, rather than his dignified king one. "It's...ah...hangin'."

"Good to hear. I can't wait to get into the fresh air." Sly fingered his lips and winced. The salve Alfric had given him seemed to have helped ease his cracked lips. Maybe an allergy of some type? He had the ointment in his pocket and decided to apply more after his breakfast.

A footman pulled out a seat for him.

"Thank you," Sly said.

The young man dipped in a polite bow but didn't quite hide his merriment. "Would you like your normal cup of tay?"

"Yes, please," Sly said. Tay was similar to tea, although the color varied from day to day. He hadn't worked out why, but it did the job and cleared the cobwebs from his mind.

The footman left to get his tay, and Sly reached for the dish of eggs. He dumped three spoonsful onto his plate, then added four slices of the pink meat that reminded him of bacon.

"Everyone likes you," Prince Liam said. "You have a knack with people. The castle seems lighter with you around."

"Polite manners never hurt." Sly shoveled a forkful of eggs into his mouth and chewed. "Ma drummed that into us from the moment we talked."

"Ma sounds like a wise woman," Liam said.

"Yeah, I miss her. I even miss Saber."

"Who is Saber?"

Sly paused, considered his answer and waited for his memory to cloud over. "Saber is my brother," he said slowly. "My oldest brother."

Iseabal paused at the doorway, alarm skittering through her. How the shoodlepoppers had this happened? Alfric had reported Sly was drinking his morning chocolate. Somehow, he'd become immune to the spell. A servant marched down the hall with purposeful strides.

"Who is that for?"

"Lord Sly," the footman answered, keeping his gaze lowered.

Something else she didn't understand. Everyone at the castle thought well of Sly, even her sister Katrina. The only person who disliked him was Calum, and that was because, come their marriage, Sly would stand between Calum and power. Oh, and the fact Sly had punched him. That hadn't helped.

"I'll take that for you." She growled when the servant hesitated. "I said I'd take that for you. Hurry or you won't like the consequences."

The cup and saucer and pot of steaming liquid—probably tay, since Sly seemed to favor it—rattled as he handed over the tray.

"Go," she ordered.

The boy hesitated again, then almost ran toward the kitchen.

Iseabal set the tray on hover, opened the pot lid, and pulled a small bottle from her pocket. The one she'd intended to give to Alfric to replenish his supply. She tipped three crystals onto her palm, frowned, and added one more. She dropped them into the pot and used the teaspoon to stir the liquid. That should do the trick. Just her luck to pick a man with a strong mind.

The head footman appeared. "Princess Iseabal. Let me take the tray. The boy should never have given it to you."

She handed over the hover tray as if it were a distasteful creature intent on biting. "No, I don't know what that was about."

"I will discipline him," the head footman said. "And confine him to the kitchen."

Iseabal nodded and sailed into the salon.

Sly spotted her and rose. "Good morning, Princess Iseabal." He seated her before taking his place again.

"Liam, are you dragging off Sly again this morn?"

"I'm hardly dragging him off, Iseabal," Liam said in an even tone.

"I don't understand why you both enjoy scrambling around in the mud. It's undignified."

"Let me remind you, Iseabal, that the farming operation gives our people work and opportunities. It gives them purpose."

Iseabal flapped her hand in dismissal. She'd heard this lecture before. Why toil when magic did everything? What was the point?

The head footman placed the pot of tay in front of Sly.

"Thank you," Sly said, ignoring the bickering between her and Liam in favor of his meal.

Iseabal frowned. He didn't need to thank everyone. It was their job to serve the royal family. "I—" She started to chastise him, then saw Liam's watchful manner. Perhaps she'd do it later, once she and Sly were alone.

The head footman settled the cup and saucer beside Sly.

"Don't worry about pouring," Sly said. "I can do it."

"It's his job," Iseabal snapped.

"I wish to eat first."

Of course he did. Obstinate male. She'd break him of that after the marriage ceremony. One final banns to read before they announced the date of their wedding.

Iseabal indicated she wanted fruit and the head footman hustled to carry out his duties. As it should be. Once she received her fruit, she nibbled at it, her belly roiling. Sly didn't touch his tay.

Impatience simmered in her, and anger built. No one made a

fool of her. *No one.*

"Something wrong, Iseabal?" Liam regarded her over the brim of his mug. The hot chocolate steamed.

"No."

"You appear upset."

"Leave me alone," she snapped.

"Liam, stop teasing Princess Iseabal," Sly said. "What are we doing this eve, Princess Iseabal?" He picked up the tay pot and poured the berry-colored liquid into his cup.

She held her breath, watching him closely, only letting her breath ease out again when he took a sip.

Ah, that should do the trick.

Middlemarch Resort

Joe stared at Sly's still body. He didn't understand it. Project *Sleeping Beauty* had been working. Sly's appearance had improved, his skin temperature warmer—until half an hour ago. He placed his hand against Sly's chest, and the cold wrung a hiss from him.

The weirdest thing. Sly wasn't losing muscle mass. They'd discussed intravenous feeding again, but Casey said he didn't require the sustenance. Ma had concurred. But this renewed coldness...that concerned him.

The physical contact with the women had helped. Each day, they had to send away disappointed guests since they limited numbers to fifty.

Joe reached for the medicated salve Ma had made for chapped lips. He placed one hand on Sly's arm while gently rubbing the salve on his mouth. Perhaps he'd arrange a morning session and pray the extra contact halted the chill spreading through his brother.

With a last pat on Sly's arm, he left Sleeping Beauty's boudoir, locked the door, and went in search of Saber.

His stomach roiled with each step, his mind a mass of knots and fatigue. They had to fix Sly, make him regain consciousness. They had to.

Castle Seelie

Sly headed for the stables with Liam, his thoughts sluggish and dull.

"Tell me about your brother," Liam said.

Sly frowned, his mind struggling with the question. "What brother?"

"Saber," Liam said.

Sly stopped. "Who is Saber?"

Liam's brow wrinkled. "Ah, I'm beginning to understand."

"About what?" Saber? He didn't have a brother. Did he? He considered the idea and flipped the thought through his mind. Sluggish fog. No, he didn't have a family. "I don't have a family."

Liam shrugged and led the way into the stable yard. "Let's go riding."

"Hey, Brigitte," Sly said, rubbing his mount on her shaggy neck. He knew everyone in the royal family. Iseabal, his fiancée. Her twin sister and her horrid husband. The names of some of the staff. A brother. No, he didn't have one. He'd remember if he had a brother, parents.

"There is that owl again," Liam said. "It follows us everywhere."

"It has pretty eyes," Sly said, and sprang onto Brigitte without the aid of a stable boy. "I like it. I enjoy working with animals of all types."

"You have a talent with them," Liam agreed, and he led the way from the stable yard. The owl followed, swooping through the air and riding the currents.

"The job today won't take long. I thought to show you some of the land. There is another lake, not quite as big as the one near the castle but still pretty," Liam said.

"Sounds fun."

As Liam had promised, they spoke with the various farmers and studied their herds of kashmore. One of the farmers offered them refreshments, and they drank mugs of hot orange-colored tay and ate crackers and cheese.

"The cheese is delicious, sharp and flavorful," Sly said as he reached for a second cracker. "Who makes it?"

"My wife," the farmer said. "She hates to waste the excess milk."

"Do you sell it?" Sly asked.

"No, we mostly give it away," the farmer replied.

"It is tasty," Liam said.

"You should try making it on a larger scale. Sell some to the folks outside of Seelie," Sly said. "Diversification is the key to farming." The words formed in his mind seconds before he spoke them, yet they seemed foreign when he tested the thoughts. He had no idea where they'd originated.

Liam gave a thoughtful nod. "Sly's idea has merit. Let me think about it and do some research. I'll come back to you and your wife soon. Will that be all right?"

"Yes, of course." The farmer was pink-cheeked and flustered.

But Sly noticed he stood taller, pride shining from his blue eyes.

Liam stood, and Sly followed his lead. "Thanks to your wife, Jonas. And yourself, of course. I'll be in touch."

Minutes later, they were away, riding swiftly across an open paddock. A screech sounded from their right, and Sly scanned the sky for the source of the raucous call.

"A hawk," Liam said. "Ferocious birds. I hope that pet owl of yours is safe."

Sly scrutinized the sky again, this time with a trace of panic. The owl barreled toward him, flying at full speed, but the hawk had her in his sights. Without thought, Sly stuck out his arm.

The owl landed with a heavy thump, hard enough to unseat him. His cambeest shied, and Sly clung with his thighs while he struggled to retain his balance. The hawk released another raucous shriek and flew over in a second pass, but the owl was safe.

"I told you that owl is following you. Not me," Liam said.

Sly ran his finger over the owl's head. The bird quivered beneath his touch, leaned into the next stroke. The hawk continued to circle overhead. Sly moved his arm. "Onto the pommel," he directed, although why he spoke to the owl, he had no idea.

"I get it," Liam said, and humor lurked in him, his dimples digging into his cheeks. "You think of the owl as a pet."

Sly ignored his friend...because the prince *had* become his friend. He liked spending time with Liam more than Princess Iseabal, which told him a lot. But he'd promised to marry her.

Sly frowned. No, he'd asked Princess Iseabal to marry him. Not that he recalled the moment.

And he should. Shouldn't he?

"Why are you frowning so hard?"

"When did I propose to Princess Iseabal?"

Liam's eyes narrowed. "You don't recall?"

Sly sifted through his memory. Holes. They were everywhere, and he made little sense of the few recollections he discovered. "No."

"What do you remember?"

"Meeting your family. Everything we've done. The places I've visited with both you and Princess Iseabal."

"Nothing earlier?"

"No."

"I see."

"You said that before." Sly stared at Liam, his scowl deepening until he felt his forehead crinkle. "*What*, damn it?"

"The lake," Liam said with a flash of a grin, yet it didn't reach his eyes. His bright blue eyes remained serious, and Sly felt as if he'd missed something momentous. "Race you there."

Liam leaned over his cambeest, galloping furiously away, his yell of encouragement for his mount floating after him.

"Hold on," Sly said to the owl, and he urged his mount after the prince. He arrived at the edge of the turquoise lake a full two minutes after the prince, the owl flying in tight formation at his side. He pulled up beside Liam and dismounted on the rocky shoreline. The owl sought refuge in the nearest tree. By habit, he stooped to pick up a pebble. He tossed the pink stone into the calm surface and followed up with a white one. A gentle plop cut through the rattle of the reeds and the faint twitter of unseen birds

Small bright blue insects flitted over the surface and a pale pink bird waded from the reeds on the far side of the lake. Sly inhaled the crisp air and released the tension from his muscles.

An animal—pure white, with an impressive set of antlers—slipped from the undergrowth and delicately picked its way to the water.

Liam hissed. "A white stag. That means death."

"A superstition?"

"No," Liam said. "We must return to the castle. Now."

Sly jumped onto the back of his mount. "I saw one not long after I arrived at Castle Seelie."

Liam flinched. "Where? You never said anything."

"At the lake near the castle. I saw it late at night. Just the once."

"I've never seen one myself, but every time someone reports seeing a white stag, someone important dies," Liam said in a grim voice. "Someone is pleading with me to return home. Can't tell who."

A lone rider intercepted them when they were halfway back to the castle. "It's the king," he gasped. "Princess Katrina sent me to find you. The king is failing."

"Hi-ya!" Liam urged his cambeest to greater speed, and Sly followed.

When they reached the stable yard, Sly slid off his mount. "Go," he said. "I'll take care of your cambeest."

Liam hesitated, since he liked to groom his mount and settle him after their rides. He said it relaxed him.

"Go. I will take care of things here."

Liam gave him a one-armed embrace. "Thank you. Meet me at Father's salon once you're done."

Sly nodded and led both cambeests toward the stables, uneasiness stalking him like a savage predator. This wasn't good.

He took his time, wanting to do a respectable job, so it was over an hour later when he entered the castle by the rear entrance. A weighty silence hung over the inhabitants, the servants scurrying past with their eyes downcast.

Sly started to go to the king's salon, then wrinkled his nose. On second thought, he changed his direction. He'd shower and change first before he presented himself. Yeah. Princess Iseabal would approve of a clean suit. One of the suits she'd picked for him.

He burst into his chamber, interrupting Alfric as he did his chores.

"Did you need something, my lord?" Alfric asked.

"Just here to clean up. Has there been any more news about the king?" He frowned, knowing this was skirting close to gossiping with staff, but how else could he learn the news?

"No," Alfric said. "From what I hear, nothing has changed."

Sly nodded, although he wasn't sure what that meant.

Clean and dressed in a fresh suit, Sly headed to the king's salon. He nodded at the two security guards outside the chamber before rapping on the door. It flew open almost instantly.

"We told you no interruptions— Oh, it's you. Why are you here?" Calum demanded. "It's family only."

"Liam told me—"

"Are you deaf? Family only." Calum shut the door in his face.

Sly stared at the heavy wood door, shook his head slightly before stepping back. "If Prince Liam asks for me, tell him I stopped by, but Calum refused me entry."

"Yes, my lord," one of the men said.

"Tell him I said sorry but didn't want to make a scene."

"Yes, my lord."

Sly retreated and decided to get something to eat from the kitchen, then head down to the lake. Something about the castle oppressed him, and he was happier away from the place.

Maybe things would improve once he and Princess Iseabal married.

Later that evening

The instant Cinnabar experienced the tingles foretelling her shift to human form, she flew to the ground and waited.

Sly already stood on the lakeshore, his restless pacing taking him across the pebbles and back.

As usual, the process disoriented her, and she wobbled before she regained her balance. Her gaze went straight to Sly.

He hadn't noticed her, and concern made her steps slow. "Sly?"

He turned. "Ah, hi. Is Princess Iseabal asking for me?"

She stared, her throat tight. She swallowed to force out a reply. "Sly, it's me. Cinnabar."

"Cinnabar?" He offered a polite smile, as one would to a

stranger. "Have we met before?"

Everything inside Cinnabar froze. He didn't recognize her. Just her, she wondered, or had he lost every memory?

"Do you remember your family?"

A furrow formed between his brows. His jaw clenched, and he rubbed his temple. "I don't... Princess Iseabal's family?" His confusion cleared. "There is Prince Liam, Princess Katrina, and Lord Calum. The king, of course."

Cinnabar wanted to cry at the injustice. The princess had either shored up her spell or created a new one to deepen her hold on Sly. "Have you met Princess Iseabal's friends?"

He sent her an odd look, as if he wondered at her impertinence. "Yes, of course. I am finally matching names with faces."

"What about the servants?"

"Why are you asking me these questions?" he demanded.

"Please, I don't wish to anger you. One more question. "Have you visited the island of Ione? It's not far from the Tiraq mainland."

His forehead puckered, and he shook his head. "No, I don't believe so."

"Thank you. I'll leave you in peace now." Cinnabar forced herself to leave, forced herself to silence, forced her anger down when she wanted to rail and shout and stomp her frustration. Somehow, Princess Iseabal had managed to make sure that Sly recalled nothing of his life prior to his arrival in Seelie. He didn't remember his home. He didn't remember his family. And he didn't remember her because they had met for the first time at the resort.

Princess Iseabal's spell had made them strangers again, and Cinnabar had no idea of how to fix this wicked tangle. She needed to think, and...

Before her brain could overrule her heart, she stomped back to Sly. "My name is Cinnabar, and we are secret friends. I'm sorry you don't remember me, but please heed this warning. Take care of what you eat and drink. Watch the prince. Eat what he eats. Drink only what he drinks. I believe this might help your headaches—"

"How do you know my head is aching?"

"You are rubbing your temples."

"Oh." His hand fell to his side.

When he said nothing else, Cinnabar turned and walked away. Maybe, if she put her mind to the problem, she'd think of another way to help Sly. She'd done what she could tonight.

CHAPTER THIRTEEN

"The king is dead. Long live King Liam!"

The cries echoed over the courtyard and through the Great Hall the next evening. Inhabitants from the surrounding properties and the village had been arriving since the release of the news earlier in the day. Now, they crowded the courtyard, all facing King Fionnghall's tower.

Cinnabar watched the royal family as they stood at the top of the tower. Liam, the new king. Princess Katrina and Lord Calum. Princess Iseabal. Where was Sly?

As she wondered, King Liam turned and spoke to someone out of sight. Sly appeared and strode to the king's side.

He didn't remember her.

Not a scrap of recognition had flitted over his face when they'd met by the lakeside.

Princess Iseabal had won.

Sly hovered in the doorway, reluctant to draw attention. Calum winged a glare in his direction. It was obvious the man objected to his presence. Liam had explained that once Sly and Princess Iseabal married, he would hold more power than Calum, and if anything happened to Liam, he and Princess Iseabal would rule Seelie.

Until their marriage took place, Calum stood above Sly in ranking.

Sly's mouth pulled firm, revulsion filling him. Politics. Power. Not for him. He'd prefer to spend time on the land. Animals didn't care about society and their proper place. He shifted his focus to Princess Iseabal. Her mood drifted like a dark cloud about to unleash a storm. Every muscle in her body quivered with angry tension, and she replied in clipped syllables whenever anyone spoke to her.

She was pissed because the reading of the final banns would not occur on schedule. The period of mourning—four weeks of official grieving and respect—trumped wedding procedures.

A sense of relief filled him, along with confusion. He spent every afternoon with Princess Iseabal, every evening. Sometimes they went dancing. Some evenings, they attended private parties. Yet, he and the princess didn't appear compatible. Their relationship seemed more about appearances. Without thinking, he'd called her by name yesterday, omitting her title, and she'd thrown a wobbly fit, ordering him to address her as Princess Iseabal. She insisted on formalities, unlike Liam, her older brother. Hell, now the king.

Then, he'd kissed her good night—a fiancé should be able to kiss his lady—but she hadn't enjoyed that either. Nor had he. It had been like embracing a wooden statue. No, he didn't understand the woman he was to marry and welcomed the delay in their nuptials.

Liam held up his hand and waited for the crowd to quiet. "It is with deep regret that I announce the passing of my father,

King Fionnghall. The funeral will take place in four cycles." He paused, his chest rising and falling before he continued. "I, my sisters and brother-in-law, wish to thank you for your attendance today, for your condolences and messages of sympathy. We invite you to attend the funeral wake to pay your last respects. The wake will take place on the cycle before the funeral. I... Thank you," Liam said. "Announcements of the program will be posted in the courtyard this eve." Liam dipped his head, then retreated into the tower.

The rest of the family followed. Sly too, but he kept to the background. Princess Iseabal didn't require his presence, and Lord Calum hated his inclusion.

He'd slip away. With that in mind, he edged to the door, intending to escape to his favorite spot by the lake.

"Where are you going?" Princess Iseabal demanded as he reached the door.

"I thought to leave the family alone," Sly murmured.

"At least he admits he isn't part of the family," Lord Calum remarked to his wife.

Sly didn't hear her reply, but the truth—he rattled around like a spare player on the reserve bench. He scowled because he had no idea where that thought came from or what it meant. His mind was a foreign entity. Strange and peculiar. And when he pictured a woman at his side, he didn't think of Princess Iseabal. He pictured red hair and sad blue eyes, feathers...

"I need fresh air," Sly added. "My head is aching and I thought a walk might help."

Princess Iseabal's expression softened. "I'll make you a potion."

"I have a headache, too," Liam said. "Come, Sly. Let us walk in the gardens."

"But we have friends coming. Relations. They expect you to greet them," Princess Katrina objected.

"I will," Liam said. "But meantime, Sly and I will walk. We'll return in time to greet our guests."

Liam gestured at Sly, and they left the salon together.

"Sly." Liam's mouth relaxed, quivered in a tiny show of amusement before firming again. It was as if he'd momentarily forgotten his father's death and had returned to the teasing prince.

"What is it?" He caught a flash of black behind him. "Aw, crap. They've given me a tail."

"And whiskers," Liam confirmed.

Sly fingered his face, felt the stiff catlike whiskers. "Lord Calum, most likely. He takes immense pleasure in his pranks. Can you magic them away, please?"

Liam muttered a few words, and the whiskers disappeared.

Sly glanced over his shoulder in time to witness the tail evaporate.

"I had to get one of the servants to magic them away earlier. Every time I attend parties with Iseabal, I develop strange appendages or get weird spots on my face or hands. My clothes change color, and my eating utensils drop to the ground without my help. Yesterday, my entire meal turned to blue bugs. No one wants me here."

"No talking," Liam barked.

Sly fell silent, anger squeezing his chest tight. He didn't fit in at the castle, so why did the princess insist on marriage?

Liam led them down a path Sly hadn't explored yet. With nothing better to do, he followed the new king. King-in-waiting. It wouldn't be official until after King Fionnghall's funeral, when they'd hold the coronation. He recalled Lord Calum's nasal explanation to his questions.

"Don't you know anything?" Lord Calum had demanded. "Where did Iseabal find you? Under a mushroom?"

If Sly stuck up for himself, he ended up with clawed feet, tails, or cloven hands. Then there were the subtle rashes in all the colors of the rainbow, the attacks of insects and birds. So he'd folded his arms and bitten his tongue, just as he was doing now.

"The old king is given a sendoff to Utopia before he is buried. The new king is addressed by the title, but nothing is official until the coronation, where he is bestowed with the crown and the ceremonial orb, the seat of the king's power."

Sly had taken the peaceful option. "Thank you for explaining."

Lord Calum had sneered—as usual—and minced away to whisper with his wife.

No, Sly didn't belong in Seelie.

The path widened and wound through a tangle of trees, their many branches reaching out like grasping fingers. Liam paused, waiting for Sly to reach his side.

"Sorry I was short before. I didn't want anyone to overhear our discussion."

"I see."

"I thought that was my line," Liam said with a conspiratorial smile.

"A figure of speech. Nothing makes sense to me. I have huge gaps in my memory. I don't like your sister, but I seem to be marrying her, anyway. Only the servants speak to me in the castle."

"I speak to you."

"Mostly when we're away from the castle," Sly said.

Liam nodded.

"Your friends, your relations dislike me—no, that is too strong a word. They hold me in contempt and treat me as a nuisance. They enjoy making me the butt of their jokes and snigger behind their soft hands and perfect manicures about my lack of powers. And then there's your sister. Princess Iseabal treats me like a hard-won possession, but now that she's won me, she's lost interest. It was the chase that excited her."

A bird flew into the trees and perched above their heads. The owl. The bird followed him everywhere.

Liam observed the owl. "Go on."

"She acted as if I had cooties when I tried to kiss her good night in front of Princess Katrina and Lord Calum. I mean, if we're getting married, shouldn't we have some sort of affection between us? If I suggested making love, I'm sure she'd give me warts."

"The royal princesses are expected to remain chaste until they are wed," Liam explained. "If anyone can prove improper behavior, the princess can lose her place in the royal line."

"Your chain of command is confusing. The way I understand it, should anything happen to you, Princess Katrina and Lord Calum are next in line, followed by Princess Iseabal."

"That is correct, but once you wed my sister, she'll become next in line to me because she has a husband and the ability to have a royal heir."

Sly made a scoffing sound deep in his throat. "I'm a possession. A means to an end."

"I like you, Sly. I enjoy your company."

"I'm not marrying *you*," Sly said.

Liam barked out a laugh. "That wouldn't work. One of us needs to bear a child to secure the line."

"You can have the kid," Sly said instantly. "I don't mind."

They reached the lake. A different viewpoint from Sly's favored evening spot. An old log formed the perfect seat, and they sat, studying choppy waves that tumbled onto the stony shore.

"The wind has come up," Sly said. "Does it ever rain here?"

"When the winter king visits."

"Ah, I've heard him mentioned. Tell me more. Who exactly is the winter king?"

"Calvin. My cousin. He rules over Unseelie. I am—or will be—the summer king. I visit his lands and take over his castle while he comes here to Seelie. Our moves bring on the changes of seasons. It's a symbiotic relationship and brings prosperity to both kingdoms."

The owl flew from the tree it had claimed as a temporary roost and settled on the far end of the fallen log with them.

"I've seen that owl with Iseabal," Liam said without warning.

"Oh?" Sly regarded the bird, its russet-red feathers and big blue eyes. "A spy?"

The owl hooted as if in protest.

"I've watched her feed it micelets."

The owl hooted again, and this time managed to sound distasteful.

"Have you eaten today?" Liam asked.

"I wasn't hungry."

Liam waved his hand, and bread and cheese appeared in front of them, along with a bottle of something. "Eat with me now."

"Liam," Sly whispered. He touched Liam's arm to draw his attention and pointed.

The white stag had appeared on the opposite bank of the lake. The creature lifted its heavy head and stared at them for an instant before taking a drink. Thirst slaked, it watched them for a moment longer before ambling into the forest.

"That doesn't bode well." Liam ripped off a hunk of bread and handed it to Sly.

"Do you wish to return to the castle?"

"Not right now."

The owl hooted and took to wing. It darted away into the trees.

"Is that owl a spy?" Sly asked. "Is that possible?"

"Anything is possible in Seelie. You've developed a case of green spots on your face," Liam said in a mild voice.

"At least it's not stinging bugs or pecking birds. Princess Iseabal doesn't seem to care if her friends pick on me. I'm confused. I still don't recall our first meeting. I know nothing of my life before. Did I hatch from an egg and start life here in Seelie?"

"I want to do an experiment. Try not to eat or drink anything in the castle."

"I have to eat," Sly said.

"I'll provide food for you. If you're forced to dine, only eat what I eat or drink what I do. If you must leave your plate or cup at any time, don't eat or drink from them on your return."

"You think someone is drugging me? Why? I don't understand." He rubbed his forehead to smooth away a stab of pain. "Wait, could it be another suitor trying to get rid of me? Could Princess Iseabal wed someone from the court of the winter king?"

"There are men from the winter court who have shown interest. She rejected their suits." Liam chewed on his bread and cheese, drank from the bottle, before handing it to Sly. "Remember, eat or drink nothing unless I have consumed it or given you the food."

Sly frowned. "Someone else told me that."

"An unscientific test to see if your mind clears."

"Can't you use your magic?" Sly asked.

"This is more than a practical joke. Memory loss is difficult, tangled. My help, however admirable my intentions, might worsen the problem because I have no knowledge of the subtleties. It's possible someone is giving you a drug rather than applying magic."

"Why are you helping? You don't know me. My history."

"You're a decent man. You treat the servants well. The men at the stables and on my farms like you. You listen, ask questions, and give suggestions. You don't talk down to them. You can tell a lot about a man from how he treats his servants, and you have reminded me of this. My cousin, the winter king, rules with a firm hand, yet he is fair and listens before acting. That is the way I wish to rule."

"Is your cousin the same age as you?"

"Yes, his father... Don't mention or discuss this with anyone, because it will cause trouble. His father was a despot. A tyrant. My cousin fought to take over as king, and my father helped him. Having the two kings together for too long causes chaos with our weather, but my cousin had the throne by the time the summer storms had died down."

"I have much to learn. Are there books to study about your

history?"

"You read?"

"You sound surprised. I read, but whether I can understand the written language here..." He shrugged.

"Not many of our people bother learning. Our history is passed between the generations in oral form, so it's unnecessary, but we do have scribes. If you have the ability to read, I can magic a pair of glasses to make sense of our language. Where were you educated?"

"I..." Pain darted through Sly's head as he fought past the blocks in his brain.

"Stop," Liam ordered. "Don't worry about the answer. It's not important."

A muffled grunt came from the bushes. A squeal.

"Wild boar," Liam whispered. "We should go. They're vicious creatures, and we don't wish to come across any when our weapons are back at the castle."

"Weapons?"

"We hunt them with bow and arrows. 'Tis excellent sport. We'll go for a hunt. Fresh pork for the wake. Our visitors will enjoy the entertainment."

Sly followed Liam, retracing their steps to the castle. At least a wild boar hunt would alleviate his boredom and get him out of the way of his tormentors.

Cinnabar flew back to the castle the instant the two men reminded her her spy status. The viewing of the white stag worried her. She'd thought—hoped—the death ended with the king. Another sighting meant more death, more suffering.

The men's discussion. She'd heard enough for her anxiety to rise. Prince Liam knew or suspected his sister had bespelled Sly.

Pride. Stupid pride. Princess Iseabal despised rejection, and the moment Sly had turned away from her to favor those blue women had been the moment he'd sealed his fate.

Princess Iseabal bore a mean streak. She'd never experience guilt for her actions. Sly was a means to an end. She'd play by the most important rules until she wed and bore a child. Once she had her precious child and had cemented her position, Sly's life would mean nothing.

He would die. Disappear.

Her eyes stung, and her vision blurred. A sharp squawk escaped her. Feeling sorry for herself wouldn't help.

Sly was lost to her now. Always had been. The princess would never lift the spell and free her. She knew this and accepted her fate.

She flew to her normal perch near the princess's chamber. Hardly had she settled when the window flew open and the princess stuck out her head.

"What took you so long?"

Alarm skittered through Cinnabar, and she froze, wishing she could flee the coming tirade.

"I don't understand why Liam has taken such an interest in him. He is nothing. Nobody. The man has no magic. He is a tool. *My tool.*"

Princess Iseabal's words emerged in staccato, along with spittle. The fine spray struck Cinnabar's feathers, but she quashed the urge to groom her plumage.

Masculine laughter filtered up from the gardens. "They're back. I thought they might be gone longer. At least that is something. I want a report of their discussion. Write it for me this eve and leave it in the usual place. I want you to pay close attention to our visitors. If anyone discusses Sly, add that to your report. Understood?"

Cinnabar hooted and departed, thankful to leave. The princess's temper, always volatile, seemed worse today. Cinnabar glided over the gardens until she knew she was out of sight and settled on the branch of an old tree with a broad, leafy canopy. What should she do? She thought about this for a brief second. Now that she'd started her duplicity, she had no option but to continue walking the delicate line of deceit. The princess would receive her reports, but Cinnabar intended to censor them, as she had since Sly's arrival in Seelie.

She'd protect both herself and Sly.

Safe for now.

Chapter Fourteen

The day of the boar hunt arrived, and Sly couldn't wait to leave the heavy atmosphere of the castle. This morn, when he woke, bright orange and purple spots adorned his face. He combed his purple hair and ignored that and the spots. Might as well leave them, because the so-called friends and nasty relatives would only give him another enhancement. Cheap entertainment for them.

Sly entered the family salon to break his fast. His stomach rumbled, hunger a constant companion, but at least his mind didn't swim with fog. These days, he pretended to sip his hot chocolate in front of Alfric and took it with him to his bathroom suite. Once there, he tipped out a healthy measure. He thought hard before he spoke and attempted to appear dim-witted. Only with Liam did he act himself.

Once his court duties ended in the eve, he read the books Liam gave him and walked to the lake. Sometimes he saw the owl, but not always. The white stag he saw most nights, although he didn't inform Liam.

Liam reminded him of his brothers. Saber would like Liam, and he thought Liam would do well with Saber too.

His brothers. A memory had come without forcing.

Flushed with success, he attempted more. Shards of pain drove away the recollections, and the windows of his mind slammed shut. *Crap.* "Freakin' magic," he muttered, aggravation tightening every muscle. He halted, closed his eyes, breathing shallowly until the slashes of pain reduced. Only then did he resume walking.

"Good morning." Sly greeted the two security guards at the door.

"My lord. Your face," one said with a gesture.

"Your hair." The second grimaced.

"Orange and purple spots. Purple hair. I know. I've decided to leave them be. People keep giving me extra appendages and a series of spots." As he spoke, he felt his ears growing. He reached up to stroke long, furry ears, much like a donkey's. "And it seems today I must be an ass."

"I'm sorry, my lord," one of the security guards said. "Ah, your hair is now orange."

"It doesn't matter," Sly said with a roll of eyes. "Let them have their malicious entertainment. At least if they're picking on me, they're not hurting others."

"You are an honorable man," the other guard said. "I believe I'll join you in dressing up today." He flicked his wrist, and purple and orange spots appeared on his cheeks and chin. He went with matching streaky hair.

The second security guard sniggered. "I think I'll go with matching ears." He waved his hand, the air vibrating in what Sly knew was a power boost from the ley lines. Purple spots. Orange spots. One purple ear. One orange ear.

Sly grinned, and his ears flapped and twitched as he nodded.

"Lookin' good."

Liam strolled down the passage toward them and did a comical double take. "What's going on?"

"My color scheme for the day." Sly gestured at his face. "The guards decided to join the fashion."

Liam cocked his head, waved his hand, and Sly watched his face turn a delicate purple. Then orange spots popped out on his cheeks. His ears grew longer. One purple ear flopped forward while the other stood at attention.

"I'm hungry," Liam said.

Sly's belly rumbled at the mention of food.

"How's the head?"

"A few twinges. Not too bad."

Liam wriggled his ears. They were mesmerizing in a tick-tock kinda way. "Excellent. Take care today."

The security guards opened the door, and Liam sailed through with Sly on his heels. The chatter died as everyone stared. Lord Calum sniggered.

Liam halted abruptly, glowered at the amused faces and smirks. "Why aren't your faces decorated? It was on the entertainment schedule this morn. Aw." He stomped his foot.

Sly covered his grin with his hand at the show of pouty temper.

"It spoils the fun if you don't play." Liam clapped his hands three times. "Quick. Party faces. Last one decorated must help the latrine servants."

With that, spots popped and ears sprouted. Hair changed color. Laughter rose as each attempted to outdo the next.

"Sit by me," Liam said. "And remember my orders regarding food. Hello, lovely ladies. May we join you?"

Liam ignored the renewed whispers and claimed the two empty spots with a pair of elderly ladies, eschewing his usual seat at the head of the high table. "Aunt Jasper, you don't have your funny face. Would you allow me the honor?"

"You're a young scamp," the other elderly lady said with a titter. "Your nephew has always been a scamp. It won't be long before you take a wife," she added. "Ooh, that's pretty. I'd like similar spots to match my outfit."

"Your wish is my command," Liam said and murmured a few words.

Liam's aunt clapped her hands in eagerness. "Do we fit now?"

"Yes. Very dignified, yet part of the fun," Sly said. "May we join you, or are your boyfriends coming to sit with you?"

Liam smiled broadly as the elderly ladies tittered again.

"Sit. Sit." The lady with a coronet of steel-gray hair and lilac spots on her face gestured them toward the empty seats.

A footman arrived and waited gravely, his manner at odds with his face freckled with bright pink spots.

"We'll have a large pot of chocolate," Liam said. "A pot of tay for Sly plus a dish of eggs, vegetables and fried wild boar. Just place everything on the same platter, and we'll serve ourselves. Ladies, have you ordered?"

"Not yet," his aunt said. "We'll have the same, and we'd like a platter of fruit, please."

"Perfect," Liam said with a conspiratorial wink at Sly.

"Where are you from, lad?" Liam's aunt asked. "We've heard much gossip but little fact about you. Iseabal ignores my questions."

Liam sent him a warning glance, and he took heed. Best to pretend cluelessness.

"Oh, Aunt. Would you mind interrogating him another time? We intended to discuss the wild boar hunt. Sly and I heard some in Landos Wood yesterday. Do you hunt with us?"

"Not these old bones," his aunt said, successfully diverted. "I thought to explore the floral gardens. I understand your gardeners have produced some unique Saratoga blooms."

"And you, my lady?" Sly asked.

"Call me Beatrice," the elderly lady said and patted his hand.

"I am Lady Jasper," Liam's aunt said. "I told you my nephew is a scamp. He didn't even do formal introductions."

"I understood Iseabal introduced you to our family members," Liam said.

"She was busy with her duties yesterday during and after the funeral announcement." Sly aimed for tactful. In truth, the princess had chattered with her ladies-in-waiting and entertained her newly arrived friends. She'd left him alone and hadn't spoken up when one of the guests—he suspected Calum's younger brother—gave him a long black tail. It made sitting difficult until another guest had taken pity on him.

Their food arrived, and after Aunt Jasper, Beatrice, and Liam tucked into the eggs, Sly followed suit. The tay was hot and sweet and perfect.

The salon door flew open, and Princess Iseabal stormed inside. She came to a screeching halt. "What is the meaning of this? King Fionnghall has died. We should not spend time on frivolity. Fix it at once before I lose my temper!"

"I knew this would happen." Liam's chair scraped across the flagstone as he stood.

"Liam!"

Sly had never seen his betrothed at a loss for words.

"What is happening?" she demanded.

"Merely a little fun. I decided everyone was too serious this morn." He gestured at the dozens of diners. "Those who are interested in a wild boar hunt, we leave in one hour. Meet at the stable courtyard. If you require a weapon, speak with the armorer."

"Do you shoot, my lord?" Beatrice enquired.

"No, I hunt on foot."

"On foot?" Aunt Jasper asked. "Is that not dangerous?"

"I..." Sly's thoughts tangled the instant he focused on the retrieved memory. In lieu of an answer, he ate his eggs.

"Where did you say you come from?" Lady Jasper asked.

Sly helped himself to more vegetables. "Earth."

"Earth?" Beatrice queried. "I've never heard of it. Is it far?"

"Yes, Aunt. It is many, many annum cycles of journey." Liam set his cutlery on his plate and wiped his mouth. "That was delicious."

"Yes, it was," Sly agreed. "My stomach has stopped rumbling."

"Sly!" Princess Iseabal hailed him.

"Go over," Liam murmured. "Do not eat anything she offers you. I will be along to rescue you shortly."

Sly rose and approached the high table.

"Good morning, Princess Iseabal." As he waited to learn the reason for her summons, a pair of cat's whiskers grew below his nose. Strange that they seemed so natural. He noted no one had dared magic the princess. Her complexion remained golden and clear.

"What kind of name is Sly?" one of Princess Iseabal's friends asked.

"It is short for Sylvester." Huh, he knew that. Hadn't hesitated. A mistake.

The princess's eyes narrowed, and she waved at the seat to her right, currently occupied by Lady Majorca. "Sit there."

At least Sly thought that was her name. The ladies-in-waiting dressed the same, and during the eve, they wore the same white gowns as Cinnabar.

Sly froze as a memory of the woman flitted through his mind. His lips tried to smile, but one glance at the princess suggested restraint. Not the place. Even so, a rumble of a purr vibrated his chest.

"Your lady-in-waiting hasn't finished her meal," Sly said.

"Sit there!" Whip-crack words.

The hair at the back of Sly's neck lifted.

The salon fell silent, the princess and her end of the table the focal point.

"You're losing weight. You need to eat," the princess gentled her voice. "I don't wish you to sicken."

"Sly ate a huge breakfast with me, Aunt Jasper, and Beatrice," Liam said.

Sly's held breath eased out. Hell.

"Then why is he so skinny?" Princess Iseabal thundered. "He is my betrothed. I worry about him."

So why did she let everyone pick on him, make him the butt of their jokes when he had no way of reciprocating? His misfortune amused her. He'd seen her laughing at his cloven feet as he tripped, suddenly off balance.

"Iseabal." Liam patted the back of his sister's hand. "Sly is fit and healthy. I'll summon the medicine crones from the winter court if you wish. We have eaten and are heading to view the yearling cambeests. Just a quick look since the wild boar hunt commences soon. Anyone who wishes to hunt is welcome. Father used to enjoy hunting and eating wild boar, and I think it will be fitting if we send him off while eating his favorite dish."

At King Liam's invitation, the dozens of relatives and friends broke into excited chatter.

Relief struck Sly until he glimpsed Princess Iseabal's flaring nostrils and flinty gaze. That wasn't good. He needed to stay far, far away until her temper cooled.

At that moment, someone zapped their sneaky magic into prominence. Turquoise-colored dots sprang out on Princess Iseabal's temper-red cheeks.

"Whoever did that, cease." Ice coated the crisp words.

Sly's donkey-size ears suddenly reduced to small pointy ears to match his whiskers, and he grew a tail.

"I said stop it! Everyone looks ridiculous. This sort of behavior would shock Father. It's disrespectful. This is his wake, not...not a p-party." Tears formed in her beautiful blue eyes, and Sly stared, unsure if her breakdown was genuine or manufactured.

"Iseabal, this is not about you," Liam said, every inch of him a king. "You let everyone poke fun at Sly and play practical jokes on him. It's not fair since he can't respond. Instead, your friends laugh behind his back. You let them because it amuses you. You speak of respect, yet you show *none* for your fiancé. Stew on that while we're gone. Come, Sly. I told the men we'd arrive early. They have other things to do this day."

Liam waved his hand, and Sly's tail, ears, and whiskers vanished. The extra appendages and colorful spots disappeared from friends and family until only Princess Iseabal stood out with spots—no they were warts—on her cheeks.

Sly blinked. Frak it. Was her nose bigger than before?

The nearest lady-in-waiting clapped her hand over her mouth.

Princess Iseabal's nose *was* larger, and pointy at the end like a storybook witch.

She gasped and whispered a quick magical chant. Her magic didn't stop her nose growing, didn't stop the warts growing on her cleavage, didn't stop the tail from forcing through the back of her gown.

"Liam, stop!" Princess Iseabal ordered.

"No." Liam cocked his head to the side. "I want you to taste an absence of magic."

"But our family from the winter court starts arriving today," she wailed, finally ceasing her chants.

"The warts, nose, and tail will reduce during the day," Liam said.

"But you never said anything before." Princess Katrina came to the aid of her twin.

The first time Sly had ever witnessed their sisterly bond. Normally, they were standoffish toward each other. He'd never do that to his twin. Joe would never—

Shock broke off the thought.

He had a twin brother.

"I shouldn't have to intervene!" Liam barked. "Respect for

others. Our mother taught us that. She'd be ashamed of your behavior. All of you! A few practical jokes are fine. A sense of fun, but it is never right to crush someone weaker, someone who can't fight back. Think on that while I'm gone." He jerked his chin toward the door. "Come, Sly. We're late."

Sly trailed Liam from the silent salon. As soon as they turned the corner, the whispers started. When they reached the halfway point of the passage, a furious scream rang out.

"Magic it away!" Princess Iseabal shrieked.

Sly didn't hear any replies, but as they exited the castle, the next scream that rippled from the salon held enough fury to scare the owl from her roost. She flew to Sly and perched on his left shoulder, her entire frame quivering.

"Shush." Sly stroked the russet feathers. "It's all right, Cinnabar. The princess is angry at Liam."

Liam halted and pivoted to face him. "Cinnabar?"

Sly blinked, and the owl squished closer to his neck, trying to burrow beneath the collar of his gray shirt.

"Why did you call the owl Cinnabar?"

Sly crashed against one of those invisible walls in his mind. A frown etched into his brow, but pushing his brain sent shards of pain darting to his temples. "I don't know." He brightened, though, as a loose thought jumped to the forefront. "I have a brother," he announced. "A twin."

Now it was Liam's turn to glower. "As far as I know, Iseabal and Katrina are the only twins in the kingdom. There are none in the winter court. Where did you come from? Iseabal must've brought you through the main entrance, yet no one saw anything. I made inquiries."

An idea fluttered before a wall slammed up, and the vague memories exploded into dust. "I've got nothing."

"Damn." Liam recommenced his determined path to the stable yard. "I wish the wise medicine crones were here. They spend six months in each court."

"Why? People must have need of them. Get sick."

"There is little illness in the kingdom."

"The king?"

"Father was old. We live long lives. I know he missed my mother and pined to join her in Utopia."

"But how do you know it wasn't something serious? Something other than old age?"

"What are you suggesting?" Liam asked.

"Well, could it have been poison? You've told me not to eat food unless you deliver it to me. If something in my food is causing my memory loss, then perhaps a similar drug was administered to the king?"

"No one would dare," Liam snapped, and his eyes morphed into a fiery red instead of the normal tranquil blue. "Everyone loved my father."

Sly raised his hands in surrender and backed up a step. "I didn't mean to anger you. I'm still learning the ways of your world and reading through the history books you've lent me. But previous kings have died from poisoning."

"When? I don't recall reading that."

The red of Liam's eyes reduced and Sly lowered his hands. "Not in Seelie's recent history, but two thousand years ago. Three of your kings were poisoned, and it got so diabolical the court hired a food taster. Two of them died before the Council of Balance captured the culprit. Do you still have a Council of Balance?"

"No, they were disbanded as obsolete. Who did it?"

"The younger brother and sister worked together because they desired power."

Liam gaped at Sly. "You think one of my sisters... No, they wouldn't. Why would they?"

"The king has absolute power. His magic is strongest in the kingdom, thanks to the staff of power. For some people, power is an aphrodisiac. It's a lure. All I'm saying is you should take care. Set procedures to make it difficult for others to unseat you in this manner."

"I'll think about it," Liam said as the stable lads led out their cambeests.

"I'm probably wrong," Sly offered. "But you're my friend. I'd hate anything to happen to you."

"The court is always full of intrigue and secrets, maneuvering for position. You're right to warn me. I spend—or have spent—much time away to avoid the petty backstabbing. I enjoy working the land and helping our people prosper." He rubbed his hand over his face. "It's not such a big jump to murder."

"I'm sorry. I didn't want to spoil your day."

Liam lowered his voice. "I never wanted to be king. If I could trust Iseabal to behave with integrity, I'd consider handing the staff of power to her."

Once away from the castle, Sly relaxed. The owl continued to perch on his shoulder, appearing to enjoy its roost.

"You realize my suspicions will work overtime now," Liam said as they cantered past the lake. "Crap, that white stag is there again. I don't like the way he's hanging around. It's an unlucky omen."

"I spend my entire day looking over my shoulder, but terrible things still happen. Do you know how difficult it is to control a tail while in human form? I've never had to do that before."

"What? What did you say?"

"I said...ah...I don't remember. What did I say?"

"You said something about controlling your tail, as if you were used to having one."

"But I don't have a tail. Not unless some idiot magics one there. Your friends find it amusing."

"I wonder," Liam said. "I wonder if that is possible."

"Wonder if what is possible?"

"Maybe you're an animal. But no, that wouldn't make sense.

You're too intelligent. Animals can't read." He tapped his chin, his thoughts turning inward. "I need to check a few things. Don't want to raise your hopes. Do you wish to marry my sister?"

"I don't like her," Sly said, going for honesty. Damn, his mouth was sore again. He patted his pocket and found the salve container. He'd apply some once they arrived at their destination. "I keep saying I don't understand why I'm here or why she wishes our marriage to go ahead."

"My guess." Liam tapped his chin. "She desires a biddable husband. One of Calvin's security guards asked her to marry him."

"A security guard?"

"Trevelyan comes from a powerful family. He's strong. Intelligent. Decisive. Your lack of magic presents a unique opportunity. Iseabal can strengthen her position as my heir without a husband getting in her way."

Sly snorted, insulted at the portrayal, even though Liam spoke the truth. "Which leads right back to my original discussion. Is it possible that someone murdered your father to place themselves in a better position to seize the throne?"

Chapter Fifteen

Middlemarch Resort

Each day that Joe entered the *Sleeping Beauty* boudoir, fear slithered with him, performing a war dance at his heels. Some days, Sly appeared improved. Other days, he deteriorated, becoming so cold that Joe's fingers tingled with frostbite.

Joe caught his breath as he approached, missing his twin so much he ached. He'd lost his confidant, his sounding-board for ideas, stupid or not. Sly had no trouble telling him to pull his head in if he behaved like a dick.

He tugged back the warm coverings and placed a trembling hand on Sly's shoulder. His breath hissed out, and tension dissipated from his shoulders. Not as serious as yesterday.

"How is he?"

Joe spun to face Saber. He smiled wryly as his pulse resettled. "He's a little better today."

Saber touched Sly's lean face, his arm. "You're right. His core temperature has improved. Do you still want to do two sessions with the guests? You could drop it to one."

"No." Joe suspected Sly would tell him to continue, even with the chapped-lips danger. "We should keep to two sessions while demand is high. If the novelty wears off, we'll go back to daily."

"No show of that happening." Scarlett stalked into the room, her black hair styled in its usual donut bun.

"Eavesdropping again?" Saber asked.

"Nope. You're getting old and your hearing is going," Scarlett retorted, green eyes sparkling with mirth.

Joe grinned. His sister was feisty, and he didn't envy the man who battled her hijinks or thought to restrict her freedom.

"Joe." Scarlett placed her hand on his forearm and Sly's. "I added *Sleeping Beauty* to our promotional package. Some of the links have picked up the news as an entertainment novelty. Eva told me she heard lots of her customers discussing *Sleeping Beauty* when she visited her restaurants on Dalcon. Bookings are up." She stroked Sly's cheek. "Hmmm, chapped lips. Are you sure none of these women are doing the nasty with his mouth?"

Saber spluttered. "The nasty? When did you speak to Eva?"

"You know. Tongue." Scarlett poked out her tongue and waggled it in illustration. "Eva called me about half an hour ago. I asked her to pick up jewelry-making supplies, and she wanted to check she was getting the right thing."

"Oh," Saber said.

"Eva is away for the day," Scarlett said, her exasperation clear. "Come on, Saber. You can do this. Go cold turkey."

Saber scowled. "Wait until you have a mate. You'll understand my position."

"Nope. Not going there. I've seen you and Felix bossing around your mates. Leo does it too. I refuse to get me a bossy man."

Joe listened to his brother and sister bickering, the constancy lightening his frustration. Sly would get better. Somehow, they'd fix whatever ailed him. "Go," Joe said when Saber and Scarlett continued to discuss the likelihood of Scarlett finding a mate.

"No sane man will have you," Saber predicted, glowering at his sister.

"I don't need a man," Scarlett said sweetly. "I have my sex—"

"Stop," Saber barked. "Do not continue."

Scarlett chortled as Saber practically scuttled from the boudoir. "Conversations about sex fluster him every time. How are you doing, Joe? And Sly?"

"Discuss your sex toys with Sly. I'd be thrilled if you embarrassed him into an escape attempt."

"Aw, Joe." Scarlett gave him a one-armed hug. "Sly is strong. We're doing the best we can. Casey is still checking her sources. Your idea to use the guests to keep Sly warm is pure brilliance. Don't worry. Somehow, we'll pull him through."

"Thanks." Joe hugged his sister back. At least the weird erections had ceased. Even stranger was the way Sly's erections had occurred at the same time each day. Not a discussion for sisterly ears. "It's time to open the boudoir. I'd better get moving."

Scarlett left, and Joe went through his daily routine, making sure Sly was clean and comfortable. He retrieved the lip salve and applied it to Sly's cracked lips. Maybe Saber was right, and they should cut back to one session while Sly was doing well.

"Sly, I don't know what is wrong with you, but I hope you can hear. Come back to us, to me. It's no fun without you around."

Seelie Castle

Excitement about the wild boar hunt filled the castle. Laughter.

Chatter. Sly had never heard such a kerfuffle. Even the princess bubbled with high spirits, despite sporting warts, a big nose, and a tail. Both nose and tail had reduced in size, although Sly wondered how she'd manage to ride a cambeest in comfort.

"Mount up," Liam called. "The stable lads will help those who need aid. Meet at the edge of the King's Forest."

Sly urged his cambeest forward and trotted beside Liam. The other riders followed them from the stable courtyard with much noise and hilarity.

"Everyone seems happy," Sly said.

"A change in routine," Liam agreed. "It makes me realize how much things need to change in Seelie. My position allows me to do as I please, and I chose to focus on our farming production and increasing our export earnings. Most of our population don't have the same opportunities. There is nothing for them to do and they get bored. They argue. They play practical jokes. They plan revenge. That's one of the reasons I'm eager for my cousin, the winter king, to arrive. His kingdom is more successful. Calvin stepped away from tradition and has more contact with the outside world. Unseelie accepts visitors without check. It works for them."

"If it wasn't for you letting me tag along, I would've gone nuts. I'm used to staying busy."

"What do you like to do in your spare time?" Liam asked.

"I hang out with Joe. He's my best friend as well as my brother. We—my other brothers and I—work together at the resort..." Sly trailed off as he heard what he was saying. "I have a family. Where are they? And why can't I remember them properly?"

"I suspect my sister has something to do with that." Liam shot him a grim glower. "I will get to the bottom of this. You haven't mentioned a resort before."

"No." Sly scanned for other riders and decided they were out of range of eavesdroppers. "I don't wish to marry Princess Iseabal.

Hell, she refuses to let me call her by her first name. And even the servants can tell she has no respect for me. A married couple should respect each other."

Liam rubbed his cambeest's hump and his mount rumbled in contentment. "Somehow, I'll fix this. Meantime, continue to take care with your food and drink."

Half an hour later, their party halted on a grass knoll at the edge of the forest.

Liam held up his right hand for silence. Their group neared thirty in number, with both men and women. In addition, Liam had organized stable lads and the head groom to join the hunt.

"We'll split our group into three and each will hunt in a defined area, known to the staff. They'll brief you on the boundaries and where you can and cannot hunt. The most important rule—identify your target before you fire your arrows. One funeral is enough. Is that clear?" Liam scanned faces to ascertain everyone understood the importance of this directive. "Princess Iseabal will lead one group. Princess Katrina and Lord Calum will lead another, and I will lead the third. Dougal, you go with Princess Iseabal."

Intrigued by Liam's casual manner, yet his undisputed leadership, Sly watched as first one group peeled off, then a second, leaving him with Liam's group of seven plus two stable lads.

"Have you shot a bow and arrow before?" Liam asked.

"I don't think so," Sly said. "I'll enjoy the ride and search for signs of wild boar."

Liam unfastened his bow and tucked it against his side. "Move out," he ordered. "Remember, double-check you're firing at a boar. Check your prey."

Liam directed his cambeest over the sun-dappled ground and into the shade cast by weathered trees with drab green leaves. The trees clung to the soil, thrusting upward in their search for light. Sly squeezed his thighs around the barrel body of his mount, silently urging Brigitte to follow the king.

Others shadowed him, their cambeests crunching dead leaves and fallen twigs underfoot.

Sly relaxed, enjoying the ride. Bright red mushrooms grew in a tight circle, in a spot where light forced through the tree canopy.

Over to his right, Sly heard the trickle of water. Other noises tickled his ears. The creak of leather as riders shifted on their mounts. The snort of the cambeests picking their way along the forest paths. The tweet of a bird. The flutter of wings. The drone of an insect. He did a visual sweep for the owl but didn't find the bird.

Another noise snared his attention. A snort. A grunt. A squeal.

"Hold," he said.

Liam tightened his reins, ceasing his progress through the forest. "Do you hear something?"

"Yeah." Sly pointed in front of their group, slightly to the right. "Can't you hear them? It sounds like pigs to me."

Liam's brows rose. "Pigs?"

A squeal rent the air. And a second, almost straightaway.

"Mine," a man from the back called. "I will target this boar."

"Sounds as if there is a singular of wild boar," Sly said.

"A singular?" Liam's brows rose in askance.

Sly shrugged. "That's what you call a group of wild boars."

"Interesting. Enjoyable day for a ride. Ah, your owl." Liam radiated humor as he signaled two men to peel from their party to track the boar. One of the stable lads followed Liam and Sly while the other stayed with the rest of the party.

Another memory frisked him, darting from reach. Something about the owl. Sly cursed under his breath. He retrieved one memory, and another slipped through the cracks. His mind resembled a sieve with more holes than substance.

A sharp squeal came from behind them. Undergrowth rustled and crackled as a boar thundered through the bushes.

"Watch out," Liam warned. "They're dangerous if they're cornered. Their tusks are lethal."

A charcoal-gray boar shot onto the track, shrieking in alarm. An arrow poked from its hairy side and blood spotted the ground as it tore past Sly. Two more boars darted after the first, crowding and jostling for space. Liam's cambeest reared as the boars rushed him.

For an instant, Sly thought they were fine, but the boars—stupid animals—charged Liam's cambeest. The cambeest shied, bucked, and lashed out with its hooves, bounding again like a rabbit before Liam regained control. A third determined leap unseated the king. He thumped to the ground, and the boars charged over the top of him.

Sly scrambled off his mount and thrust the reins at a pale-faced stable lad. "Hold him." *Crap.* Liam couldn't die this way, not as they prepared to bury his father.

Sly raced across the uneven ground and crouched beside him. "Liam. Liam!"

Liam groaned and turned laboriously onto his side. He winced, his nostrils flaring as he attempted a full breath.

"Holy crap. You okay?" Sly ran his hands across Liam's back, his arms, and legs, checking for injuries. No blood. That was encouraging. "Let me help you up." He turned to the stable boy. "You'd better go and catch the king's cambeest before it reaches the stables."

The boy tied Sly's cambeest, leaped on his own and hustled along the path after Liam's steed.

"Liam, speak to me," Sly ordered.

"I feel as if I've been run over. Do I have footprints on my back?"

Sly chuckled, relieved Liam had cracked a joke. Hell, that he was speaking at all. "The boars galloped over you."

Liam let out a pained groan as Sly gripped his arm. "Holy wild boar. That hurt."

An understatement. He bet Liam would sport a colorful batch

of bruises on the morrow unless he used his magic. He eyed Liam's face, his jaw. It was gritted. Pain etched into the king's eyes. "You sure you're not gonna faint like a girl?"

Liam snorted. Winced. "Don't make jokes. Help me up."

"*Ooh*, that sounds like a royal order."

Liam attempted to stand. "Ow, ow, ow."

Sly slipped his arm around Liam's shoulders and aided his struggle to his feet.

A stick crackled behind them. Sly stilled. Cast out his senses. Liam hadn't reacted, but everything in Sly screamed a warning.

Danger.

He edged in front of Liam, eyes watchful. Scanned the tangle of bushes. The vines. The trees.

Nothing.

But that weird preternatural awareness gripped him, prodded him, cautioned him.

Three seconds passed, and his breath eased outward. Nothing out here except his vivid imagination.

As he turned back to Liam, a stone rattled. A leaf crunched beneath a foot.

The owl shrieked. A flurry of movement came from the bushes.

"Get down!" Sly shoved Liam behind him.

Something whistled through the air and struck his biceps. Fire sizzled through his arm.

What the hell? He gaped at the black feathers on the shaft of the arrow piercing his limb. The blood. After all Liam's warnings, some idiot had shot him.

The crack of a branch grabbed Sly's attention. He searched the trees and again saw nothing.

But the bastard was out there hunting them. Did they look like bloody wild boars? Should've worn the bright suit Alfric had laid out for him. Unwise decision, overruling his valet and grabbing his favored dull colors.

"Hey! Stop. You're shooting at the king."

His cambeest grunted and called a greeting, big ears twitching.

"The stable boy must've found your cambeest. Let's get back to the castle," Sly said. Crap, his arm stung like a bitch. At least the bleeding wasn't too copious. Should he try to take out the arrow? Nah, leave it till later. He crouched beside the king. Hell, his mind...dizzy. *Hurry.*

A whistle warned him.

He threw himself over Liam and grunted as another bloody arrow pierced his shoulder from behind. *Just call him pin cushion.*

The stable lad raced toward them and slid from his saddle. At least the cambeests blocked the shooter now.

"Stop shooting!" the stable lad called.

"He's a poor shot," Sly muttered. "He's not hitting the king."

Beneath him, Liam laughed. Cursed. "Get off me, you big lump. You're heavy."

Yeah, he should probably try to move. *Muscles don't work. Focus. You can move.*

Shades of light and black burst behind his eyes. Sly gasped. He refused to faint. Liam would never let him hear the end of it. He forced his legs to move. His right arm dragged, didn't work. *Move.* His fingers twitched.

"Let me help, my lord," the stable boy said.

Sly struggled with his feet. He felt like an old man with shaky balance. Once he rolled off Liam, the stable lad helped the king to rise.

"You saved me," Liam said.

"Nah, I was unlucky and got in the way of the arrows," Sly answered, aiming for humor. It fell flat. *Too bad. Best I can do.* "Help Liam onto his cambeest."

"Should I go for help?"

"Wait," Liam gasped out.

Sly flinched at a flash of movement from above, then relaxed.

The owl. It landed on his saddle pommel and stared at him with its round blue eyes.

"Your owl didn't warn us," Liam said as he struggled to mount his cambeest.

"It did," Sly said. *Keep your eyes open. Don't pass out like a girl.* Joe will tease. Wait. Joe wasn't here. Where was he? Why wasn't his brother coming for him? Hell, damn if he knew.

"Help, Sly," Liam ordered, sounding more alert now.

Sly pushed to his knees, bit back a groan. "Legs not working."

"He's going into shock. We need to get him back to the castle," Liam said.

"Lean on me, my lord."

Sly bit back a strangled laugh. Black humor. He towered over the stable lad. He'd flatten him.

But the boy never faltered. He slipped his arm around Sly's waist, taking care not to knock the arrows protruding from his body.

The lad hid muscles in his scrawny frame.

"I'll ride ahead and get help," Liam said.

"Careful." Sly tried to lift his head and failed. "I'm sure they were shooting at you."

"I'll return soon," Liam promised.

"Can you walk, my lord?"

"Yes." No stupid arrow was going to beat him. Sly gritted his teeth against the darting jags of agony. Sweat prickled his skin, ran beneath his shirt. Or maybe it was blood. He shivered. Pushed his limbs to action. *Move, dammit. Liam isn't safe alone.* He wobbled along the uneven path and stumbled over a tree root.

His vision faded in and out, blurring the scenery.

Time slowed, measured in beats of pain.

One. Two. Three. Another step.

One. Two. Three. Step.

Wetness soaked his shirt. Sweat beaded his forehead.

A thunder of hooves raced toward them. The stable lad tensed. Sly tripped and almost tumbled them to the ground.

"Hellfire. His shoulder is bleeding," someone said.

Sly tried to acknowledge the speaker. Couldn't force open his eyes.

"Sly." Liam slipped his arm around his waist, aiding the lad. "Maybe I can magic him back to the castle."

"No," someone said. "You've had a fall too. Lift him onto his cambeest. The stable lad can go up with him and keep him safely balanced. It will be faster. No disrespect, but he's a big man."

Sly wavered. He didn't care how he arrived at the castle. Just craved a flat surface. Rest. His legs buckled. He groaned. Nausea had him swallowing, swallowing, swallowing. His mind drifted to fog, the holey walls fading to black. Darkness spread, covering the fog until only a pinprick of light remained.

The last thing he remembered.

CHAPTER SIXTEEN

C innabar perched in a tree. Two arrows. *Two*. She hadn't seen the shooter but had heard them and glimpsed the top of their bow. He or she had known they weren't shooting wild boars. By the time she'd thought to discover the shooter's identity, they'd vanished.

Sly lurched without warning.

"He's out," King Liam said. "Let's get him onto a cambeest while he's unconscious."

They managed to lift him, and the stable lad leapt astride the cambeest to hold Sly in position.

Cinnabar flew from branch to branch, tremors shaking her feathers. She should have warned them sooner and signaled the danger. What if Sly died, and she never had a chance to speak with him, touch him again?

They arrived at the stable yards and Liam bellowed for help. The other groups hadn't returned yet.

"We'll take him to his chamber—"

Cinnabar squawked and ruffled her wings. She stepped from foot to foot and issued a sharp shriek.

The king paused, his contemplative gaze connecting with hers. *Please don't leave him alone. It's dangerous.*

"No, on second thought, we'll carry him to my chamber."

Cinnabar relaxed a fraction as King Liam and the stable boys lugged Sly to the castle.

"The side entrance," King Liam ordered.

As they approached the door, the two security guards rushed to help. Cinnabar shifted course and flew to the other side of the castle. She settled on the ledge outside King Liam's tower chamber. Frying fungus, she had turned into a peeping Tom. Hopefully, King Liam wouldn't rip off his clothes. She blinked. Seeing the king naked might be a punishable crime.

She waited until the men carried Sly into the chamber and set him on King Liam's bed. The king noticed her immediately. She stiffened, ready to take flight if the king approached. He did, and she lifted into the air, flapping her wings to hover out of reach.

King Liam pushed open the window. "We're removing the arrows as soon as we have medical supplies. Hopefully we won't need them, and my magic will still his bleeding." He paused and grimaced. "Although why I'm telling you, I have no idea." He turned his attention to Sly. "Where are the medical supplies?"

Cinnabar took a risk, worry urging her to move closer. Her talons curled around the stone window ledge, and she fluffed out her wings, settling in to watch the proceedings. Sly had to be all right. He had to. He should've regained consciousness by now.

King Liam's valet appeared with an armful of bandages and salves. He disappeared and returned with a basin of water.

"Right. Let's get those arrows out and the bleeding stopped before he wakes," King Liam ordered.

"Too late," Sly mumbled from the bed. "Jeez, my shoulder hurts like a bitch."

"Okay, Sly," King Liam said. "Inconvenient of you to wake now, but let's get this done."

Sly checked the room until his attention fastened on her. He grinned, or tried to. It was more of a grimace of bared teeth. "Hell, yeah."

The king gripped the shaft of an arrow and yanked while muttering a quick booster spell. The arrow emerged a bit at a time, Sly's groan tortured.

Cinnabar ached to offer comfort, but what could an owl do? Nothing. This curse cut like a knife, attacking her again and again, stabbing her in the heart.

This wasn't living.

This was a hellish punishment with no end.

Cinnabar's agitation ruffled her feathered breast. She hopped through the window and alighted nearer the bed.

"Your Majesty," his valet protested. "Why is the owl inside?"

"It's Sly's pet. Let it be," King Liam said.

Pet? She was no one's pet, but she did belong to Sly. That part was true.

Cinnabar ached in her anguish. She needed human fingers to massage away the pain. Instead, she blinked and watched the proceedings.

The king mumbled a spell as the second blood-tipped arrow emerged from Sly's arm with a horrid sucking whoosh.

"Damp cloth," King Liam ordered.

The valet handed it to him. "You shouldn't be doing this, Your Majesty. Let me do it for you."

"Sly deserves nothing less than my personal attention. He saved me from an arrow. Whoever shot him was aiming for me, and Sly pushed me out of the way. Damn, the bleeding has stopped but the flesh isn't knitting together as I'd expect."

"Is he gonna be all right?" the stable lad asked, the one who had been with them during the attack.

"Shush, lad," the valet ordered. "Get back to your duties. The rest of you, too."

"Thank you for your help," King Liam said as they departed. "I'll send a message to the stables later and let you know how Sly is doing."

"Thank you, Your Majesty." The stable lad lifted his chin. "We like Sly. He's a respectable man and doesn't deserve this."

Cinnabar agreed. The king's expression indicated a like mind.

"Can you magic the salve, Your Majesty?" his valet asked.

"I'll try. At least the bleeding has stopped. I intend to change things around here, Gilbert. Once the winter king comes, I'll discuss my ideas with him."

Determined footsteps clicked on the stone floor outside the king's chamber. Cinnabar lifted her head, hooted, and fled to the open window. She took flight seconds before the door thumped, but she guessed the new arrival's identity.

Princess Iseabal, and she'd want to know why Sly wasn't in his chamber.

Princess Iseabal stomped through the door. Damn her brother for interfering! He knew something. No, he suspected she was up to something. That was the difference. She had to get the priest to complete the banns. No one would object then. They wouldn't dare.

Sly lay on Liam's bed while her brother attended him.

"Why are you treating him?" she demanded. "Why didn't you send me a message?"

"You were still on the hunt," Liam said without glancing up. "I didn't want to spoil your enjoyment."

Iseabal ground her teeth together and bit back the angry words festering for release. Liam would *not* derail her plans. She stuffed tension-stiff hands in the pockets of her hunting gown. "Sly is my betrothed. Of course, I am concerned. Why bring him to your tower? What is wrong with Sly's chamber?"

"Someone shot two arrows into him. I want him safe, and my personal security team can provide protection."

"No one would dare attack my betrothed within the castle."

"Someone shot him in the royal forest." Liam stood and glowered at her, eyes red and flashing with ire.

Iseabal took half a step back, such was the force of her brother's fury. "You think this was intentional?"

"We called out after the first arrow struck Sly. The archer knew he'd hit one of us rather than a wild boar. What other conclusion is there?"

"You think I— Why would I want Sly dead? I intend to marry him. And if it wasn't for Father's wake and the funeral, the priest would've called the final banns. The final banns will be called on the first service after the mourning period. Sly and I *will* marry." She refused to fail. Her plan must continue if she was to rule the kingdom. Calum gloated, reveled in his new position. Bastard. She had no idea why her twin had wed the weasel.

Marriage to Calum had changed Katrina. She was quieter. More proper and never offered an opinion. And Liam...her brother let his soft emotions rule him instead of using a cool head.

She packed away her goals, planted herself in the present. "Is Sly conscious?"

"Just," Sly croaked.

Liam's expression told her she'd blundered. She hadn't asked after Sly, asked about his injuries. Should've done that first. *Shoodlepoppers.* "Are you hungry? Let me order soup from the kitchen. I'll feed Sly while you clean up. Our cousin should arrive soon for the wake."

"I'm not hungry. Just wanna sleep," Sly said.

Iseabal circled the bed. His eyes fluttered closed, his breathing evened out. Blast. "He has lost weight. I've noticed he's not eating much." Which was a nuisance. The dual spell she'd placed on him required a top up. She could do this. Hold things together until the wedding.

Liam straightened, cocked his head as the watchman blasted his horn three times. "Calvin approaches. Come, let us leave Sly to sleep and greet our cousin."

Iseabal retraced her footsteps and stood at the end of the bed. "Do you know if Trevelyan is attending the funeral?"

"As far as I know, Calvin intended to bring his security team with him."

Blast. Trevelyan thought he owned her, had asked her to marry him. The time he'd kissed her... No, she refused to forfeit her rights for a man. Trevelyan would boss her around, expect her to cede power to him.

No. No, she refused. Sly was the better option for her plan to succeed. Somehow, she'd get spelled food into Sly and make sure he didn't regain his memory. "I'll fetch a warm wrap. You'll need a jacket too. The temperature will drop."

"Excellent point. See you in the courtyard."

"No, you're the king. You—"

"I expect both you and Katrina in the courtyard to greet our guests." Liam stalked off to find a jacket.

She stiffened, and the blood rushed to her head. Her skin heated, then a chill swept her. Should she do a sneaky counter spell to boost her power over Sly? A vibration tickled her arm. Liam returned. Damn and blast, there was no time.

With a last glance at Sly, she swept from Liam's tower and detoured to hers. She required Cinnabar. Once inside her chamber, she opened her window to search for the owl and sent her maid to bring a plate of hazelberry cookies to get rid of flapping ears. *Tap. Tap. Tap.* Where the devil was Cinnabar? Iseabal paced, sent a mental call and, as she turned, a whoosh of wings announced

Cinnabar's arrival.

"Where were you?" Iseabal demanded. "You must stay on your perch."

Cinnabar hooted—a soft acknowledgment.

"I want you to watch Sly. He's resting in King Liam's chamber. The instant he's alone, I want you to let me know. Do you understand?"

Cinnabar hooted again.

"Don't fail me. Are you hungry?"

Cinnabar blinked.

Iseabal cocked her head, smiled, warmth flooding her chest. She wanted to laugh, to share this delicious joke with everyone. Cinnabar had always done the right thing, shown Iseabal up with her proper behavior, her so-called grace. "I have a mouselet for your dinner."

Iseabal conjured a glove and plucked the wriggling mouselet from a jar she'd acquired earlier.

Cinnabar stared at the mouselet as if mesmerized, yet her eyes held a hint of dazed horror.

Iseabal laughed and dangled the gray creature in front of Cinnabar. "Don't be shy now. Eat up."

Sly pushed out a breath the instant the door closed after Princess Iseabal. But he didn't make the mistake of moving until a full five minutes passed and his senses told him he was alone. In the bedroom, at least. The low murmur of voices and the rub of fabric as the wearer shifted his or her weight sounded. Liam's security guards, he presumed.

Using his arms, he gingerly pushed himself upright. Huh. Surely, that should've hurt more. He peeled away the crisp white bandage covering his arm and blinked at the slightly red flesh where the first arrow had speared him.

The owl appeared at the window, and Sly stood, striding over to let it inside again. "Cinnabar." He kept his voice low so the security guards didn't overhear. "Check out my arm."

He showed her the healed wound.

Cinnabar hooted—an enquiring sound—and stared at the other bandage strapped around his upper chest and shoulder.

"Yes, let's check my other war wound. It doesn't throb. Not like it should. Liam worried 'cause his magic didn't work." Sly sat on the edge of the bed and removed the dressing. "That's weird. What do you make of that?"

Cinnabar sidled closer.

Sly stroked her head. "I've missed you."

Cinnabar cooed and leaned into his touch.

"My mind went blank again, but it's not at present. I have a brother. More than one. My family and I came from Earth. That's all I remember so far, but it's a start. Has Liam's cousin arrived?"

The owl whistled.

"I need to leave Seelie. I wonder if Liam's cousin would allow me to travel with him."

Cinnabar bounced up and down in place and hooted.

"Yes, you're probably right. Leaving will be tricky. Liam might help. I'll tell him everything I recall. There are still blanks. Hopefully, I'll remember more."

Sly prowled the confines of Liam's chamber, his mind busy while he considered his past and his future. "Has Liam discovered who shot at him?"

"Who. Hoo. Hoo," Cinnabar said and added a whistle.

"No? I'll ask him when he changes for dinner. Meantime, I'm stuck here. I don't want to run into Iseabal. Excuse me, *Princess* Iseabal." No mistaking that sarcasm. It said everything. He'd never respect a woman who demanded such formality. It wasn't his way.

He tugged at that string of thought and smacked into a wall. Not as solid. He'd smash through soon and find the answers he sought.

The voices outside the door grew louder. Every muscle in his body tensed as he listened intently.

"It's Liam," Sly said finally, relaxing.

The door opened and Liam stalked inside.

"You're awake." His gaze shifted to Sly's arm. He halted mid-stride, did a rapid eye blink. "Your arm. It's healed." He closed the remaining distance between them and ran his fingers over the reddened skin. "Does it hurt?"

"No, it's fine."

"The other one is almost healed too. I don't understand. My magic didn't work. Even I don't heal that fast, and my body responds to magic. Hmm, maybe I need to spend more time practicing."

"Have you learned anything about the archer who shot at you?" Sly held out his arm. The owl jumped on and transferred to his shoulder.

Liam stared, shook his head. "I've asked questions, checked with the stable lads. None of them saw anything unusual. I've arranged to question everyone on the morn."

"You need to watch yourself. Take care of what you eat and drink," Sly suggested.

"I can't believe one of my subjects is trying to do away with me. It's unthinkable."

"Someone tried to skewer you with their arrows," Sly countered, then changed the subject. "How can I leave Seelie?"

"You want to leave?"

"I don't belong here. This isn't my home."

"Have you remembered everything? Do you know where you come from? The location of this resort?"

Sly slumped. "No. All I know is that Seelie isn't home. I want to search for my family. My brothers."

"I've come to think of you as my friend. Someone I can share my thoughts with and receive a sensible reply. You don't treat me like a royal. You tell me what you think, even if you know it differs from my opinions. That's rare in Seelie. You know about farming. None of my so-called friends are interested in farming or the land, yet this is where our wealth lies."

"Just because I want to leave, it doesn't mean we can't continue our friendship. But you must understand this is strange. Somehow, your sister has done this to me. I don't know where she found me, but my home can't be far away."

The owl cooed and cuddled into his neck.

"Aye, as far as I know, she didn't leave here overnight. I must check with the guards on the gate to double check her movements. I'll contact the guards now."

The technology here seemed strange and, now, Sly considered it, unfamiliar to him. Liam stared into the distance before walking to the transparent globe in the corner of his chamber. The globe lit and glowed a pale blue.

"Yes, sire," the head security guard said.

"Did my sister, the Princess Iseabal, leave Seelie while I was away on my last business trip?"

"No, Your Majesty," the guard said. "I'm positive. I would've sent at least two guards with her, the same as usual. Let me investigate further. My guards were grumbling about boredom, so I sent them off training. As far as I know, your private guards were the only ones to leave Seelie recently."

"Thank you," Liam said. "Please send six guards to the castle. We've had trouble here, and I'd like the extra security since the winter court has arrived. I'll speak to my cousin and coordinate our security."

"Aye, Your Majesty."

Liam ended the call. "You heard what he said. She didn't leave."

"Could she use her magic?"

"She doesn't have enough power to bring you in that way."

"Could you?"

"Perhaps, but it'd drain my reserves."

"She managed it somehow." Sly threw up his hands. "Your sister brought me here, and you're putting up stop signs, trying to halt me from leaving."

"No!" Then Liam scowled. "You're right. I am. As soon as the funeral is over, I'll force Iseabal to give us answers. If I ask her, she repeats her story of meeting you at her friend's party. The friend backs up her claims."

The owl hooted in alarm. Sly tensed as he, too, heard determined footsteps. As voices became audible, the owl sped out the open window.

"Iseabal," Liam muttered.

Sly grabbed the bandage and leaped into the bed. He yanked the covers up to his shoulders and pretended sleep.

Liam cursed. "Gratafire." He stomped to the door and flung it open. "Cease your noise. Sly is asleep. How can you be so inconsiderate? The man took an arrow for me."

Taut silence fell, and Sly wished it was possible to use more than his hearing to decipher the blast of tension.

"You never said the arrows were intended for you." Iseabal broke the hush.

"I thought I did," Liam answered.

"Any clues as to who's responsible?"

Sly discerned nothing but surprise. Concern. If Iseabal had organized the archer, she was a hell of an actress. But, given her behavior to date, that didn't surprise him.

"Not yet," Liam said. "But I'm investigating."

"Please call me when my betrothed awakens," she said briskly. "I'll contact the kitchen and organize a meal for Sly."

"Thank you," Liam said. "I'll see you at dinner."

"Where are you sleeping?"

"I'll worry about that later."

Iseabal *tut-tutted*. "My betrothed has a perfectly fine bed in his chamber. I don't know why you brought him up here."

"I wanted my private security to guard him," Liam stated, his tone every inch the king.

"As you wish. You're the king." Iseabal backpedaled.

The door shut.

"You're safe now," Liam murmured.

"Iseabal hardly ever calls me by my name. I'm a possession. If I were her fiancé, she'd let me kiss her, address her informally. I don't get the no-contact rules. They're archaic."

"You remember me telling you about the rules for royal princesses?"

"Yeah. Cinnabar mentioned a few things too." Sly wrinkled his brow.

"Cinnabar ran off with a man from the winter court. Iseabal was most irked. Where did you meet Cinnabar?"

"I..." Sly hesitated, running smack into another one of those mind walls. They sprang up and down like faulty automatic gates when Liam asked direct questions. "All I recall is the name."

Liam nodded. "I'd better dress for dinner. It will be a late night. You'll like my cousin. I'll get my valet to organize a trundle bed."

"Have you told your cousin about the attempt on your life?"

"I will as soon as we have a private moment. If I hurry, we might manage a drink together before the rest of the guests come down for dinner."

"Can I read your books?"

Liam gestured at his desk and bookcase at the far side of the chamber. "You may. I've arranged for my valet to get food for you." He paused as someone scraped on the door. "Ah, there he is now. This food is safe, but don't eat anything else that arrives."

"I won't."

The prince flung off his jacket and shirt and hurried to his en suite. Minutes later, water poured against tiles, and the king warbled an off-tune song. Sly grinned. Just as well he was a king. He'd never make a living as a singer.

The evening passed as slow as dripping honey on a chilly day. A *tap-tap-tap* at his window claimed his attention. The owl. He opened the window, and the bird entered. Loud music and chatter floated up from the courtyard before he refastened the window.

"My mind is a winter paddock—full of mud and icy slush." Sly tugged his hair, frustration pressing like a vice around his head. *Thump. Thump. Thump.* He pressed his temples and rubbed, attempting to will away his brain turmoil.

Sly closed his eyes, sucked in a huge breath and released it slowly.

"I remember a place. It's in a valley and surrounded by hills. I think it is summer because the sun is warm. There are trees and paddocks. Crops in the ground. And stones. There are strange stones on the hill. They remind me of building blocks—lumps of wood and plastic that I played with as a child. It's almost as if a giant has tossed his building blocks on the ground. Do you think that is my home?" Sly sank onto the end of the bed. "Sometimes I think my mind is clearing, and then it goes murky again." He rubbed his hand over his face. "Crap, I don't know what is wrong with my mouth but it's sore. Where is my salve? Ah, there it is."

The owl flew to the tub of salve and ferried it to Sly.

"Thanks." He gingerly applied the white paste. It tingled, but the ointment helped relieve the dryness.

"It must be late. I might try to sleep."

The owl flew to the upright dresser at the side of the bed.

Sly laughed. "Bossy thing, aren't you?" He stripped off his clothes and chuckled as he noted the owl's wide eyes. "I'm healed. A miracle. I wish I knew how I did it."

He slid into bed. "Lights off."

The lights went out. Sly's eyes adjusted quickly to the gloom, and he watched the owl resettle by the bed. Tired, he closed his eyes.

He dreamed of big black cats. Leopards. They raced through the stony outcrops, chasing each other in a frantic game of hide and seek. Then, a large white ball appeared from somewhere. Other big cats joined the game. Lions and tigers. Spotted leopards. Black leopards. They played in teams, giving no quarter until the air hissed from the ball when a tiger sank in his teeth. Sly chortled, his gruff *huh-huh-huh* echoed by the others.

"Sly. Sly." A sweet, feminine voice woke him. "Sly, move over. I'm cold."

"Cinnabar?" he asked, his mind groggy but supplying him a name. At her insistent push, he shifted toward the center of the wide bed. "Yikes, woman. Your feet are cold."

She cuddled up to him. "You're so warm. I've missed you."

Sly wrapped his arms around her shivering and very naked body. His mind cleared and his body wakened as her breasts flattened against his chest. "I've missed you too." Some of their background, the memories of their past, failed him, but her presence lightened him. He liked her. Kisses. Yes, they'd done this before. Where? *Where?* Dammit to hell. He should remember more of her. More than a mere name.

"Where did we meet?"

Her hand halted his next question, his demand for answers. "We're together," she whispered. "Let's make the most of it. Kiss me."

Yes. He wanted her. Craved her touch. Her kisses. Her body. Questions later.

He rolled without warning, so he loomed over her slight body, imprisoning her within the cage of his arms.

Cinnabar's bright blue eyes twinkled at him. "That's better," she said, and her shy smile charmed him.

He lowered his head.

"Your mouth is better," she whispered.

"My mouth?"

"Yes."

She was right. Somehow that fact had slid into brain sludge. He touched his lips to hers. Yeah. A bit tender, but not too painful that he couldn't get serious.

Playfully, he nipped her bottom lip. Enjoyed her swift intake of air. The soft moan. His tongue smoothed the spot he'd nibbled. He traced the curve and when she opened for him, he accepted the invitation to explore.

Her small hands stroked his back, her touch soothing and arousing. Hellfire, she made him want to purr.

Purr? Where the hell had that come from?

Sly laughed at himself, his fanciful brain. He'd taken a path into plain weird, dreaming of cats and now purring. She pinched his arse and a rumble escaped him. Heck. Now he even sounded like a cat. And his mind was wandering. *Idiot*. Bed. Beautiful woman. Willing woman. Hard-on. He had all the ingredients for pleasure and he sank into thoughts.

Yep. Imbecile.

He shoved aside his thoughts to kiss her, diving into taste and feel and the roar of blood through his veins. His cock pushed against her belly. Better. Much better. His tongue stroked lazily against hers until the need for air had him parting their mouths.

He nibbled her neck, pausing at the fleshy part where neck and shoulder met. A strange urge to bite took him, but he ignored the notion and flicked out his tongue to taste the skin on her collarbone. Still sweet. Honey and spices.

Hurry. Oh, hell. He needed to plunge into her body. A shiver grabbed him, sped the length of his body. No. Stop. Guilt had him hauling his needs to a halt. Make it perfect. Kiss her breasts. Explore her body. Slow is better.

Sly sucked a pert nipple and gloried in the moan that escaped her. He liked it so much, he did it again. Cinnabar wriggled and parted her legs, driving him to distraction. Fast. Go. Go. *Go.*

But something in him—a gentlemanly part, the part that listened and took advice from his big brother... Huh. No! Don't pull at the thought. *Not now.*

He plucked at Cinnabar's nipple and sucked on the underside of her other breast. Her scent grew musky. Still with the honey and spice undertones, it drove him onward. *Make her mine.*

He moved down her body. Stroking. Caressing. Indulging his senses. "You are so pretty," he whispered.

"Sly." She infused the one word with so much emotion.

Sly understood without checking her expression. She wanted him as much as he craved her. He ran his fingers over the delicate flesh between her legs. Parted her folds. Stroked the silken dampness, drawing a shiver from her.

"Now," she demanded. "Please."

Yes. Sly guided his shaft to her entrance and pushed a fraction. His cock entered her warmth. Oh, yes. He took his time, invading and retreating, until they both shuddered at the exquisite friction. *Exquisite.* Hell. A girly word, yet his mind thought it, and the description fit. He centered his busy mind. *Focus, dammit.*

Sly upped the speed of his thrusts, and Cinnabar clung. She pressed kisses to his neck and urged him onward. The pleasure grew while the blood pooled in his shaft. His balls tightened to a point shy of pain. He plunged into her again, and Cinnabar cried out, the quick spasms of her channel caressing his dick.

He allowed himself one lazy stroke and another before reaching a point of no return. Faster. Faster, he plunged into her until he exploded, his dick contracting with the force of his release, and his mind found a perfect slice of peace.

"Sly?"

Aware of his weight on her slighter body, he heaved himself off her. A weak kitten would have more energy. He winked at her. "You've done me in."

"That was wonderful."

Sly squeezed her a little. "Better than that. Exceptional." That was nothing less than the truth. And he'd make sure they did it again as soon as he had the energy to move.

Sly rearranged their bodies and tugged Cinnabar against his side. He closed his eyes and drifted at peace for the first time in ages. Cute breathy whistles escaped Cinnabar, heating his shoulder. He'd tease her later. Joe would like her, and so would his other brothers. She'd fit with his family, and they'd treat her with respect, even if she did morph into an owl. Somehow, he'd make everything right. Somehow.

The door flew open without warning.

Sly's arms tightened around Cinnabar. Every muscle in his body tensed, and he opened his eyes as Liam skidded to a halt, gaze fixated on their twined bodies.

CHAPTER SEVENTEEN

"How did you find a woman without leaving my chamber? Who is that?" Liam wavered from side to side and belched.

A wave of alcoholic fumes drifted to Sly. He wrinkled his nose. "Quiet. You'll wake her."

Cinnabar stirred, and the covers drifted lower to reveal a naked shoulder.

Sly tugged the covers back into place. "Stop ogling."

"But how did you get a woman past my guards?"

"Sit down before you fall."

"Too much sweetwater," Liam said, not taking his attention from Cinnabar. "My cousin and I had a few. Who is that? One of the maids? If you get one of the staff with child—"

"It's not one of the staff," Sly snapped. "That would be an abuse of my position within your court." Such as it was.

Cinnabar stirred, her blue eyes opening. She sat up, blearily rubbing her eyes. "I can't believe I went to sleep."

"We have company," Sly said. "Eyes off!"

Cinnabar spotted the king, let out a shriek of horror, and burrowed beneath the blankets.

"Cinnabar?" Liam stared at the trembling mound beside Sly. "Iseabal told me she ran off with a group of players."

"Princess Iseabal lied," Sly snapped.

A muffled protest came from beneath the blankets. Sly scowled at Liam.

"Cinnabar, come out from under there." Liam stood abruptly and almost toppled over his own feet. "Damn and blast!"

"She can't give you the truth either."

"But I'm the king." Liam hiccupped.

"A drunk king." Sly smirked, deciding to tease. "I'm certain you're seeing mirages."

"Not," Liam said, staring at the mound as if he intended to burn away the covers. "Could use magic."

"Don't," Sly ordered.

Liam subsided with a frown. "Maybe I'll bring my cousin."

"No," Sly said. "I take it he's as drunk as you."

"Maybe."

"Turn around."

"Why?" Liam demanded.

"So she can get dressed without you gawking at her."

"Didn't realize she was so pretty."

A growl rumbled through Sly, surprising both him and Liam, judging by the king's rapt goggle. They stared at each other.

"All right." Liam meandered toward the double windows. Once there, he held on to the ledge and studied the darkness beyond.

"Close your eyes," Sly commanded. "You're checking out the reflections."

"It's not fair. You have a lady. I don't have time to indulge myself. Not unless I visit my cousin. Too many gossips. Too many expectations."

"That doesn't mean you can ogle her. Close your eyes."

"You're spoiling my fun."

"Too bad." Once Sly was satisfied Liam wasn't peeking, he lifted the covers to reveal a trembling Cinnabar. He climbed from bed and scooped up her stained white dress.

Cinnabar pulled the gown over her head, and Sly helped tug it into place.

"You can look now," Sly said.

"It *is* Cinnabar. Did you return with the winter court?"

"No, she didn't." Sly hated the way Cinnabar huddled against his side, trembling violently.

"Another mystery," Liam murmured. "Castle is lousy with 'em."

"It's all right." Sly stroked Cinnabar's tangled hair.

"Why is your gown stained?" Liam asked.

A moan escaped Cinnabar. Her breaths were short and shallow. Rapid.

"I won't let anything happen to you." Sly caressed her back to offer comfort. She'd want to escape, but Liam blocked the windows. Although pity surged within Sly, he didn't force Liam to move. If Liam witnessed what happened, he'd have answers to his questions. Even if he couldn't leave and go home, perhaps there was a way of helping Cinnabar.

With another moan, Cinnabar stepped away from him. The faint glow Sly had seen before lit her form, and the next instant, she was an owl.

Liam straightened from his slouch, anger burning through some of his confusion. "Someone cursed Cinnabar!"

Cinnabar flew from the floor to Sly's shoulder. Her russet feathers ruffled, and she scrunched up her body, hiding her head against his neck.

"Who?" Liam asked.

"Make an intelligent guess," Sly said.

"Iseabal."

Sly didn't confirm or deny.

"My sister lied to my face. Cinnabar has been here the entire time. Another item for my list," Liam said with a trace of disgust. "Iseabal is at the center of my problems."

Cinnabar let out a distressed hoot and lifted off his shoulder. She flew around the chamber as if searching for an exit.

"Open the window and let her leave."

Liam managed to unfasten the latch and stood back to allow Cinnabar's escape.

An invisible band tightened around Sly's chest. She was leaving, would always leave. Shoulders slumped in regret, he turned to face Liam.

"Have you discovered anything about the shooter?"

"I've learned Calum went missing for a time. It wasn't his feathering on the arrows, but that means nothing. Iseabal and Katrina remained with the stable lads, so I know it wasn't either of them."

"The culprit might have paid someone to fire the arrow."

"My cousin has pointed out this likelihood. He suggested I fabricate a truth spell and order everyone at court—servants and nobility—to undergo questioning."

"Can you do that?"

"Yes, but it will cost me in power. It will take time to recover, and anyone with power of their own can challenge me. If they win, I'll lose my place within the court."

"Do you trust your cousin? If he had your back, now would be the time to conduct the questioning."

Liam rubbed his chest as if it ached. "At this point, I don't care if I lose my power. It would allow me to follow my love of farming, to live a normal life."

"You'll make a decent and fair king, Liam." Sly sensed this with every fathom of his gut. "The everyday people—the servants, the farmers, the weavers, those with minimal magic—need you to champion them."

Liam heaved a sigh, weighty with defeat. "As much as I wish it, I can't walk away." He straightened and threw back his shoulders, his royal blood never more apparent. "You're right. I don't have to follow tradition. I can change things. Give the normal man a better life. Give the nobility a better sense of purpose. And all that starts with a truth spell." His eyes blazed with a tinge of red as he focused on Sly. "You will help me."

"Yes," Sly agreed. "For as long as I can."

Liam nodded. "We bury my father on the morrow. The following day, I will conduct the truth spell. I ask that you and my cousin monitor proceedings while my power is at low ebb. You will be acting king while my cousin provides the juice, should you require magic."

"Won't your sisters and the rest of the nobility grumble about that?"

"Yes." Liam's grin held mischief. "You'll like my cousin. I'll introduce you in the morn. Meantime, I need to decide how to deal with Iseabal. She must reverse the spell on Cinnabar. Do you know why Iseabal cursed her?"

"Yes."

Liam's glance was shrewd. "Let me guess. The stain on Cinnabar's dress tells an interesting tale." Liam yawned so wide his jaw cracked. "Gratafire, I'm exhausted. I forgot to request a trundle bed."

"Your bed is big," Sly said. "As long as you don't try to cuddle me, we're good."

Liam snorted. He sat on the edge of his bed and attempted to remove his boots.

"Hopeless. Let me." Sly tugged off the boots and indicated Liam should stand. He pulled off his jacket. "You can do the rest.

Remember, no cuddling."

The next morn came all too soon. Sly moaned and stood to stretch.

"Liam, it's time to get up."

Liam groaned.

"I'm going back to my chamber."

"Ask one of my guards to escort you."

Sly shrugged. "Okay."

Liam rolled to a sitting position and groaned. "I knew I shouldn't have drunk so much sweetwater. Don't eat or drink anything. Not a *thing* until you're in the salon with me. We'll eat from the same dishes. I need your head clear to take over for me temporarily."

Liam hadn't arrived when Sly walked into the salon, fully dressed in a clean suit and starving. His stomach rumbled the instant he smelled the scent of wild boar slices.

"Sly, come and join us," Iseabal said. An order.

Sly stilled, not wanting to go near the woman.

Liam's Aunt Jasper and her friend Beatrice were sitting nearby with a young man. His skin was a pale blue. Sly ignored Iseabal and let his curiosity drive his footsteps in that direction.

"Ah, Sly. Have you met Calvin, the winter king?" Aunt Jasper asked. "Take a seat, lad. Eat with us. Calvin, this is Sly, Iseabal's betrothed."

Golden eyes regarded him from an almost pretty pale blue face. Sharp cheekbones. Long eyelashes. A pair of dark blue horns that swept back from his temples in a graceful curl. "You hail from Ione Island. Your family runs the Middlemarch Resort, correct? I believe my cousin and her friends visited you recently. They had an enjoyable time and hope to return in the future."

"You know Sly?" Liam appeared behind him.

"Not personally, but my cousin showed me some of her souvenirs. Photos, I believe you call them," Calvin said.

Liam pushed Sly into the empty seat and gestured at another empty one nearby. It scooted over the floor by itself, and Liam sat.

"Calvin, please don't tell Iseabal that you know of Sly. Not to anyone else, either. I'll explain when we're in private. Sly." Liam clicked his fingers in front of Sly's face. "Pull it together, man. Iseabal is watching."

"I'm hungry," Sly said for lack of anything better to say. His mind spun, his thoughts whirring so fast he could barely make sense of them. He had a home. Family. Now there was a chance he'd manage to return. But Cinnabar... He hated to leave her trapped in the body of an owl.

"I'll order for you," Liam said, and proceeded to do so.

"Why does Calvin have horns and you don't?" Sly asked.

"No one knows for sure," Calvin answered. "A genetic anomaly. The Unseelie people came from warrior stock, while the Seelie toiled the land and kept the peace. Rumor says the horns became weapons and the people encouraged the genetic quirk."

"The Unseelie mind-speak better than us, too," Liam said. "Our mental communication isn't reliable."

"Interesting." Sly fell quiet and ate until hunger no longer rumbled his gut.

"Sly!" Liam spoke with an air that told Sly he'd attempted to snag his attention more than once.

"Sorry. What did you say?"

"I'm going to leave you with Calvin. He will protect you. Whatever you do, don't leave his side and don't go anywhere with Iseabal. I'm bringing forward the truth ceremony. We'll do it this afternoon instead. The funeral takes place in an hour. We'll go for a walk to the lake and discuss our plans. Remember, mention nothing."

"An intrigue," Calvin said. "This is proving an interesting visit."

Iseabal observed the three men sitting with her aunt, her warning antenna vibrating. *Liam knows.* Somehow, he'd discovered what she'd done and was keeping Sly from her control. Sly's mind had cleared. He was remembering things. His bright green eyes—intelligence lurked there, instead of confusion.

She cracked her knuckles beneath the table, temper sparking her magic. Her dinner plate rattled against her eating fork.

She required answers before she determined her next move.

Perhaps Cinnabar...

She hadn't seen her recently. Well, she'd hunt her down, and if she carefully phrased her questions, she'd learn at least some of the required answers.

She was too close to achieving her goal, had conscientiously practiced her magic to boost her chances for a power grab. She refused to misstep now.

Damn and blast, Trevelyan was heading her way. Too late to escape.

"We had an understanding." The burly blue security guard shot straight for the jugular.

Aware of eavesdroppers, Iseabal rose, took his arm, and marched him from the Great Hall. She pulled him into a quiet audience room and shut the door.

"You kissed me." He planted his hands on his hips, a picture of masculine outrage with his head thrown back, his blue horns making him appear taller. "Why are you betrothed to this no-magic stranger?"

Iseabal hesitated, ignored the pitter-patter of her heart, and applied her brain. A clean cut. Best for both of them. She ignored the twinge of pain, the ache of loss. Trevelyan was a handsome man, a respectable man, one who made her laugh, but he bore the dominant gene.

And he was decent. Too honorable to help with her plan.

She was close to seizing power and authority, her birthright.

"Call off the betrothal," Trevelyan ordered.

And that, right there, was why she'd ignored her attraction to Trevelyan and walked away.

She stared him straight in the eye. "I don't love you." Her fingernails dug into her palms, but she maintained her implacable gaze.

Deep blue swirled into his cheeks. His nostrils flared, and for a second, she thought he might strike her.

He didn't. Instead, he lifted his chin, disgust layering his even stare. "Have an enjoyable life, Iseabal." And with one more scathing glower, he walked away.

The door rattled in its frame as he slammed it shut.

Iseabal blinked hard, shoved aside all tender emotions. She didn't need Trevelyan. She didn't need any man...at least, she wouldn't once she seized power and became the ruler of Seelie.

CHAPTER EIGHTEEN

"A truth ceremony? Ridiculous!" Lord Calum blustered. "The ground hasn't settled over your father. You're not even the official king until the crowning ceremony. Tell him, Katrina. Tell your brother this is a preposterous idea."

Sly stood at the rear of the family salon, his arms crossed over his chest. Calvin, the winter king, leaned against the wall beside Sly.

"Is that guilt or my imagination?" Calvin murmured.

Sly liked the king, despite their short acquaintance. The blue man emanated the same confidence and authority as his cousin. "Shush, I want to hear Iseabal's reaction."

Iseabal sniffed, her pert nose rising to its imperious best. "For once, I agree with Calum. You'll leave yourself vulnerable if you insist on this idiocy. Calum would love to rule. How do you know we won't side together and toss you out on your arse?"

"Frightened of the truth, Iseabal?" Liam asked, and his eyes took on that freaky red glow.

Her hand closed to a fist at her side, her only sign of unease.

"She has a guilty conscience," Calvin murmured.

Sly agreed, but then he knew of Iseabal's perfidy. "So does Calum."

"This is ridiculous!" Calum blustered again, seconds after Sly spoke.

"It does seem an extreme way to discover truth," Katrina agreed in her usual calm demeanor. "And disrespectful to Father's memory."

"If I were Liam, I'd ask questions about his father's death, too," Calvin said. "He sickened without warning. He wasn't an old man."

"I suggested that," Sly replied in an undertone.

"Who will have your back, Liam?" Calum demanded. "No one in the court will wish to be questioned."

"Sly and Calvin stand for me," Liam said calmly. "My men are already assembling the servants."

"You can't force us to take the truth questions. Come, Katrina. We will retire to our chambers." Calum led his wife from the room.

Iseabal lifted her chin in challenge, pupils edging toward red. She paused in the doorway, right foot *tap-tap-tapping*. "Sly, a word."

Sly found his feet moving and forced his muscles to hold firm. A prickle akin to a mild electrical shock sizzled over his flesh. He exhaled, winced.

"Sly!" Iseabal barked, and steel rang in the command.

"Take care," Calvin murmured. "She is using a spell to make you comply."

No kidding. He'd love to see her on the receiving end of magic for a change. See how she liked it.

"Come with me."

Sly battled the compulsion. Failed. His steps quickened, puppet-stiff and unwilling. Once Princess Iseabal saw he followed, she strolled away in a swish of skirts, leading him like the Pied Piper. *Huh.* Who the heck was the Pied Piper? Some random dude from his memory bank.

"Start your questioning," Calvin said before Sly quick-stepped from the salon. "I'll handle Iseabal. Sly and I will be there momentarily."

"Go away." Iseabal glared red daggers at Calvin. "I wish a private conversation with my betrothed."

"Liam requires our presence in the throne room," Calvin said. "Can't you have your lovers' chat later? Come, Sly." Calvin snapped his fingers.

Sly's legs jerked and twitched. Wooden footsteps sent him right. A sharp tug on his calves directed him back to Iseabal. "Stop it," he snarled. "Iseabal, I am going with Calvin. Cease this now."

"Princess Iseabal," she snapped.

The push and pull halted. He staggered before he regained control of his limbs.

"Thank you, *Princess* Iseabal." He struggled to hold his mockery and failed. *Too bad.* He had rights, and it was time to exert himself. "I will seek you once this is over. Where do you wish to meet?"

"In the gardens, where we can be assured of privacy."

Sly dipped his head. "Of course, Princess."

He walked away with Calvin, convinced Princess Iseabal would change her mind at the last minute. For once, he was wrong and thankful for it.

A line of servants snaked outside the throne room. It shuffled forward as Liam's men checked each new arrival for concealed weapons. A pile of knives, stunners, and thin twigs filled a trolley.

Calvin and Sly bypassed the line but paused at the double doors.

"King Liam is expecting you." The head of security gestured them through.

Calvin nodded and sauntered through the right door, elegant in his navy-blue suit and lace. Wearing a plain black suit, Sly felt like a ragamuffin beside the winter king's sartorial elegance.

Of all the rooms at the castle, this one screamed royal, with an imposing golden throne toward the rear of the square room. Rich tapestries of hunting scenes hung on the walls, and an arrangement of swords and hunting knives dominated the wall behind the throne. Liam sat on the throne, golden crown atop his head, fur-trimmed cape around his shoulders, and a golden, jewel-studded staff in his right hand.

Calvin's royal guards stood on one side of the throne—a blue wall of muscle—and Sly wondered which one had courted Princess Iseabal. He scanned their faces and met the gaze of the tallest. Ah. The big blue man hated his presence. Sly studied Liam's guards—a gold wall of determination—who stood on the other side, their eyes watchful. At least Liam would remain safe.

Sly's skin prickled and buzzed. "What is that?"

"It's Liam's magic. He's divorced his body from the magic and is using his power to discern truth."

"So anyone could kill him?"

"That is why we're here. To stop that from happening. Plus, they're searching for concealed weapons. Don't worry. Everything will be fine."

"Do you know who shot Sly?" Liam's voice emerged in a register deeper than normal, and his gaze glowed with red. Compulsion—a tangible force—shimmered in the air like static electricity.

"No, Your Majesty," a trembling housemaid answered.

"Next," Liam commanded.

The housemaid curtsied and exited via the left door of the double doors at the entrance.

The next servant approached Liam. He repeated the question and received the same answer. Gradually, the dress of the servants changed as Liam interrogated the stable boys and the palace archers, the security force. While most showed nerves and unease,

SHELLEY MUNRO

all answered Liam's questions in the negative.

The line dwindled and ended.

"That is all the staff, Your Majesty," the head security guard said.

"Summon the nobility," Calvin ordered. "My people as well. Might as well do a thorough job."

The questions changed, and Sly paid close attention, despite the sneers and whispers drifting from those in line.

"Do you know where Cinnabar went?" Liam asked a young woman.

Sly didn't recall her name but thought she was one of Princess Iseabal's ladies-in-waiting.

"She ran away with the players from the winter court," the woman said.

"How do you know this?"

"Princess Iseabal told me," the woman answered without hesitation.

"Do you know who shot the arrow that hit Sly?"

"No, Your Majesty."

Calvin frowned. "Cinnabar is the russet-haired lass. One of Iseabal's ladies-in-waiting, isn't she?"

"She used to be," Sly said absently, listening closely to the replies.

Calvin tapped his chin. "Cinnabar isn't at the winter court."

"No," Sly said.

"Wait. You know. Liam knows?" At Sly's curt nod, he straightened. "Then why is Liam asking?"

"He has reasons."

Nerves skittered through Sly's belly as the line proceeded and Liam interrogated the members of his court. Calvin's people.

Lady Jasper arrived. Beatrice. Their answers were the same.

"That is everyone," the security guard said.

"My sisters? My brother-in-law?" Liam asked in a tight voice. His fingers curved around the carved arms of his throne. The bright lights caught the jeweled stones of his crown and reflected shards of purple and blue and red.

"I am here," Katrina said from the doorway. "I have nothing to hide."

"Which implies her husband and her sister do," Calvin murmured.

"Katrina!" a harsh voice called. "Do not defy me on this. Your brother does not have the right to question us in this manner." Calum appeared in the doorway.

Sly stared. Calum's blond hair stuck up in tufts and his cravat had come unfastened, hanging around his neck like a noose.

"Liam is our king. He has the right to rule as he sees fit." Katrina marched to Liam. "Question me, Your Majesty."

"Do you know where Cinnabar went?" Liam asked.

Surprise bolted over Katrina's pretty face. "She ran away with a player from the winter court."

Liam steepled his fingers under his chin. "When did this happen?"

"A while ago now. I'm not certain. I'm sure it occurred while you were away. Iseabal will recall."

Sly watched Calum. As Calum listened to Liam's questioning of his wife, his shoulders relaxed and his expression smoothed out, his panic dispersing.

"Send for Iseabal," Liam instructed. "Bring her kicking and screaming if you must. You may go, Katrina."

"He's taking a risk," Calvin murmured.

"Why?"

"He can't question Katrina again," Calvin replied in an undertone. "The spell only works for one questioning. He will have to regain his power before he can repeat this."

A furious scream echoed down the passage, growing louder as guards dragged Iseabal into the throne room.

"You can't do this!" she spat, defiant as the guards hauled her to stand in front of her brother. Her eyes blazed red, but Liam appeared unfazed.

"Sly, I will question you next."

Princess Iseabal gasped. "You can't question him!"

"I can question whomever I wish," Liam said, his manner haughty.

Sly hesitated until Calvin shoved him in the middle of the back. He staggered forward.

"Where does Cinnabar live?" Liam asked.

"Seelie," Sly said after a hesitation. Nimble fingers filed through his brain, bringing the answer to mind. Compulsion. A desire to help the king.

"Iseabal, your turn," Liam said without warning. "Did you place a spell on Cinnabar?"

Iseabal's face contorted, fury battling with what Sly suspected was a touch of fear. She opened her mouth, snapped it shut. Her entire body shuddered.

"*Did* you place a spell on Cinnabar?"

"Yes," Princess Iseabal gritted out.

"Why?"

"She—" Iseabal broke off, her teeth clacking. She jerked and twitched like a marionette controlled by an amateur.

"Iseabal, answer my question. Why did you place a spell on Cinnabar?"

"S-sh-she spilled a drink on my favorite gown."

Silence fell, and even though Cinnabar had already told him the truth, Sly gaped at Iseabal. She held not a smidge of shame. Instead, angry color bloomed in her cheeks, echoed in her red gaze. Fury at having her actions under a spotlight.

"Most people would slap their servants. Chastise them. Buy a new gown," Calvin commented.

"No one asked you," Iseabal snapped and lifted her chin.

"Did you kidnap Sly from his home and family and force him to become your betrothed?" Liam demanded.

"N-n-nooo." Every muscle in Iseabal's body spasmed and pain etched into her features.

"Iseabal!" Her name was a whiplash of fury.

"All right!" Iseabal snarled. "I did it."

"Did you bespell him so he wouldn't regain his memory?"

Iseabal shot a glower of loathing at her brother and it ricocheted to Sly. "Yes," she spat, her anger a wavering, palpable mass.

"You will undo both spells. Immediately!" Liam thundered, his flashing eyes so red, Sly took a step backward.

"No."

"*Now*," Liam reiterated. "Then the guards will take you to your chamber while I decide on your punishment."

The siblings exchanged glowers until finally, Iseabal slumped. "Very well."

"Do it now."

Iseabal nodded and murmured under her breath.

Suddenly, Sly's mind was crystal clear. With wonder, with excitement, he recalled his family, his brothers, his sister, his mother. How he'd come from Earth with other shapeshifters. His feline side...

Sly felt for his cat, the leopard that slithered through his thoughts, bunched beneath his muscles, rumbled and purred. Snarled complaints.

Nothing.

Panic unfurled like a seed pushing toward the light. Something Iseabal had done? Or something else?

"How did you get Sly into Seelie with no one else noticing?" Liam asked.

"A private portal," Iseabal said.

She seemed tired, dispirited, and didn't attempt to battle the truth spell now.

"Did you try to kill me?"

"No."

Torn from his feline concerns, Sly caught the way Calum stiffened, and Sly nudged Calvin to alert him to the behavior. The winter king gave an imperceptible nod.

"Did you order someone else to do it?"

"No."

"Thank you, Iseabal. Wait there."

Iseabal studied the floor, her imperious manner cut off at the knees.

"Calum, did you order someone to shoot me with an arrow?"

"No," Calum answered.

Liam frowned. "Calum, did you poison my father?"

"Yes."

The throne room became a cavern of silence, yet the very air pulsed with energy. Sly's hair lifted with the *oomph* of the magic at work. He curled his lip, disgusted. Poison. A coward's way.

"Calum, do you want to kill me?"

Calum lifted his chin, appearing to struggle. A drop of blood ran from his nose. "Y-yes."

The idiot was fighting the truth spell and losing.

"Did you shoot an arrow at me?"

"N— Yes," Calum snarled, his face contorting into a grotesque mask.

"Why?"

"I deserve to be king! Your father deposed my grandfather. The throne should be *mine*!" The words fired from him with the velocity of bullets. *Bang. Bang. Bang.* Spittle accompanied the gun discharge. *Ping. Ping. Ping.*

Liam's expression held disgust as he wiped his face. His form swelled, bigger and more imposing than normal. "Guards!"

His private guards, all six of them, straightened.

"Yes, Your Majesty," the head guard said.

"Take Lord Calum to the dungeons. Maximum security. No visitors."

"Liam, no!" Katrina protested. "He's my husband."

"He killed our father! He tried to kill *me*. Hell, if it wasn't for Sly, he would've succeeded."

Liam stood and wavered on his feet. "Once Calum is secured in the dungeon, please return and escort Iseabal to her chamber. She will remain confined until I determine a fitting punishment."

Middlemarch Resort

Joe kicked a pebble as he headed to check on Sly. Still in *Sleeping Beauty's* boudoir, his twin wasn't getting any better and showed no signs of waking.

Joe knocked on the door, and his cousin Sam let him inside. "How is he?"

"About the same, except his skin isn't as cold. Last time I watched him for you, it was icy cold." Sam smiled with encouragement. With his black hair and green eyes, he resembled Sly. A fitter version. "That's good, right?"

Joe crossed the floor to the bed where Sly lay. His twin bore more color, yet his eyes still hadn't opened.

"Do you want me to watch Sly for you again, later in the day?"

"Yeah," Joe said absently, his fingers gripping Sly's biceps.

"Excellent," Sam said. "There's a new arrival—one of those green ladies—who keeps hunting me down. My backside is black and blue. She gives me the creeps, and I'd be happy to hide out here with Sly."

"Thanks," Joe said.

"Have you eaten?"

"No." His appetite had vanished lately. Food held no attraction with Sly unconscious. "I'll grab something when Leo takes charge for me. I need to check the crops."

"I'm not doing anything. You want some help?"

"Sure," Joe said. "I'll probably shift and have a run."

"Even better," Sam said.

His cousin headed off, leaving Joe alone with Sly.

"Dammit, Sly. You have to come back. I miss you, talking farming with you." Joe knuckled his eyes, his throat so tight he had to swallow to speak. "You can't leave me alone."

Chapter Nineteen

To escape the tension indoors, Sly and Calvin wandered through the garden, whiling away time while Liam recovered.

"Help! Help!"

"Did you hear that?" Calvin stopped in the middle of the gravel path.

Sly lifted his head, searching for the source of the feminine cry, glad of the distraction. Yellow flowers—fluffy balls of sunshine—filled the garden beds. Another display of red flowers grew to their right. Beyond the formal plantings, large trees thrust skyward, their green canopies thick enough to block the light.

"Is someone there? Help. Please help!"

"Cinnabar!" Sly sprinted toward the trees.

Once they left the gardens, leaves crunched under their feet. More dead leaves than he recalled the last time he'd come in this direction.

"Cinnabar?" Sly called.

"Sly, is that you? Over here!"

Sly raced around the bend in the path and skidded to a halt. Calvin plowed into the back of him, almost knocking him off his feet. Sly regained his balance, moved closer to the tree trunk, and looked upward.

"Sly! Thank the goddess." Cinnabar clung to a tree branch, awkwardly sitting on another. "I don't understand what happened. I-I have been avoiding Princess Iseabal as much as I can. And...and I was perched in the tree, and suddenly, I regained my form. I almost fell on my head, and now I can't get down."

"Cinnabar, listen to me. I want you to climb farther out onto the branch—"

"I'll fall."

"Yes, you will, but I'll catch you. I promise, sweetheart. I won't let you hit the ground. No. Don't overthink. Just do it, Cinnabar." Sly injected an order into his tone. "I guess you weren't expecting to change forms so suddenly, huh?"

"No."

"Cinnabar, you're not moving."

"If I fall and kill myself, Sly Mitchell, I will come back and haunt you."

"That's fine, sweetheart. I expect nothing less."

Sly watched anxiously while Cinnabar inched along the branch. "Good. That's right. Now let go and I'll catch you." The fear digging into her features gutted him and blasted him with adrenaline. "Ready?"

"Y-yes."

"Let go."

He caught his breath as she hesitated, then her fingers relaxed and she dropped. She landed in his arms in a whoosh of white skirts, momentarily blinding him.

"You caught me," she whispered.

"I promised, didn't I?"

"That's a very fetching pair of legs," Calvin said, having remained silent until this moment.

Cinnabar gasped and wriggled frantically. Sly set her on the ground and helped her right her skirts. "Oh! Your Majesty." She bobbed a quick curtsy.

"This is turning into a most diverting holiday," Calvin said. "I haven't had such fun for...I don't know. Many, many solar cycles."

"Calvin, this is Cinnabar."

"I heard," Calvin said languidly. "You know, I could've used my magic and had her down in a blink."

Sly muttered a curse. "Why didn't you say?"

"You didn't give me a chance." Calvin nudged Sly with his shoulder, mischief glimmering in his strong features. "Besides, you had everything under control."

"Knock that smile off your face." Sly took half a step before he controlled the urge to help him.

"Sly." Cinnabar tugged at his arm. "That's the king of the winter court. You can't punch him."

"Someone should," Sly said as Calvin's smile broadened to smart-arse and toothy.

"Why did I change forms?" Cinnabar tilted her head to the side. "What's happened?"

"Liam did a truth spell," Calvin said.

Cinnabar gasped, seeming to forget her awe of the king. "But that's dangerous. Is he all right?"

"He will be," Calvin said.

Cinnabar shivered, and Sly wrapped his arm around her waist.

"It's a bit cooler now that I have arrived in Seelie," Calvin said. "Come, let us resume walking."

Sly shrugged out of his coat and helped Cinnabar don the charcoal-gray garment.

"I don't understand. Will I turn into an owl again?"

"No, sweetheart," Calvin said. "Liam discovered his sister's treachery and stopped it."

"Enough with the endearments," Sly snapped.

"Sly, he's the king of the winter court," Cinnabar chided again.

"He's a pain in my arse," Sly countered.

Calvin wiggled his eyebrows, golden eyes dancing and teasing. "Yes, a most diverting holiday. Shall we finish our walk and check on Liam? Is there a back entrance? I tire of people bowing to me."

Sly rolled his eyes at Calvin, and the infuriating man laughed. "Someone should kick your butt."

Cinnabar moaned and trembled against his side. "Sly!"

Calvin guffawed harder, hunching forward and holding his belly.

Sly shoved Calvin off the path and guided Cinnabar past.

"Hey, don't go without me."

"He's annoying. Keep walking," Sly directed, as Calvin, still smirking, trotted to catch up.

Guided by Cinnabar, they ambled down paths Sly hadn't yet discovered. Many of the leaves were turning color. Greens transforming to red and gold. Pink changing to fiery red and a hotter pink.

"Are you staying for long?" Cinnabar asked timidly.

"Not this time. Only until Liam recovers and is officially crowned king. The plants should recover."

"Princess Iseabal is confined to her room," Sly said. "She won't bother you again. Calum admitted to killing the king and attempting to murder Liam."

Cinnabar gasped, her hand flying upward to cover her mouth.

"What will Liam do with him?" Sly asked as the path ended and they emerged by the lake.

The white stag stood under a tree, chewing its cud. Sly stared at the beautiful creature, its antlers curved with age.

"He has no choice. Calum will be executed. It is what I'd do." Calvin jerked his head at the stag. "His presence confirms a death."

As they watched, the stag ambled into the trees. A somber quiet fell over the threesome as they turned and retraced their footsteps.

"I want to check on Liam," Calvin said.

"We'll come with you." Sly ignored Cinnabar's quiver. He'd ask Liam if Cinnabar might go home with him. That's if Cinnabar wanted to stay with him. He wanted to learn more about her, spend time with her without fear of the ticking clock or Princess Iseabal.

Cinnabar's tremors increased as they approached Liam's royal security men, stationed at his tower entrance.

Sly lowered his head to whisper in her ear. "It's all right, sweetheart. I won't let anything happen to you."

"Princess Iseabal—"

"She can't hurt you."

"King Liam will see you now," the security guard said, opening the door wider for them to enter.

Sly exerted force at Cinnabar's back to propel her forward.

King Liam lay on his bed, his normally golden face tinged with blue. His smile seemed forced, and Sly frowned. He hadn't realized the truth spell would sap so much of his energy.

"Ah, Cinnabar. The housekeeper has arranged a chamber for you near Sly's." He paused. "No sharing chambers or rumors will fly."

Cinnabar flushed. "I understand, Your Majesty."

"I don't," Sly said.

"Liam and I can't share our beds with lovers without much pre-planning, so neither can you," Calvin said. "Our people do not have sex before marriage. No, let me correct that. The women should not have sex before marriage. Those are long-standing rules." His focus fell on Cinnabar, drifted to Sly.

"Your rules suck."

Calvin rolled his eyes. "Our ancestors wished to ensure they didn't end up with another man's child in their nest."

While Sly understood, he preferred to keep Cinnabar close. "What can we do to help you regain your energy?"

"Only rest and time will help."

"I want to go home," Sly said. "My family will be worried about me."

"Can you wait a few days? The journey to Ione Island via our main entrance point will take four days, but you will arrive home sooner if I can recover and open the portal Iseabal used."

Liam's suggestion made sense, and he owed the king for helping him. "All right."

"And you must promise to visit me. I consider you a friend," Liam said.

"I, too," Calvin added.

"You *are* a friend, Liam, although I'm not so sure about your cousin. He keeps winding me up."

Both men stared at him blankly. "An Earth saying. It means that he teases me," Sly added. "We sometimes say, 'Can you feel the key in your back?' to indicate winding up."

Calvin laughed. "Tell us more about this place. Liam, order refreshments so we can listen and revive ourselves after our exercise."

Sly seated Cinnabar on a padded chair and squeezed her shoulder. His sister or one of his brothers' mates would've demanded clothes, a shower. Not Cinnabar. She perched on the edge of the chair, ready to bolt. Sly retrieved two more chairs and arranged them near Liam's bed.

He claimed the one next to Cinnabar and reached for her hand.

Once a pot of tay and small cakes arrived, Sly started his story.

"My family comes from a planet called Earth. We lived in New Zealand, a small island nation. A feline disease struck, and many of our people died."

Liam blinked. "Wait. Feline?"

"Yes, we are a shapeshifting race. We have this form, and that of a black leopard."

"Show us," Calvin demanded.

Worry slid through him like a slithering snake. Voicing the truth made it real. What if he could never shift again? It'd suck. "That might be a problem. I haven't felt my other form since you got Iseabal to lift the spell and my mind has become clearer."

Calvin and Liam exchanged silent messages.

"It might be something to do with the spell Iseabal used," Liam said finally.

"Or it's possibly the veil over Seelie," Calvin suggested. "Intriguing. I have heard of shifter races before but never met one."

"I saw big cats when I was at the resort," Cinnabar blurted, drawing their attention. She hunched her shoulders, obviously trying to look smaller.

"Don't fear," Liam said. "Neither Calvin nor I will harm you. You have suffered enough at Iseabal's hands. I understand you've been forced into owl form for a long time."

"She fed me micelets." Cinnabar swallowed hard but couldn't prevent her dry retch.

Sly growled, the sound distinctly feline. "I've a mind to feed *her* micelets. See how she likes eating them."

Liam expelled a choking gasp. He stared at his hands, shoulders quivering. "M-micelets? Iseabal?"

"Maybe you should eat one," Sly said in a distinct warning. No one made fun of Cinnabar. Hell, no one blamed her for her skittishness. She'd spent at least three years—according to Liam, since he hadn't seen her for that long—cursed to her owl form. Cinnabar didn't feel safe yet, but she showed sparks of independence, traces of the woman she could be. Sly craved that woman, one who'd stand up to him and give him hell if he deserved it.

"Sorry, it was the vision of Iseabal and micelets, which set off my inappropriate humor. Iseabal shall receive her punishment," Liam promised. "Continue. Tell us about your family."

"I have a twin brother. Joe. I have three other brothers, all older. Saber is the leader of our people. It was his idea to leave Earth when the virus became prevalent. Felix and Leo are next. All three of my older brothers have mates. Our mother is still alive, and we have one sister. Scarlett."

Again, Liam and Calvin shared a glance, and Sly *tsk-tsked*. "Scarlett is impossible. She's stubborn. Outspoken. Intelligent. A smart-arse."

"Describe her physical traits," Calvin ordered.

No. Bad idea. Both men resembled slobbering wolves. "She has the Mitchell black hair. Long, in her case. Green eyes. And that's all you're getting. I'll be warning her about the pair of you. How you live in the middle of intrigue and magic. Scarlett likes her freedom. Her independence. She designs jewelry, collects semi-precious stones. She uses tools and fire."

"I'll gift her with as many stones as she wishes," Liam purred.

Sly threw up his hands and turned to Cinnabar. "Did you meet Scarlett?"

"She checked Princess Iseabal into the resort." Cinnabar lifted her chin. "She is beautiful and full of life. Sly is right. She speaks her mind and would hate the restrictions here."

"A challenge," Calvin mused.

"You may escort me home and I'll introduce you to my family," Sly said. "You are welcome to visit anytime."

Cinnabar went silent, hunched into herself. Crap. He wanted to take her home with him. He'd take her for a walk after dinner, go to the lakeside where they'd spent so much time together. Ask her to live at the resort or at least visit. Give her a place of safety to regroup, regather her confidence. And he'd date her. Dinner. Dancing. Long walks together. He'd get to know her again without

Princess Iseabal getting in the way.

Yeah, that sounded like an excellent plan.

"It's not advisable for me to absent myself from the kingdom for too long." Liam's disappointment swirled through the air, smelling like old boots and holey socks.

Cinnabar coughed, swallowed. "Ah, the portal is close. I can show you where it is but can't open it. Princess Iseabal told me it will open only for those of royal personage. If you use the portal, you can visit for a few hours and return before anyone realizes you're missing."

Liam perked up, and the air quality shifted to a piney green.

"Is this true?" Calvin demanded of Sly. "I hadn't thought much about the practicalities of leaving Seelie for too long."

"I don't recall," Sly said.

Cinnabar straightened, pushing back her shoulders. "It's true."

"It's settled then. We'll go as soon as I regain my strength," Liam declared.

Sly sipped his pale green tay. "I thought you wanted to wait until you were officially crowned king."

"With all that has happened, I've decided to waive that tradition and start in the way I mean to go on. Calvin has agreed to make the formal announcement, naming me king of Seelie, two cycles hence. I must deal with Calum and Iseabal, and I think it best if you go sooner rather than later. I hate to say it, but I don't trust my sister. I intend to bind her magic, again, with Calvin's help. No one should prey on those weaker. Iseabal has made it a game, and no one has ever informed me or our father for fear of reprisal. This stops."

"Hush, cousin. You require calm to regain your strength."

Sly nodded at Calvin. "Liam, let me tell you about a game we played on Earth. We haven't had time to organize games here, but it occurred to me that the grass paddock near the stables would make a perfect rugby pitch. It would be a friendly way for your people to interact with my family and friends. If my brother Saber agrees, of course. There are fifteen men per team plus six reserves…"

Sly noted Liam's and Calvin's intense interest as he explained the rules and the history of the game. They didn't know it, but he, his brothers, and cousins would crush them. Fun times ahead.

Sly was leaving.

Cinnabar's fingers pressed against her breast, willing the empty ache to fade. She'd known he'd want to return home. Understood it, even. But, oh, she'd miss him. Tears pricked her eyes. She refused to let them fall. She wore a clean blue gown and a pair of comfortable leather shoes. Things could be worse. Micelets were worse. A shudder momentarily usurped the throb in her chest.

The courtiers at the neighboring table—two elderly women and two younger ones—kept staring at her. Whispering. And they weren't the only ones. Most had avoided her since her reappearance, but one or two bolder ones had approached and asked pointed questions. Where was her husband? Had she run away from him? Why was she here?

Cinnabar might no longer fly as an owl, but Princess Iseabal's curse continued to exact revenge.

She placed the spoon back in her bowl, no longer hungry. Not even the rich scent of vegetable and grain soup tempted her appetite.

Sly was leaving, and he'd take her heart with him.

"You're quiet," Sly said, touching her arm for attention.

She jerked. The spoon jumped from her bowl and clattered, striking the bowl, the table and finally the floor.

Heads turned in the big salon. Whispers heated the air. *More gossip.* Her cheeks burned and a self-conscious sweat heated her skin. Hot. Too hot.

"Sorry," she whispered. "It's so noisy. So many people. Their hungry stares are pecking me."

"Don't let them see your distress," Sly commanded.

"He's right, my dear," Lady Jasper said.

Beatrice, their other dining companion, tut-tutted but not in a mean-spirited way. "Sly is correct, my dear. Lift your head and stare them in the eyes until they grow uncomfortable. If you act guilty, they'll believe you culpable."

The two elderly ladies were incredibly supportive and friendly.

"I'll try." Cinnabar lifted her head, turned it slightly, and met the regard of Merry Jacobs, one of the worst gossips in the kingdom. Might as well start big. She forced a cool think-what-you-want smile and stared down her nose until the bosomy matron huffed out a breath and returned her attention to her heaped plate of wild boar.

Lady Jasper patted her hand. "Oh, well done."

Tiny steps. She could do this. The king had told her nothing was impossible. King Calvin had offered her a home at the winter court. Sly had said nothing.

Confusion sapped her bravery.

She drew in a shuddering breath and felt the weight of a stare. Sly. She forced a smile, one which Sly returned with a heat that brought warmth to her face, her private places. Yet her mind remained cool. She'd given him her body. Gone with her desires, even though she'd known no other man would want her—accept her—after she'd been with Sly.

A mistake.

Yet, at the time, she'd thought she would remain an owl for the rest of her life.

And the truth. Even now, she'd make the same decision.

"Would you like to go for a walk after our meal?" Sly asked. "The gardens are beautiful."

"Too cool for me," Lady Jasper said. "Always the same when King Calvin visits."

"I do better when the winter court goes home," Beatrice agreed.

"That east wind is icy. Cuts through my bones, it does."

Cinnabar caught Sly's momentary shock and realized he meant a private walk with her. He hadn't meant to invite the two elderly women.

A laugh burst free, attracting attention. This time, she didn't care. "I'd love to go for a walk."

"Take a coat," Lady Jasper ordered.

"Of course. It *is* cold with the winter court here." Cinnabar's smile fit her mouth better this time. Sly had asked her to go for a walk. Maybe he'd kiss her too. A moment for her to remember later, once Sly returned to his family.

And she could visit from wherever she decided to live.

The long meal ended. Thank sugarplums. The king left the salon with King Calvin, ostensibly speaking to him about a personal matter, yet, with her inside knowledge, Cinnabar noticed the way King Liam leaned and King Calvin propped him upright.

At least the gossip about her had halted closer scrutiny of the king. A positive point.

"Are you ready for our walk?" Sly asked. "You get a coat, and I'll meet you by the side door, leading to the gardens."

Cinnabar nodded and hurried away to get a jacket. Habit led her footsteps to her old room in the servants' quarters. A wise choice, since she didn't have a coat among her new clothes. Her old room, not much more than a broom closet, remained undisturbed. Dusty, with the pervading scent of kitchen greens, since it shared a wall with the scullery. So small and crowded with the bed, none of the other servants had wanted it.

Ah, her coat. She pulled it from a wall peg and shrugged into it. Although tatty and well-worn, it was warm.

She found Sly waiting.

"I thought you might've gotten lost."

"I had to get my coat from my old chamber. I didn't have enough magic to summon it, so it took longer."

"Sorry," Sly said, reaching for her hand. "I assumed you'd have warm clothes."

"Most residents at the castle promenade through the rooms within the castle, especially during visits between the courts. They don't require warm clothes."

"Never mind. You're here now. Let's go." He tugged her past the two security guards at the door. "We're going for a walk."

"Yes, my lord," the tallest of the two guards said, his manner cheerful yet his blue eyes alert. "My lady."

Respect. She didn't often garner respect. Sly's doing. She elevated her chin, feeling better about herself than she had for a long, long time.

The icy breeze lifted her hair, and she raised her collar to cut the chill. Dried leaves, newly fallen, littered the gravel paths winding between bedraggled blooms. When the path allowed them to walk side by side, Sly drew her closer and wrapped his arm around her waist. He smelled of soap and honey and citrus. Delicious and enticing. She breathed in his scent again because she enjoyed the process. Memories. She'd hoard them now because soon she'd be alone, probably in Unseelie, since she'd hate to be at the mercy of Princess Iseabal again.

She'd never survive a second curse.

Princess Iseabal didn't make mistakes twice.

It was time to face her fears head on. "Are you looking forward to going home?"

"Yes. I miss my twin. Now that I remember Joe, it's weird he's not with me. We do most things together. My day isn't right without him around."

"I know he is identical, but does he enjoy the same things?"

Sly's quick glance sliced and diced and dissected until she quivered with awareness. Even though they hadn't known each other long, she liked him so much. He was honest. A loyal friend. He didn't treat those weaker than him as objects. He spoke to and asked them questions, and she noticed the king did the same. No longer did the staff scuttle around the castle with their heads down, avoiding eye contact.

"Joe loves farming, and our tastes in women are similar. Just as well I met you first."

"Me?"

Sly came to an abrupt halt. He turned her to face him, his dark brows furrowed in a deep frown. "I thought you'd come home with me. Don't you want to? Would you prefer to stay in Seelie?"

"You want me to go with you?"

He stroked her cheek with the tips of callused fingers, his pretty green eyes serious. "I do, but if you'd prefer to stay here, we'll make it work. I can visit you. I want to introduce you to my family, and it'd be pleasing to make love with you in my own bed. I'd like to wake up with you and go to sleep with you by my side."

"Yes. Yes," she whispered, her pulse beating fast and thundering in her ears. He wanted her to go with him. Joy spread through her, her smile more natural.

"Excellent." He dipped his head and captured her lips with his. He devoured her, holding her so close her breasts flirted with his chest. Tiny tingles of excitement radiated from the point of contact, and she moaned, craving more physical contact.

Sly pulled back with a groan. "One touch and I forget everything. Come on, let's continue our walk. I'll kiss you again when we get to the lake."

"Promise!"

Sly gave her a one-armed hug and grinned. "My mother will love you."

Cinnabar swallowed, attempted to moisturize her dry throat. Yes, nerves skipped in her stomach, but it was because she scarcely believed she'd escaped the curse. Okay. Not quite true. The idea of meeting Sly's family stressed her a little. She had no standing. A lady-in-waiting. A glorified maid with little to contribute. What would they think?

"Ma will enjoy meeting my girlfriend."

"I'm your girlfriend?"

Sly groaned. "I'm not doing a decent job of this. Walk. We'll talk at the lake."

A future. A potential future with Sly. Away from Seelie and the princess. She sought Sly's hand and laced her fingers with his. Her smile—elusive earlier—refused to quit. He truly wanted her. Something broken inside her mended at the realization, and she had the absurd desire to sing and dance.

The lunar star peeked from behind clouds, and wind whistled over the lake, whipping up choppy waves on the surface.

Sly tugged her behind a rock formation, and instantly her hair settled, the chill cut by the shelter of the stones. "Now I get to kiss you properly."

"Yes, please," Cinnabar said, and went into his arms to meet him halfway.

"But first," he whispered. "I want you to understand exactly what I want for the future. I want to have dinner with you and dance. I'd like to walk in the moonlight and show you my feline side. I intend to woo you and hopefully, you'll share my bed. I find I sleep better with you next to me. I want to get to know you better and show you what the future could be between us. How does that sound? Are you willing to try that?"

"Yes to everything." Cinnabar nodded emphatically.

"Thank the stars," Sly said.

He studied her for a long moment, groaned, and kissed her. They didn't come up for air for a long, long time.

CHAPTER TWENTY

I seabal stood at her chamber window and watched Sly and Cinnabar stroll hand in hand through the garden before they ambled past her line of vision.

The traitorous bitch.

Cinnabar had spoiled her plans even while cursed to an owl form. She'd decided her lady-in-waiting was too cowed to act independently, but she'd been wrong. Now she thought about it, once they'd returned from Middlemarch Resort, she'd seen little of Cinnabar. The owl had kept her distance, only presenting herself when Iseabal ordered.

Now she knew why. The mouselet had gained courage.

Well, she'd soon stop that.

Iseabal continued staring out the window from her vantage point and spied the pair as they rounded a bend. They stopped to talk, then merged as one.

She hissed, her eyes narrowing while anger lent rigidity to her muscles. It was worse than she feared. Cinnabar had sunk her claws into the weak man. No wonder he'd spurned her company and preferred the outdoors, either walking or spending hours with her conniving brother.

All that time, they'd laughed behind her back.

And her plans to oust her brother had turned to dust.

"Ooh!" Iseabal stamped her right foot, a vein ticking to life in her neck. She stomped back and forth. Back and forth. She should've insisted on an immediate reading of the banns. She shouldn't have allowed him time to recuperate. And she shouldn't have misjudged the initial spell.

She'd pay to get her hands on that hussy Cinnabar.

Iseabal prowled a circuit of her chamber, testing the magical spells trapping her within her prison. Unfortunately, they were strong and stable, since their horned cousin had lent assistance. Liam had stationed two guards on the door with orders to freeze her, should she cross the threshold without authorization.

There must be a way to escape.

A weakness.

She'd find it—and make Cinnabar sorry.

Sly.

Her brother.

Her cousin.

She would punish them all because no one treated her this way. *No one.*

She'd heard Sly intended to leave on the morrow. If she failed to escape before Sly returned home, she'd live with that. Cinnabar, however, would pay. And this time, she'd suffer. She'd rue the day she'd betrayed Princess Iseabal.

But first, first she must discover an escape path to break past the enclosure spell.

She needed to act swiftly, before Liam regained his strength.

She'd practiced faithfully for this day and was confident she could out-magic her weakened brother. Calvin, though, presented a problem.

Yes, a plan. Time to think of a plan.

Iseabal studied her door and commenced a systematic scan for weak points. Escaping her jail was a starting point. Revenge came next.

Evening fell, and after dinner with Calvin and Liam, Sly bid them good evening and left Liam's chamber.

Liam had almost recovered. A relief, since Sly hated leaving Liam vulnerable. The castle housed too many backstabbing courtiers for his liking. At least he'd noticed those with power had ceased torturing the servants. He hadn't worn spots or a tail since the truth spell.

"Are you retiring for the evening, my lord?" one of the two security guards asked.

"Yes," Sly said. "It's been an eventful day."

He strode down the passage toward his chamber, but took a right into another corridor, pausing to sneak a fresh bloom from one of the urns. He grinned. He wasn't lost this time and had a destination in mind.

He tapped on the second door, opened it, and darted inside.

"Sly." Cinnabar straightened, a brush in hand.

"I came to brush your hair for you."

"Oh." Heat crept into her golden cheeks, delighting him.

He'd kiss her there to taste the spicy heat of her cheek.

"And I thought I might stay. I'm frightened of the dark."

Her lips quirked in an almost smile, as if she guessed his devious plan. "My reputation will suffer."

"You're coming home with me to Middlemarch Resort. My family will like you because you're my girlfriend. They're good that way. But, if it will make you happy, no one saw me arrive, and I'll sneak out in the same furtive manner. No one will know I've spent the night with you."

"Do men and women sleep together where you come from? Without censure?"

"Yes, although it wasn't always that way. Over history, habits and customs have changed, which means my family and friends won't bat an eyelid if I stay with you overnight or we share a room."

"It's not the Seelie way."

"Too much talking." Sly prowled closer. "I missed you at dinner."

"I ate with Lady Jasper and Beatrice."

"Perfect." He'd asked if they'd keep an eye on Cinnabar. Rumors were rife, and he hadn't wanted her alone. *Moving on*. He placed his hands on her shoulders. "You're wearing too many clothes."

She wrinkled her nose at her ruby-colored robe.

Cinnabar had gained in confidence, and he enjoyed the change. "You think I'm wearing more clothes than you?"

"Yes." Her cute nose wrinkled again.

Maybe he'd kiss her nose first. "That won't be an issue. Not at first."

Her beautiful eyes glowed with humor. "Why?"

"I'll show you." Sly slipped her robe off her shoulders, and it pooled at her feet, leaving her naked.

Her hands rose to cover her breasts.

"No, don't hide from me." He backed her toward her narrow single bed. She toppled, and he caged her beneath him. Her mouth shaped into an O, and he couldn't resist. He kissed her, tasting her, moving against her softness. He gloried in the sensations, the feel of her, and he groaned when she wrapped her arms around his shoulders. Her mouth was hot and wet, her lips tempting. A hungry little noise escaped her as he increased his erotic assault and caressed her arms and hip with his fingers.

He slid his hands over her shoulders, then cupped one of her breasts, shaping the weighty globes. Lovely. He trailed kisses down her neck, lingering at the fleshy part between her shoulder and neck. That part of her tasted delicious and made him want to nibble. It was his feline instincts at work—or at least a hint of them. He pushed aside the niggle of worry about his missing feline self, and he moved lower, cupping both breasts and tasting her nipples.

"Sly." She tugged at his hair to the point of pain.

"Hey," he protested.

She grinned and lightened her grip, her captivating smile warming him through. Once she regained her self-assurance, she'd be mischievous and playful. He knew it. She'd relaxed already since Iseabal had reversed the curse.

He returned his attention to her nipples, sucking and teasing and pushing her while his own body heated in a slow burn. He ran his hands over her rib cage, the elegant curve of her hip, before moving lower and parting her thighs. Cinnabar tensed as he pressed a kiss to her inner thigh.

"Relax, sweetheart. Let me make you feel good. Do you trust me?" He waited, happy to exercise patience.

But she never hesitated. "Yes."

Proud of her brave spirit, he stroked her hip and kissed her inner thigh again. Once. Twice. Three times. She quivered, her breathing harsh.

His hearing had improved, seeming sharper. His ability to discern scent. Cinnabar's honeyed scent with the overtones of cinnamon spices deepened as he kissed closer to her pussy. He parted her folds, ran his tongue down her slit. Her flavor burst over his tongue, and when he skimmed her clit and hummed, she moaned. Desire, liquid and molten, smoothed his way. He nuzzled and sucked, his fingers teasing. Then, he cupped her bottom and lifted her to his mouth. He strummed with his tongue until she cried out, trembling.

"Please, Sly! Please. Stop torturing me."

"But it's so much fun."

As he tongued the sensitive nub, he slipped a finger inside her channel. In. Out. In. Out.

She lifted her hips, taking his digit deeper. She cried out again, and he curled his forefinger inside her, a deliberate, probing stroke.

"Yes." She made a dark sound as sexual hunger and pleasure claimed her. Her clit vibrated beneath his tongue while her sheath contracted around his finger.

"Sly!"

He grinned against her flesh. Yes, with her confidence in place, he'd need to fight off the single men at the resort. His brother. His cousins. His friends. They'd flirt with her, give him hell. He couldn't wait to witness her bloom and shine as he introduced her to his world.

When she quieted, he shifted up the bed, taking her mouth in a possessive kiss. The more he touched and kissed her, the more he wanted her.

While he intended to woo her and give her a chance to grow, he'd stand aside for no man.

Cinnabar was his woman.

His mate.

The next morning

"Are you going to eat your fruit?" Sly asked Cinnabar.

She shoved it away with a moue of distaste. "I'm nervous. My stomach is churning."

"You can stay in Seelie if you want," Sly said, forcing out the words when everything inside him protested in a vicious *haka*. It seemed he retained some of his New Zealand roots if he wanted to do a war dance. "Liam will protect you." He received a nod from his friend.

"Or move to the winter court," Calvin offered, leaning back in his chair.

Sly snorted. If the man got any more comfortable, he'd need popcorn.

"No." Cinnabar lifted her chin. "I want to go with you."

"Good girl," Calvin said. "Nerves are normal. Liam and I hold some anxiety when it comes to meeting Sly's family."

Sly barely smothered his snort, turning it into a cough at the last second.

Liam grinned. "It's true. We're worried about Scarlett."

"I'm worried Liam's confidence is misplaced, and he won't manage the portal," Calvin said.

Sly *did* snort this time, and Cinnabar giggled.

"I think we're ready," Sly said. "Do you have our luggage?"

"Yes, I had enough magic to shrink our belongings. Everything is inside my bag." She pointed to a small bag on a long strap that she'd draped over one shoulder.

"Nifty trick," Sly said. They hadn't discussed magic. He figured Cinnabar didn't possess much, and he'd gradually learn of her abilities. That trick would come in handy around the resort.

As they stood, a servant approached. He bowed to Liam. "Your Majesty, a messenger has arrived from Dalcon for you."

"Ah," Liam said. "I must speak with him. Why don't the three of you meet me at the portal? I know roughly where it is, since Cinnabar has described the area to me."

"You can use a location spell," Calvin suggested.

"It seems strange, leaving Seelie," Cinnabar said. "But the resort is pretty. I want to swim in the pool and try one of those fruity drinks."

"I can arrange that." Sly contemplated her curves, highlighted in her pale blue gown, and a rakish grin bloomed. "I can't wait to see you in a bikini."

"Maybe I should cover my eyes and ears," Calvin said as Liam departed with the servant.

Sly grinned. "Let's go."

The sun blazed overhead as they exited the castle. The season hovered at autumn, a combination of summer and winter. Sly found this fascinating and made a note to mention crop manipulation to Liam and Calvin. Right now, he was eager to leave Seelie.

The portal wasn't far from the castle, but in a wilderness area where few ventured. Cinnabar led him and Calvin along a narrow path, sometimes turning sideways to squeeze between piles of rocks and scrubby pink trees.

"It's here," Cinnabar said. "Right by the tree with the purple leaves."

Sly frowned. He'd imagined a shimmering circle, not an impenetrable wall of trees.

"Ah, yes," Calvin said. "I sense it. I wonder if it will open for me. Have you tried, Cinnabar?"

"I couldn't open it from the other side. I had to wait for Princess Iseabal to let me into Seelie."

Calvin stepped forward and held up his hand. For an instant, it appeared to Sly that he held his hand against nothing, then a golden glow appeared around his fingers, expanding until it grew outward into an oval.

Beaming with satisfaction, Calvin stepped back. "Behold, a portal."

"Smart-arse," Sly muttered.

"That's King Smart-arse to you," Calvin said in a regal tone, his horns glinting in the light.

237

Sly rolled his eyes, ignoring Cinnabar's horrified gasp. "Someone needs to keep you and Liam humble. Can we go through?"

"Sure. Liam will find us." Calvin opened the portal fully and stood back with a flourish of his hand. "After you."

Sly indicated Cinnabar should precede him and stepped through after her.

He staggered suddenly, his entire body jolting. Pain struck his head, his chest, his limbs, and he cried out, falling to his knees since his legs refused to bear his weight.

Cinnabar screamed, scrambling to kneel beside him.

"Sly," Calvin said urgently. "Take shallow breaths. Somehow, I believe Iseabal split your personality. I know you've worried about your feline side. I believe he remained trapped here, and the two parts of you are colliding. Breathe, man. It must hurt like hell."

Sly closed his eyes and focused on filling his lungs, breathing through the crashing agony. After long moments, the discomfort eased to a low-level headache. His legs trembled like a newborn calf, and he pushed upright with Cinnabar's aid.

He opened his eyes to meet Calvin's concerned gaze.

"How do you feel?" Calvin asked.

"Like I've fallen off my cambeest and got stomped on." Sly sucked in a breath, the rise and fall of his chest coming more naturally now. He focused carefully, groping for his feline, despite the hammers beating in his head.

Ah. There he was, snarling and testy and fighting for release.

With regret, Sly beat him back. *Soon. Soon we'll go for a run.*

"Do you think Liam will be long? I—" He broke off to gawk at the portal and the curls of smoke creeping through. "What is that black smoke?"

As Calvin turned, the smoke poured through the portal and darted around him. It formed in a stack, growing taller and more prominent.

Cinnabar whimpered and scuttled behind him. Sly blinked as

the smoke shaped into a form.

"How the feck did she manage that?" Calvin murmured a quick spell, the foreign sounds meaning little to Sly.

Calvin cursed, and a feminine laugh came from the midst of the smoky form. It took on more substance until even Sly recognized the threat.

"You didn't think I'd let a little thing like a locked room stop me, did you?" Princess Iseabal stood before them, hands planted on her hips, a gloating expression displaying her ugliness. She chortled, the sound tinged with amusement, a touch of madness, as Calvin attempted another spell. Then, her attention shifted to Sly and Cinnabar. "Nothing like a little revenge for motivation."

Middlemarch Resort

Joe blinked. Sly. He'd been there seconds before, lying on the bed. He'd spoken to him, told him about the seeds they'd brought from Earth and how some had failed, but the ones that had germinated were doing better than he'd expected.

Sly had vanished.

Joe sprinted from the room and tore through the resort. He found Saber with Ma and Eva in the resort kitchen. He skidded to a halt. "Sly is gone."

"Someone is playing a trick on you, son," Ma said.

"Saber, I am *not* fucking around. Sly is gone. He was there. I was talking to him. I walked over to the window, and when I turned around, he'd disappeared. I didn't hear the door. Not a thing. He's truly gone."

"We'll organize a search party," Saber said. "Pass the word to the staff."

Joe sprinted out and started a systematic search of Sly's favorite spots.

"Any luck?" Leo appeared behind Joe as he scanned the beach.

"No. I've searched everywhere I can think of." Joe saw Saber striding toward him. "Have you found him?"

"No," Saber said, and worry lines bracketed his mouth this time. "We'll have a meeting and widen the search."

Joe nodded. "I'll check the implement and storage sheds."

"Right. I want to organize the rest of the searchers before I join you."

"I'll go with Joe," Leo offered.

Saber waved them away and jogged toward the main meeting room. Joe and Leo strode through the resort to the private accommodations and followed the gravel path to Joe and Sly's storage sheds and greenhouse.

Joe darted into the greenhouse while Leo checked the first storage shed.

"Anything?" Joe asked when they met up again.

"Not a sign. Do you think he would've gone farther than this?"

Joe frowned at his older brother. "I don't know anything anymore."

"Let's check in with Saber first," Leo suggested.

Joe nodded, uneasiness leaving him faintly nauseous. His feline stretched beneath his skin and yowled a protest. Joe wanted to howl along with him. "Okay. I might check on the grapevines—just in case."

"Sly hasn't eaten. He'll be weak, and his legs wouldn't take him that far." Leo squeezed Joe's shoulder.

The silent commiseration made Joe want to cry. Instead, he let his brother lead him back to the resort.

At the last second, he halted. "You go on. I can't explain it, but something tells me to go to the vineyard."

"Let's go then."

"You don't have to come with me."

"I'm your brother. I'm going with you."

Joe swallowed. Hell, his thoughts darted around like a swarm of hyperactive bees. Where the devil was Sly? Where had he gone? Why had he left? Questions. All he had was questions.

They retraced their steps and entered the grass paddocks he and Sly had developed after hacking down trees and ploughing the land until it was suitable to plant their precious grapevines.

They scanned the land and walked up the hill, following the line of the vines. When they reached the brow of the hill, they paused to scan the landscape.

"There's someone down there," Leo said.

"Where did they come from?" Joe tried to make out faces, but they were too far away.

Chapter Twenty-One

"Iseabal," Calvin warned. "Don't make this worse. Sly and Cinnabar are leaving Seelie. Let them go. Neither has done anything to you."

"Nothing to me?" Iseabal spat, her voice rising. She poked her finger toward Cinnabar. "She stole him! Sly belongs to *me*."

"I do not belong to you," Sly snapped. "You kidnapped me from my home and kept me drugged so I didn't remember my family and my previous life. You made me a prisoner."

"As is my royal right." Iseabal swiftly reached into her pocket and hurled a purple ball of energy at Cinnabar.

Sly tried to shelter her, but the energy ball blasted him in the chest and struck Cinnabar in the face. She screamed and dropped, her hands covering her eyes. Sly saw double.

At the same time, a shout came from the portal. Liam sprang through and let rip with a scarlet energy ball. A second energy ball, blue in color, zapped from Calvin's fingertips. The two collided, strands of color twirling around Iseabal. She laughed, a maniacal sound that raised the hair at the back of Sly's neck.

His vision wavered in and out, and he started to view everything through a white film.

Iseabal teetered, and Calvin caught her the instant the energy strands ceased glowing hot around her body. Although no longer bright in color, the strands remained in place, trapping her. Her eyes fluttered, her chest rising and falling in tiny increments.

Sly crouched beside Cinnabar. "Sweetheart, are you okay? Can I check your eyes?" He pried her fingers from her eyes and sucked in a hasty breath. Whatever Iseabal had done to Cinnabar had changed her eyes, lightening the cornflower blue. He blinked twice. His vision wasn't too flash either.

A cunning, crafty laugh escaped Iseabal, jerking Sly's attention back to her.

"What did you do to her?" *And to him.*

"I took her sight. My right," Iseabal taunted. "She'll never see you again."

Sly peered into Cinnabar's eyes, concern filling him with each sharp, fear-tinged gasp. Hellfire, the white film was growing deeper, shrouding the stunning blue of her eyes. "Sweetheart, can you see me?"

A full body tremor told him no. Her shaking head confirmed it.

Sly lifted his head, tears filling his eyes at Iseabal's casual cruelty. "Haven't you made her suffer enough? She tripped over one of your friends and spilled a drink on your gown. It wasn't even her fault." He clenched his jaw, his fists. A pity they weren't around Iseabal's scrawny neck. The bitch. "Take pity."

"Why would I?" Iseabal demanded. "She must learn. I am a princess and have the right to punish those of lesser rank."

The woman had no heart.

Sly swallowed his curses, his tears. Neither would help. "Liam?"

Iseabal cackled. "He can't undo my spell. No one can apart from me."

Sly turned to her brother. "Is that true?" God, this wasn't fair.

"Iseabal, reverse the spell," Liam ordered.

Calvin knelt beside Sly. "Look at me."

Sly thought Calvin frowned but didn't trust what his brain was telling him. A hand gripped his chin, tilted his head. "Liam, she zapped Sly too."

"Gratafire. Reverse the spell now, Iseabal! Stop mucking around."

"Or what?" she scoffed. "You already intend to punish me. I can tell by your face."

Calvin stood, looking immense albeit fuzzy, with his head and horns thrust high. Fury spilled from him. Energy sizzled, snapping and popping. A sharp, acrid scent filled the air.

The dry leaves beside Iseabal burned and smoked.

Sly frowned and thought he saw Calvin yank on the lines of energy holding Iseabal prisoner. They burst with a brilliant cobalt blue.

"Reverse the spell," Calvin ordered.

Iseabal laughed. "No."

Dispirited, Sly's shoulders slumped. The woman was plain malicious and smug. Evil enough to fill a dozen fairy tales.

"Can't you make her?" Sly groped for Cinnabar and tugged her against his chest. Her shoulders heaved, and dampness soaked through his shirt. Tears. He felt like crying himself.

"Priceless," Iseabal scoffed. "Tell you what. You let me go and I'll restore vision to one."

"Iseabal!" Liam sounded shocked.

"Choose who regains the use of their eyes, and I'll gift it back. In return, you let me go."

"And you give your word, you won't attack either of them again?" Liam asked.

"Don't trust her," Sly said.

"Choose," she taunted.

Sly swallowed. From what he knew of Iseabal, she'd set her mind and wouldn't shift. "Fine," he said. "Give Cinnabar back her sight."

"So gallant," Iseabal mocked. "Last chance to ch-ch-change your mind."

"Return Cinnabar's vision," Sly snapped.

"Very well. Liam, do you promise to let me go?"

Liam hesitated. "Yes."

"Very well. Turn her to face me," Iseabal said, her tone imperious.

Sly bit back the retort tingling for release. *Don't antagonize her. She has no honor.* She'd renege at the slightest excuse. Gently, he turned Cinnabar in the direction of Iseabal's voice.

"Release the energy bonds, so I can return her vision," Iseabal ordered.

There was a moment's pause. Sly saw nothing, the film screening his vision fully now. It was the strangest thing. The film reminded him of the night sky. A deep black-blue with pinpricks of stars.

"Liam, do you want me to do this or not? Doesn't matter either way to me." Iseabal sounded amused.

The silence bloomed again, and Sly imagined Liam and Calvin in silent communication.

"Liam." Iseabal's tone grew sharp.

Liam cursed. "Release the bonds, Calvin."

"There, that wasn't so difficult, was it?" Iseabal derided.

Sly felt rather than saw Iseabal's magic, the prickle in the air as she tugged the ley lines.

Cinnabar groaned, and his hands tightened on her shoulders. "Are you okay? Can you see?" He kept his voice low while he used his feline senses to gauge what was happening. He didn't trust Iseabal not to attack in another way.

"Cinnabar, can you see me?" Liam asked.

"Y-yes."

"I'll be going now," Iseabal said.

The air crackled and an acrid scent of burning bark with a hint of amber wafted to Sly. Every muscle in his body tensed, his instincts screaming danger.

"No. No!" Iseabal screamed.

"What's happening?" Sly asked.

Iseabal screeched in fury. "You promised!"

"I didn't." Calvin's voice held finality. "You're out of control. You've abused your position, and Liam shouldn't have to worry about your treachery. Neither should your sister wonder if you'll murder her in her bed to ensure your victory."

"I wouldn't. Tell him, Liam!"

"You would," Liam retorted. "We both know you're hungry for power. That's why you captured Sly."

Iseabal cursed, and Sly imagined madness flowing across her face.

"If it weren't for Calvin, I would have ousted you, brother! You are weak. *Foolish.*" She cackled, flaying her brother with a vicious tongue. "Concentrating on farming instead of practicing your magic. Foolishness! I will win. I will discover a way."

The pressure on the ley lines intensified. Iseabal screamed again, the shriek cutting off abruptly, the complete silence terrifying.

Sly gripped Cinnabar's shoulder. "Cinnabar, please. Tell me what's happening."

"King Calvin used his magic to trap Princess Iseabal inside a bottle. Liam added his power, and she turned to smoke. The bottle...it sucked her up. Oh, frying fungus—he has affixed a stopper."

"Sly," Liam said hoarsely.

Sly turned toward Liam's voice.

"Your eyes," Liam whispered. "They've turned a deep blue. I can see pinpricks of stars. Are you truly blind?" He sounded broken.

Sly swallowed. Time to admit the truth. "I can't see you. All I see is the night sky."

Clothing rustled, and Liam's fingers curled around Sly's forearm. "I'm so sorry. I'd undo it if it were possible." Liam's voice broke.

His feline pushed in his mind, grabbing Sly's attention. "Stand back and give me room to shift. Shifting to feline helps heal injuries quicker. Perhaps it will repair my sight."

Liam stepped away, and Cinnabar released his hand. Sly fumbled with his footwear and clothing. A frustrating process. He'd never realized how much he relied on his eyes.

Eventually, he stripped and called up his feline. The beast stretched beneath his skin until the pressure grew painful. His bones in his body, his face, popped and crackled as they changed shape. A grunt escaped him, and a memory from the past flickered into prominence.

Don't fight the change, son. It makes it more painful. More chance of getting caught in between.

His father. Peace fell over him, and Sly ceased struggling. He relaxed, and the transformation flowed through his body. He toppled forward, and big paws held him steady. He flicked his tail and opened his eyes.

His vision...he was still blind.

A hand stroked along his back, soft and tentative. The floral and spicy scent told him it was Cinnabar. A purr erupted, her touch diverting the tendrils of panic threatening to overtake him. She repeated the caress over his shoulder.

"Did that help?" Liam asked.

Unable to communicate in this form, Sly gave a testy growl and shook his head.

"I have a suggestion to get around the spell," Calvin said from Sly's right. "It's not perfect, but it might help until Liam and I can research for a way to break Iseabal's spell."

"Do it," Cinnabar said.

Despite the circumstances, Sly wanted to smile. She hadn't realized it yet, but she was ordering around a king.

"Hold still," Calvin warned. "This might burn."

Sly caught a whiff of pungent amber seconds before a blast of energy seared him. A snarl ripped up his throat. The energy ball consumed the air, and a sneeze erupted from him. His eyes watered, and he blinked rapidly and again when the heat dispersed.

"Sly, are you all right?" Cinnabar crouched beside him and ran her hand over his head. "Can you see?"

Her face was wet with tears, and he pressed his nose against hers, his tongue lashing out to gather a tear.

"Your eyes. They're green again." Joy suffused her voice, and she threw her arms around his neck and hugged him.

"It worked," Liam said. "Hellfire, Calvin. Thank you for thinking of it. I thought...I thought Iseabal..." He shook his head, seeming young and broken. "It's bad enough now. I don't know how Sly can ever forgive us."

Sly gently shunted Cinnabar away and shifted to speak. His return shift wasn't quite as painful. It was as if his body had taken time to remember his identity and abilities.

As the transformation completed, his vision faded to midnight blue.

"Sly! Sly!"

That sounded like Joe. Thrilled, Sly turned toward the shout, his feline rumbling at the familiar voice. "Liam, describe them."

"They resemble you," Liam said.

"Sly, your clothes," Cinnabar said in a soft voice.

"Hold still. I'll dress you," Calvin said. An instant later, clothes covered his body.

"Joe?"

"Sly, it is you!" Joe sounded excited. Happy.

Sly found himself in a solid embrace, the familiar scent of his twin filling his nostrils. Tears ran down his face, so great was his relief.

"Sly, where the hell have you been? You vanished! We've been searching everywhere for you."

That sounded like Leo. Joe moved away, and another hard hug told Sly he was right.

"He was here?" Calvin asked, seeking confirmation of his theory. Leo stepped back.

"Yeah," Joe said in a who-the-hell-are-you tone. "You were in the *Sleeping Beauty* boudoir. What's wrong with your eyes?"

"He's blind," Cinnabar whispered, a distressed sob bubbling through. "It's all my fault."

"It's not your fault," Sly said gruffly, and slid his arm around her waist, relishing her closeness.

"He's right," Calvin said.

"These are my friends, King Liam from Seelie and King Calvin from Unseelie. And this is my girlfriend, Cinnabar. What's a *Sleeping Beauty* boudoir?" he asked as an afterthought. He didn't recall any *Sleeping Beauty* room at the resort.

"You were unconscious. Have been for almost a month." Joe sounded plain confused. "What happened to your eyes?"

"Can we do this back at the resort?" Sly asked. "Then I can tell everyone at once."

"Sure." Joe's voice indicated he'd moved off.

Cinnabar gripped Sly's arm. "We're walking uphill. I'll try to describe the obstacles."

Joe must've heard her speak. When he spoke again, his voice sounded by Sly's ear. "You really can't see?"

"I have vision while I'm in feline form."

"Well, that's something." Joe gripped his forearm. "God, Sly. I missed you so much, and I've been worried. Are they really your friends? Even the blue dude with the horns?"

Cinnabar gasped.

Behind him, Calvin chuckled. "I keep telling you. King Blue Dude with the Horns."

Sly took a step and tripped over a protruding stone. Joe hauled him back up.

"Your lady is pretty," Joe said.

Sly imagined Cinnabar's blush and smiled. "I know. I'm glad she met me first."

"Where did you meet my brother?" Joe asked.

"At the resort."

"Oh, wait. I remember. I saw you together," Joe said.

Sly grinned. "Yeah, you did. She is my mystery lady—the one who disappeared. It's brilliant to be back home."

"I'm the handsome twin," Joe said. "You should have bypassed Sly and headed straight to me."

Calvin snorted from behind. Liam snickered. Or it might have been the other way around.

"Sly is fine for me," Cinnabar replied. "I like him."

"He snores," Joe said.

"No, he doesn't," Cinnabar protested.

Sly smiled again, this time in Joe's direction, and promptly tripped.

"He really is blind." Leo sounded surprised.

"You tripped him on purpose," Cinnabar accused. "I saw you stick out your foot."

"I'm sorry," Leo said. "I thought Sly was joking."

"Not kidding," Sly said drily. A fact that was only starting to sink into his mind.

"Saber is coming," Joe said.

"Look who we found," Leo called.

"Where did you get those clothes?" Saber asked. "Where have you been? We've been turning the resort upside down to find you."

"Calvin, what did you dress me in?"

Liam chuckled. "The clothes you were wearing when we left the castle. They're different from those of your brothers. Now I understand why you complained about Iseabal's suits."

"Saber, can you call everyone together?" Sly asked. "I'd like to introduce my friends and tell my story just the once."

The story took a while, but Sly managed to answer all the questions with help from Cinnabar, Liam, and Calvin.

"You'll never regain your eyesight, son?" Ma asked, and her tone told Sly of her concern.

"Not when I'm in human form," Sly answered. It hurt to push out the words, yet he'd do it all over again. He didn't regret helping Cinnabar. She had suffered more than him. For an instant, he worried his handicap might repulse her, or she'd prefer Joe or one of his cousins. He'd need to ask her, set his mind to rest.

The last thing he wanted was her sympathy.

"There is hope yet," Liam said. "Calvin and I will search for a spell to restore your sight and check with the medicine crones. I refuse to let Iseabal win this war."

"We intend to search every alternative," Calvin agreed, his tone determined. "We can't promise a cure, but we will try everything, including interrogating Iseabal again."

"Young man, I will cook you a special meal every week if you can restore my son's sight," Ma said.

There was a brief silence, and Sly imagined his two friends exchanging a glance.

"That sounds delightful," Calvin said, and he sounded sincere.

"It does," Liam agreed. "It will allow us to get to know Sly's brothers and sister better. I'm sorry we missed Scarlett during this visit. Sly has told us much about her and her liking of rocks, and about the rest of your family, of course."

Sly snorted, and Cinnabar giggled, the warmth of her body seeping into his side.

Mate. *Mate.* His feline twisted beneath his skin. Cinnabar

251

might be his mate—hell, she *was* his mate. Now that he'd returned to his world, he knew it for certain. No. Stick to his plan. A slow courtship. Give her a taste of freedom, a chance to learn herself. He wanted that for her.

To give her a choice.

At absolute worst, he had a friend.

And with his new handicap... Yeah, the future might suck for him.

"Young man, your sister sounds like a terrible woman. Are you sure that bottle is strong enough to hold her?"

Sly smiled inwardly. Only his mother would dare lecture a king.

"Calvin and I will take it back to Seelie for safekeeping," Liam promised.

Over two hours later, after Ma had fluffed around after him and shed tears on him, Liam and Calvin departed with promises to visit. Saber allocated Cinnabar a room in the staff area, and Joe led them to her new quarters.

"Do you want to show Cinnabar around the resort by yourself or would you like me to come with you?" Joe asked.

"Cinnabar has been here before. I'll shift so I can see. Is that okay, sweetheart?"

"Of course," Cinnabar said. "I'll unpack our clothes while you speak with your brother."

"Where are your bags?" Joe asked.

Cinnabar patted her bag, or at least it sounded like it to Sly.

"Show Joe," Sly said. "Start unpacking."

Sly cocked his head, listening and letting his imagination roam. It was easy to picture his brother's shock.

An instant later, Joe whistled. "Have you taken to wearing lacy bits of nothing, Sly?"

"Not that," Cinnabar said, her tone half-horrified and half-embarrassed. "That's mine. Here. This is one of Sly's suits."

Sly grinned at his brother's teasing. "You didn't tell me you'd packed lace."

"Shush," Cinnabar said, sounding mortified.

"It's hard to believe this princess spirited you away. Lucky for you we're shifters, and she didn't realize we are dual-natured. We're fortunate that part of you remained at the resort. I admit it." Joe cleared his throat. "I was worried. I thought you'd die. It was better after we did the *Sleeping Beauty* thing."

"It's no wonder my mouth was sore, with all that kissing. The servants gave me salve to help the dryness."

Joe gripped his shoulder. "I didn't know what else to do. But on the plus side, we have enough currency to purchase cattle."

"Really? I fetched that much? That's brilliant. We'll research the Scothage people on the mainland to learn more before we approach them. Liam has contacts too."

"King Liam and King Calvin both gave me message globes. We can contact them at any time," Cinnabar said.

"I liked them," Joe said.

"They're first-rate men, although Scarlett should take care if she wishes to remain single. They were disappointed to miss her. Cinnabar, are you ready to go for a walk?"

"Wait, I need to change my gown."

"Whoa," Joe said. "How did you do that? I didn't see a bit of skin."

"Magic," Cinnabar said. "My magic isn't powerful, but I can do the basics."

"You'd better not have seen anything," Sly growled.

"I'll collect you both for dinner. Eva and Ma are organizing a celebration meal for you and Cinnabar."

"For me?" Shock and disbelief colored Cinnabar's words.

He fumbled for her hand and squeezed it. "You're my girlfriend. They want to get to know you and introduce you to the rest of the relations."

"Oh."

The wonder in her voice caused a constriction in his throat. She hadn't received the same opportunities as him. He'd make up for that lack.

"Catch ya later, bro," Joe said. "Don't disappear again. My heart can't take it."

"Promise," Sly said with feeling.

His brother strode from the room, his footsteps sure and confident.

"I like your family, although your big brother is scary."

"Saber?"

"Yes."

"He has a lot of responsibility. Eva, his mate, is perfect for him. Can you magic off my clothes for me? Pack them in your bag, so I can dress—no wait. We'll pick up shorts and a T-shirt at the bungalow I share with Joe."

An instant later, he was naked. This time his shift was smoother, easier. And Cinnabar. She was so beautiful with her russet hair and bright blue eyes. They shone with tears. He wanted to say so much to her, but it was impossible while in feline form. Instead, he licked her hand and ambled to the door. He waited for her to open it and led the way to the bungalow.

With his clothes in Cinnabar's magic bag, he trotted through the resort with Cinnabar at his side. The pink foliage seemed brighter than usual, the tree bark holding more texture. The scents. The panorama. He'd never appreciated them more.

He headed to the private part of the beach reserved for family and staff. To his relief, it was empty. The briny scent filled his lungs, and the gentle swish and retreat of waves soothed him.

"It's so pretty. I like the lake, but this is lovely," Cinnabar said.

Sly stood back and shifted, the lack of vision an abrupt shock. "Can you magic on my clothes for me?"

"Of course." Her bag rustled and clothes slid across his skin.

His stomach did a twirl. Anxiety. Hell, he had it bad for her. If

254

she didn't want the same thing...

No point dragging his feet. He'd ask her if he had a chance with her, if they might have a future. He sank downward until his backside met the warm sand. Cinnabar settled beside him, her body heat comfortable against his side.

"Do you think you'll want to stay here?"

"If I'm allowed."

Sly floundered, unable to read her body language. "Of course you can stay. Even if you don't want to be with me."

"You don't want me?"

"No. Yes. Wait, I can't interpret your body language, and it's making it difficult for me." Hell, he was making a mess of this. He sucked in a deep breath, hoping to quell his anxiety. "I want you to stay here at the resort, for you to be happy and safe and to choose the path of your future. The last thing I desire is for you to stay with me because of what Iseabal did."

She took his hand and squeezed it. "Sly, you gave up your vision for me. No one has ever cared about my well-being, but you've shown me kindness and friendship from the moment we met. You gave me self-worth. Because of you, I'm no longer cursed to spend my life as an owl. I would be an idiot if I walked away from you."

"I'm blind."

"For now," she said, her tone determined as she squeezed his hand again. "King Liam and King Calvin will find a way to restore your sight. I know they will. You stood with me when I was powerless, and I will do the same for you."

"But my blindness will make things difficult when I am in human form."

Her fingers tightened around his. "Stupid man. Don't you understand? I am happiest when I'm with you. It doesn't matter if you can see or not or if Iseabal managed to turn me back into an owl. My feelings for you won't change. I love you, Sly."

Every muscle in Sly's body relaxed. *She loved him*. Joy and contentment curved his lips to a smile. "I love you too. But I want to take things slowly, get to know you. I need to explain to you about feline mates and what it means. But most of all, I want you to enjoy your freedom."

"What will I do here? I can't laze around while everyone else works."

"Don't worry about that. If you want to do something useful, you can spend time with each of my brothers' mates until you discover a job you enjoy. You can help Joe and me with our farm or Scarlett on reception once she returns. She'd love a helper, so she can concentrate on her jewelry."

"Oh, Sly. That sounds perfect."

To his relief, she sounded thrilled. She cupped his face and mashed her lips against his. He fell back against the sand, taking her with him, taking over the kiss.

Hope. Love. A future.

He tasted all these things in the kiss.

He still intended to take things slowly, but now confidence filled him as he directed their kiss into tender and sweet. Cinnabar's presence made him whole, despite his lack of sight. She gave him purpose. He was under no illusions. Adapting to his blindness would take time, and no doubt bring frustrations, but at least he had hope. Together, they'd beat Iseabal. Liam and Calvin would do their best to discover a way to restore his sight, plus he had Cinnabar. A beautiful woman full of courage, willing to stand at his side and love him as he loved her.

The owl and the pussycat—the perfect mates.

A match made in fairy tales.

Thank you for reading Sly and Cinnabar's story. Joe is the

next Mitchell sibling to find his match and his journey is one of action and adventure with a determined heroine! Visit my website to learn more about Journey With Joe. (https://shelleymunro.com/books/journey-with-joe)

Also By Shelley

Middlemarch Shifters
My Scarlet Woman
My Younger Lover
My Peeping Tom
My Assassin
My Estranged Lover
My Feline Protector
My Determined Suitor
My Cat Burglar
My Stray Cat
My Second Chance
My Plan B
My Cat Nap
My Romantic Tangle
My Blue Lady
My Twin Trouble
My Precious Gift
My Grumpy Wolf

Middlemarch Gathering
My Highland Mate
My Highland Fling
My Elusive Mate
My Valiant Princess
My Highland Wedding
My Highland Billionaire

Middlemarch Capture
Snared by Saber
Favored by Felix
Lost with Leo
Spellbound with Sly
Journey with Joe
Star-Crossed with Scarlett

House of the Cat
Captured & Seduced
Claimed & Seduced
Merry & Seduced
Stranded & Seduced
Seized & Seduced
Hunted & Seduced
Festive & Seduced
Betrayed & Seduced
Enticed & Seduced

Dragon Investigators
Blue Moon Dragon
Blood Moon Dragon
Black Moon Dragon
Snow Moon Dragon

About Author

USA Today bestselling author Shelley Munro lives in Auckland, the City of Sails, with her husband and a cheeky Jack Russell/mystery breed dog.

Typical New Zealanders, Shelley and her husband left home for their big OE soon after they married (translation of New Zealand speak - big overseas experience). A twelve-month-long adventure lengthened to six years of roaming the world. Enduring memories include being almost sat on by a mountain gorilla in Rwanda, lazing on white sandy beaches in India, whale watching in Alaska, searching for leprechauns in Ireland, and dealing with ghosts in an English pub.

While travel is still a big attraction, these days Shelley is most likely found in front of her computer following another love - that of writing stories of contemporary and paranormal romance and adventure. Other interests include watching rugby (strictly for research purposes), cycling, playing croquet and the ukelele, and curling up with an enjoyable book.

Visit Shelley at her website.
https://shelleymunro.com/

Sign Up for Shelley's Newsletter
https://shelleymunro.com/newsletter/